Running Toward Home

BETTY JANE HEGERAT

Library and Archives Canada Cataloguing in Publication
Hegerat, Betty Jane, 1948-
Running toward home / Betty Jane Hegerat.

(Nunatak fiction)
ISBN-13: 978-1-897126-01-1
ISBN-10:1-897126-01-8

I. Title. II. Series.

PS8615.E325R85 2006   C813'.6   C2006-902994-6

Editor for the press: Lynne Van Luven
Cover and interior design: Ruth Linka
Cover image: "Tiger with Volcano, From Forbidden Subjects," by Chris Flodberg
Author Photo: Artistic Impressions

 Canada Council   Conseil des Arts
for the Arts   du Canada
 Canadian   Patrimoine
Heritage   canadien
 edmonton
arts
council

NeWest Press acknowledges the support of the Canada Council for the Arts, the Alberta Foundation for the Arts, and the Edmonton Arts Council for our publishing program. We also acknowledge the financial support of the Government of Canada through the Book Publishing Industry Development Program (BPIDP) for our publishing activities.

NeWest Press
201–8540–109 Street
Edmonton, Alberta T6G 1E6
(780) 432-9427
www.newestpress.com

NeWest Press is committed to protecting the environment and to the responsible use of natural resources. This book is printed on 100% post-consumer recycled and ancient-forest-friendly paper. For more information, please visit www.oldgrowthfree.com.

1 2 3 4 5 09 08 07 06

PRINTED AND BOUND IN CANADA

*This book is dedicated to children in care
and the foster parents and social workers
who keep them safe.*

1 WILMA STOLE SIDELONG GLANCES AT HER FOSTER SON. He trudged along like he was on the way to the dentist, or a math exam, rather than a sunny afternoon with the mom he hadn't seen in months. When they were abreast of the baleful brontosaurus who keeps watch over the south perimeter of the Calgary zoo, Wilma paused and squinted through the wire grid of the fence. Dinny the dinosaur, she thought, was only slightly more stony-faced than the boy at her side. The statue was roped off, untouchable for his own good.

Corey had stopped too, but looked as though he wanted to bolt. In which direction, Wilma wasn't sure. "When I was a kid," she said, "Dinny wasn't fenced in." He turned to her with a polite pretence of interest. "I tried to climb him once, but I only got halfway up the tail before someone hauled me down."

This time Corey's long-lashed eyes widened for real. "He's as tall your house," he said.

She put a hand on his shoulder. "We'd better get moving. You'll be late." Through the skimpy T-shirt, his collarbone felt as sharp and fragile as china.

Half a block away, a stream of people flowed across the road to the ticket booth. A busy afternoon at the zoo. The kind of day Wilma would normally have avoided. She'd prayed for rain, for Corey's mother to be called in to work, for some benign reason for this visit to be cancelled. She'd felt a guilty surge of relief this morning when Corey came listlessly to the kitchen with flushed cheeks and the unmistakably bright eyes of fever. She'd tried to send him back to bed. But it was too late to get in touch with his mom, he'd said. It was nothing. He'd be fine.

"Are you sure you're meeting here? If your mom rode down on the train she'll come in the north gate." She tried to keep in step with him, but the path was busier now and they were forced to single file.

Each time Corey glanced over his shoulder at Wilma, the wind lifted a silky fringe of hair, exposing his pale forehead. "We meet at the tigers," he said. "You don't have to wait with me."

At the entrance they joined the ticket line, all those mothers and their children. Wilma resisted the impulse to stroke Corey's arm, to measure the warmth of his body. "I wish you'd brought your jacket, especially with that fever you're running. It'll be cold later." She'd bitten her tongue this morning when he appeared in washed-out shorts and faded T-shirt. Clothes that must have been buried in the bottom of his suitcase.

He jerked his chin, raised his arm like a marionette. "There she is. You can go."

So many young women beyond the gate, and no one waved back. Wilma looked hard at Corey. "You're sure? Sure she knows you're staying with her overnight?"

"The social worker said she talked to her about it."

"When?" She struggled with the nasty edge of disbelief in her voice. "When did the social worker tell you that? We haven't even met the new one yet. I've only talked to her on the phone."

His face was flushed. He flicked the hair from his eyes. "Yesterday. She came to school. I got called out of science class to go to the guidance office."

"With the guidance counsellor?" Now it was high-pitched paranoia and she couldn't cover it. A conference? And she and Ben didn't know about it?

"No. Just her and me. Look, I'll see you tomorrow. I can buy my own ticket."

He turned, stepped forward to catch up with the queue. Wilma lunged, grabbing a handful of T-shirt. "Wait!" She scrabbled in her purse. "I should have taken you to the mall to buy your mom a birthday present. Pick out something at the gift shop." She let go of his shirt. He hesitated, but then plucked the bill from her fingers. She wanted to reach out and smooth the wrinkle she'd left in the thin grey cotton. Instead, she lifted a hand in farewell and stepped aside.

No wonder she hadn't spotted Tina. There—finally she'd dared to say the woman's name. When Corey moved beyond the ticket window and past the wooden slats in the fence, Wilma stared at the girl who ran to embrace him. Dressed in shorts and a skimpy white top that showed at least six inches of bare midriff when she lifted her arms around him, she looked more like a teenage sister than the mother of a twelve-year-old. Without question, this was the girl in the small photo in Corey's room. The girl whose picture had caught Mark's eye on his last visit home.

"Wow! Who's the hot babe on Corey's dresser?" he'd asked.

"Shush!" Wilma had hissed at him and pulled him out of earshot. "How'd you like someone to call your mother a 'hot babe'?"

He'd grinned and wrapped his long arms around her. "Happens all the time, Mom."

Now, slim arms reached for Corey and the two figures merged. Wilma pulled her sweater tight across her chest and retraced their steps along the river path. She'd bring Corey back to the zoo on another day. This was the best time of year, all the baby cats curled in beside their mothers, the wobbly baby giraffe hardly daring to step away from his mother's shadow. On a long ago spring day, when both her boys had finally insisted they were too old for the zoo, Wilma had wandered down alone and crouched by the snow leopard's enclosure. The family of cats basked in the sun on their platform, the mother licking each cub, inch by inch. Wilma's toes had curled in her sandals with each swipe of the leopard's tongue.

Any time now, Corey would decide he was too cool for the zoo. She'd bring him back soon, next weekend. Saturday morning when Ben was golfing. If Ben was along, he'd take charge and hustle them straight to the gorillas and insist they read every page in the book that hung on a post by the enclosure, identifying each animal in the troop. The cuteness of the little gorillas notwithstanding, Wilma's eyes would be riveted to the oldest female, with her flaccid breasts swinging, and that look about her as though she was carrying the entire gorilla world on her sloping shoulders. "Run!" she always wanted to call. "Run before you're knocked up again and there are even more of those little gorillas chasing after you!" And there'd be the old silverback staring at Ben as though he recognized his brother, even after all this time in captivity.

After the gorillas, Ben would march them through the prehistoric park explaining the construction and the funding and the politics around it all. By the time they got to the tigers, both Wilma and Corey would be pleading to go home. A day at the zoo with their dad, Mark and Phil had always said, was too much like school.

She wondered where Corey and Tina were at this moment, and if they planned their destinations the way Ben did, or had a meandering style like hers. When she paused to stare through the fence, she was across from the brontosaurus again, and there was no sign of Corey in the moving throng of children. Dinny stared at the sky, blind as ever. *Time to bury the lonely old dinosaur,* she thought. He never had been a work of art.

2 TINA KEPT HAVING THIS FUCKIN' AWFUL NIGHTMARE THAT some day she'd walk by Corey on a street, another scruffy kid slouching by, and she wouldn't know him. In the dream he tried to grab her arm; when she pulled away and broke into a run he came after her screaming, "Mama! Mama wait!" The voice was shrill, a tiny child's voice; he'd never called her Mama, but still she woke up in a sweat.

She didn't recognize Corey when she saw him through the fence, waiting in line with the woman in the ugly sweater. Not until he waved. Even then she thought he could be signalling to someone else. With her eye on the crowd, crawling out of her skin because she was dying for a smoke, although she'd promised him last fall that she'd quit for good, she schemed about what she'd tell him. As soon as he came through the gate she'd say that things weren't working out so well. That something had come up and he'd have to call his social worker and ask her to pick him up at four instead of in the morning.

The big problem was Simon and his shitty timing. Which could have been even worse if he'd shown up half an hour earlier. Tina hadn't met Corey's new social worker until she'd come pounding on the door at nine this morning.

"I'm Kristel Maclean," she'd said, as though Tina should stand up and salute.

Kristel had rattled off a list of rules for the visit, said she was coming to pick up Corey at nine o'clock sharp tomorrow morning. And then, "Do I have to remind you about the restraining order? What will happen to your access to Corey if Simon Miller is around?" She was trying to look past Tina, into the apartment.

Tina had stepped out into the hall and closed the door on the snoopy bitch. "He's in jail," she said. Instantly she regretted her words. Every social worker who'd had their clammy hands on Corey's file knew Simon was a two-bit criminal. But she didn't have to give them the pleasure of admitting it herself.

Her face was so close to Kristel's, their eyelashes almost touched. They were the same height, the same size. The woman stepped back as though she'd smelled something bad. Looked at Tina for a long time, up and down.

"That's not what I heard," she said. She blinked behind glasses as big as picture frames. "You know, I've read every single thing there is to read about Corey, and about you. A lot of people think you're a pretty smart woman. That you really care about your kid." She shifted the big bag hanging from her shoulder, crossed her arms. "My theory is that none of that matters so long as your boyfriend is in the picture. You'd better make sure he's not around in the next twenty-four hours."

She'd stomped away, without looking back to see Tina give her the finger.

The door had barely closed when Simon was thundering against it, all sexy grin and "Happy Birthday Mama, I'm home!" In two minutes flat he had his clothes off and was working on hers. It had been such a long time, now what the hell was she supposed to do?

When Tina looked again, the boy in the line-up seemed to be arguing. The woman finally stepped away. Only she didn't go far, stayed lurking next to the fence just out of Corey's sight. Tina felt her lip curl as she watched. One more neurotic foster mommy trying to steal her kid.

All her nightmare fears about not knowing Corey dissolved when he came past the gate. One glimpse of him trying to slip through the crowd as though he was invisible, and she was walking with her arms out, knowing as soon as she felt the bones rest against her own that she would never mistake Corey for anyone else. He was taller, his hair longer and darker than before, but he still had that funny rabbity smell she would've been able to sniff out in a whole zoo full of kids.

Only a few hours to hang onto him. But he didn't know that yet, and as soon as he squirmed free of her hug, she lost her nerve. A scrawny, big-eyed kid who jumped at his own shadow, but had this way of looking at his mom like a little old man. Not judging like everybody else, but quietly watching. Corey knew too many things he shouldn't know, and mostly about her. No, even though it wouldn't surprise him, she couldn't tell him that she'd screwed up. Not yet.

She pulled Corey to her for one more hug. "Hey! Wish me happy birthday, you little shit!"

3 EVERY SIX MONTHS, RIGHT BEFORE HIS VISIT WITH his mom, Corey was afraid that he wouldn't know her. That she'd dye her hair blond, cut it short, and start to dress like a woman instead of like a girl. Tina grabbed him and squeezed his face into the hollow of her throat. Her skin was damp against his cheek, as though she'd just showered. A crinkly cloud of hair tickled his ears. She smelled of coconut, of the shampoo she'd used forever, or at least as long as he could remember. When she spoke, the breath of cinnamon gum—always the sugarless kind in the red package—didn't quite cover the trace of cigarette. He wondered how long she'd try to hide the fact that she was smoking again.

"Holy crap! You grew another six inches." She spun around behind him and stood back to back, her hand levelled and patting to find the top of his head. "Get a load of this! You're as tall as I am."

"No way. You're still taller than me. I'm still the shortest one in my class." Corey's gaze travelled beyond the fence, through the long grass, around the pond. He'd glimpsed the pacing tiger when he was first inside the gate, but now the cat had disappeared.

"Good. I don't want you to turn into a gorilla." Looping a cool arm through his, she pulled him into the flow of people on the path. "I'm cold. Let's find some sunshine and sit down." She broke away and ran, her hair lifting in the wind like the tail of some exotic bird, with Corey following, zigging and zagging and then grabbing her arm and tugging to the right.

"Hey, Tina, there's a new gift shop. Let's look."

"For Chris'sake, we just got here. Do we have to buy something already?"

He pulled away, stung. He never asked her to buy him stuff. Never. She must have been with somebody else's kids lately to be so crabby. Paulette's probably. One of the things he could be glad about, living away from Tina, was that he didn't have to hang out with that bunch of losers anymore.

Every sunny bench was occupied, so Tina kept moving, never looking back to be sure he was still with her. Finally, they sprinted over a large expanse of lawn across from the elephant house, and he caught up with her at the edge of a bed of flowers. Breathing hard, she doubled over for a few seconds, and then sat cross-legged on the grass. "Let's talk," she said. She pounded the piece of lawn beside her.

Corey sank onto his knees. His legs had been doing funny things when he ran. Moving on their own. All he could feel was a rubbery ping like elastic bands. When he looked down, it was like watching someone else's legs pumping away under him. He'd woken up this morning with a taste in his throat that made him want to puke. Now he tried to stop the gulps of air that were like sandpaper on his throat. He shifted so that he was sitting cross-legged like Tina. Spread his arms out at his sides and ran his shaking hands over the grass, balancing himself. Breathing slow and careful. "What do you want to talk about?" he asked.

"Duhhh? I haven't seen you since your birthday. Maybe, how are you? What's new? Are those new people treating you good?"

"They aren't new. I've been there almost six months. That's like some kind of a record."

The thick grass, when she ripped at it with clawed fingers, made a sound like fabric tearing. "Thanks, Cor. I love being reminded that you're kicking around foster homes because everyone thinks I'm a lousy mother." She trailed her hand over their bare legs, anointing them with a drift of green.

Corey stared at his thighs, too tired to brush them clean. Good start. Five minutes and she was already pissed off. "Sorry." He mumbled the word again. "Sorry." Sorry, Tina. I didn't mean it, Tina. Don't worry, Tina. Must have been the first sentence he ever said. Sorry, sorry. Sorry Corey, that was him.

She pulled her knees up to her chin, snippets of grass clinging now to her arms and throat. "Hey, it's okay. It's this birthday thing, you know? I don't want to get old."

"Twenty-six isn't old." He reached with the toe of his running shoe to tap a blood red tulip in the bed beside them. Again, the leg seemed to be disconnected from his brain. "These are like Opi's garden."

She wrinkled her nose. "Bloody old Dutchman cares more about his stupid tulips and lilies than he does about us."

Mostly, Corey couldn't remember his grandfather's face. Only the voice.

What kind of a mother . . . leaves her son with strangers . . . gets picked up by police . . . hangs around with criminals, drunks, drug addicts . . . sleeps with strangers . . .? What kind of a mother? That thick sound had rubbed on his ears like the rough grey mittens the old man wore in winter. Even now, Corey wanted to put his hands over his ears to stop the pounding. It felt as though there was an ocean in his head.

On the other side of the wide lawn, kids were swarming over a giant spiderweb of ropes. Beyond them, tucked against the trees, Dinny stretched his neck to puffs of cloud. When Corey squinted, he had the creepy feeling that the old dinosaur was watching him.

"Hey, wake up." Tina's fingernails, shimmery with silver polish, danced like butterflies on his arm.

A fat bumblebee crawled out of the scarlet cup of one flower, quivered in the sunshine, and then buzzed to the next. "Have you seen Opi?" Every time he saw her, he asked the same question, and every time she shook her head. "So he doesn't know we're at the zoo?"

"How would he know if I haven't talked to him?"

Corey's eyes shifted toward the screen of trees beyond the large mammal house, toward the river on the north side of the island and the road back home to Opi's house that he and Tina had walked so many times. Then to the back of the building where one lone giraffe reached to the top of a wooden pole and pulled at a clump of green branches. As though it could feel Corey's gaze, the giraffe turned its pointed face and watched Corey, head nodding gently as it chewed.

Three girls had flopped down on the grass a few feet away. They were laughing hysterically and acting as though there was no one else around, the way the girls at school behaved in the hall. Like they were the only ones on the planet, but they knew everyone was watching. One of them looked familiar, like that girl in his band class who cried because she could never get any decent music out of her French horn. She was tall, way taller than him, and skinny, and always wore white T-shirts. When she blew into the horn, her tits showed. Unless you looked really close at Tina's face, she didn't look much older than those girls. He wondered what they thought. That she was his sister, maybe? Or that he was the kind of guy who brought a girl to the zoo?

Tina dug her elbow into Corey's ribs. "That chick's giving you the eye, Cor. You might be one of the shortest guys, but I bet you're the cutest."

When she stood up and the girls stared, Corey wished that Tina had changed. That she was dressed in pants that covered her ass cheeks where the bits of grass were clinging, and that she had a sweater like the one Wilma was wearing today. Tina's shirt had oval cutouts along the bottom. Even when her belly was covered, her skin winked through the holes like small, brown eyes. He stood up and took quick steps sideways so that when they walked away, she couldn't link her arm with his.

4 WILMA HAD INTENDED TO GO STRAIGHT HOME AFTER she left Corey at the zoo, to plant the flats of petunias that were growing leggy in the greenhouse attached to the garage. Planting, though, was a reflective task and she knew that she would spend the time on her knees worrying about Corey. With each hole she dug, each sprinkle of bone meal, each gentle spreading of roots, she'd be mulling over this visit with his mother. Twice a year, on his birthday and his mother's, he was delivered to the zoo for a visit. When he'd come to them last fall, his birthday was past and they'd missed the chance to meet his infamous mother. Which was their good fortune, the social worker had said, because a meeting with Tina—and when he said her name his voice had an edge like a rusty shovel—usually meant another move for Corey.

"Every year at the zoo?" Ben had asked. "Don't these people have anywhere else to go?" When Wilma tried to imagine the unimaginable— that her own boys had been torn from her when they were small—she was at a loss about where she'd choose to meet them, but Ben reeled off a long list of venues. Museums and parks and hockey games. All places, she didn't dare tell him, which were as crowded as the zoo with Saturday fathers. Her one comfort in the months they'd been trying to fit Corey into their lives was that for once it was Ben's heart and not hers that had dragged them into the drama of the past six months.

Ben had come home one day, livid with a story about a foster child one of his partners was throwing back, and two minutes into the tirade Wilma knew where he was leading. He'd been saying, since Mark left, that the house was too quiet, that she seemed too lonely. When she guardedly agreed with Ben that they could "at least ask," in her mind she'd already conjured the boy and bound him to her as tightly as Mark and Philip.

This morning, Wilma had wished Ben was home to deliver Corey to the zoo. Ridiculous, but the responsibility of returning him to his mother's care, even for one night, had seemed excessive. Something better handled by Ben, who wouldn't have hesitated to march through the gate and ask Tina to give him a detailed itinerary for the evening. Ben, however, had been out of town all week. He'd be home this afternoon. Might even be home now.

Watching Corey move through the gate and into his mother's arms, Wilma finally named the fear that had followed her to the zoo. She didn't think the fence, not even with the slanting row of barbs at the top, would be enough to keep him safe. When this visit with his mother was over, when morning came, he would have vanished. Chances were he'd be found, as he had the other two times he'd run, but this would be strike three.

No, if she knelt in her garden, that fear would hang over her shoulder and whisper in her ear the whole afternoon. Instead, she detoured to the grocery store, to the library, to the bank. When she arrived home at three o'clock, Ben's car wasn't in the driveway, but a blue Honda was parked across the street. Wilma was almost to the front door when she heard the car door open and then slam shut. She turned and watched a diminutive figure sprint across the street, a patchwork leather bag hanging from her shoulder, slapping against her side as she ran. The woman was wearing black leggings, a gold turtleneck sweater that fell straight to her knees, and soft black leather running shoes that were so tiny they looked like ballet slippers and hit the concrete with soft but determined thuds. "Mrs. Howard?" She stuck out her hand. "I'm Kristel Maclean."

 Wilma put down the grocery bags she was carrying. How could Corey have forgotten to mention her visit to the school? This woman was unforgettable. Kristel Maclean's hair was buzzed to about an inch and a half, and gelled. Her scalp flashed white through black spikes. "I've been trying to call but you weren't home." The tone was accusatory. The absence of hair, of a frame for her small face, made her dark eyes enormous behind the square glasses. The rims glinted red in the sun. Rows of small gold circles flashed in the cartilage of both ears, with one larger hoop in each lobe.

"I had to run some errands after I dropped Corey at the zoo." Wilma felt ridiculous explaining herself to this girl. The breakfast dishes were stacked on the counter, and she was exhausted. The front step seemed like a perfectly fine place for a brief conversation, but clearly Kristel expected to be invited in.

Wilma gathered up her bags and pulled a stack of letters out of the mailbox on her way through the door. Inside, she dumped everything she was carrying onto the floor in the hallway and motioned toward the living room. "Would you like something to drink? Juice or a coke?"

"I don't have time." Kristel tapped her wristwatch, a red disc the same colour as the frames of her glasses, and roughly the size of a bread plate. "I have two more calls to make, and I need to pick up my son at the babysitter's by five o'clock."

Wilma let herself be led into her own living room, where Kristel settled in the rocking chair by the window. The room was stifling, the afternoon sun illuminating every dusty streak on the glass. When Wilma stepped past to close the blinds, Kristel thrust a business card into her hand. "My home phone number's on the back," she said. "In case you need to call me about tomorrow. I don't usually give it out."

"No, I suppose that wouldn't be a good idea." Wilma squinted at the black letters. She sat on the couch. Was she supposed to eat the card in the morning, to keep the secret safe? When she looked up, the young woman was staring at her. Wilma tried to smile. To rise above her instant dislike. "That's a different spelling—of your name, I mean. I noticed it on some mail we got from your office." She caught herself before she started to babble about all the people she'd known who were Crystal or Cristal, but never Kristel.

"My mother couldn't read and she couldn't spell." Kristel's voice was flat with a thin layer of grit. "I told Tina Brinkman I'd pick Corey up at nine o'clock tomorrow. I'll call you before I leave for her house." She produced a rolled-up sheet of paper from the patchwork bag. "You need to make a doctor's appointment for Corey. For his camp application. The deadline's next Thursday."

"Camp?" Wilma took the form and pretended to read. Her glasses were in her purse.

The paper wanted to curl against her fingers.

"Yeah." For the first time, a flash of animation showed in Kristel's face. "Wilderness camp for Native kids. Didn't Corey tell you we talked about it yesterday?"

Admit that Corey didn't communicate with them? Not a chance. Not to this woman. "Yes, he did." Wilma said, nodding. "Yes." She tried not to hiss, to unclench her teeth. "But a camp for Native kids?"

"What part of that don't you understand?" A shaft of light through the blinds glinted off Kristel's red frames.

"First of all, nobody's ever told us Corey was Native."

"Oh." Kristel folded her arms and leaned back. "Would it have made a difference?" The edge of the coffee table pressed sharp against Wilma's knees. "It wouldn't have made a difference if Corey was from the planet Jupiter."

Kristel's laugh was halfway between a snort and a bark. "A kid from Jupiter would have a better chance in the system than an Indian kid with a string of middle-class foster homes behind him." Her eyes didn't seem to move at all behind the lenses. "No one mentioned it because, even though it's pretty obvious from his social history, no one ever figured it was important. I do. If nothing changes, I give him about as much chance as a dog that chases cars. Maybe we should back up a few steps, Mrs. Howard. I didn't come here to start a fight."

One of Wilma's fingernails snagged in a loop of the upholstery where she was clawing at the edge of the cushion. She held her breath, listening to the sound of a key rattling the sticky lock in the back door. "Corey hasn't run in two months." Exhaled when she heard the door open.

"And by the stats that means he's about due for another one." Kristel stood up, anchored the bag on her shoulder.

With a tug and a wince, Wilma ripped her nail free just as Ben walked into the room. She pointed at Kristel. "Corey's new social worker," she said, handing Ben the card.

He raised his eyebrows. "And Corey? He's at the zoo, right?"

5 TINA STOOD OUTSIDE THE LARGE MAMMAL HOUSE TAPPING her foot. Corey was off in the bushes, puking his guts out. They'd barely made it inside the door before he bolted.

When he straightened, Tina pulled a wad of Kleenex from her bag and walked across the path. Pasty-faced, he swiped at his mouth with his wrist. "It stinks in there." His chin wobbled like it used to when he was about three years old, trying hard not to cry.

"What a wuss," she said, but she curved her arm around his shoulders. "You must have inherited the old man's nose." Opi kept the bakery doors open in all kinds of weather because even the good smells—yeast, and cinnamon, and hot bread—made him gag if they were strong. "You're a real pretty shade of green. Come on."

She led him to bleachers facing a dirt enclosure outside the elephant house. Thank Christ they'd missed the show. Tina had watched these elephants roll barrels and count with their feet enough times to last her lifetime. This was where she and Opi used to sit on warm days when she was a kid.

"Lie down," she ordered. With Corey sprawled on the bottom bench facing the path, she sat beside him, lifted his head onto her lap, smoothed his forehead. Poor little bugger. His skin was slick and clammy. With each stroke of her hand his thick eyelashes fluttered like insects against the greeny-white skin. "What'd you eat before you came?"

He rubbed his nose with the back of his hand and started to sit up, but she held him down. "Toast," he said. "It was the smell in there. I'm okay now."

Still, she kept one hand on his chest. A few more minutes. She wanted a few more minutes to feel the silky tickle of his hair, the weight of him on her thighs. It had been years since she'd held him for this long. She leaned over him and pointed, as the strips of leather in the huge doorway of the building parted. The old male elephant plodded into the yard.

Corey sprang up, grabbing the edge of the bench as he sat. "Look! What happened to his tusks?"

In place of the long, yellow tusks, there were now two stumps capped with shiny stainless steel. Tina shrugged. "Weird, eh? Guess he had an accident." Wouldn't this give Opi something to yak about? He was like a one-man fan club for that old elephant.

She grabbed Corey's hand, pulled him to his feet. "I'm tired of elephants." And then she tugged at him until he followed to the other end of the bleachers, where they had a perfect view of a pair of snow leopards sprawled on a high platform.

"You okay now?" Tina lifted his chin with her thumb. When he nodded, she fluttered her fingertips at the leopards. She liked to make sparks of sunlight fly off the end of her fingers. A snoopy visiting nurse had told her, when Corey was a baby, that she should be careful not to scratch him when she was changing his diaper. 'I don't change him', she'd said, just to push the woman's buttons. 'I don't want to break my nails.' After the nurse left she'd daubed Corey's tiny fingernails with red. The old man almost had a stroke over that.

Tina watched the mother leopard licking her kittens. She stuck out her own tongue, trying to imagine the feel of the thick fur. A tangle of ropes hung from the underside of the platform, a muddy puddle on the far side of the pen, and that was it for toys. "Hey, Cor, check out the swimming pool. We're having one at our next house for sure." She joggled his skinny chest with her elbow. "What a coat you could make out of these guys, eh?" A family on the path beside them turned to glare at Tina. Mom, Dad and two princesses.

She grinned. "Just kidding." Mom and the kids went back to reading the signs, but Tina could feel the sneaky sideways gaze of the man slide from her face, to her chest, down her legs, and back up again. She winked. First at Corey and then, turning her head slightly, at the daddy of the perfect blond kids. But before she could see the look on his face, Corey stepped around to the other side of her. Between her and the man.

"I feel better now," he said, but he was still as pale as unbaked pie dough.

6 COREY'S STOMACH HAD SETTLED DOWN. HE'D BE OKAY
until they got to Tina's and then he'd sleep. "Can we go see the
tigers now?" he asked.

Tina dug into her bag, fumbled and then pulled her hand
out, empty, fingers spread, tapping her thigh as she walked. Pretty good.
She'd gone a whole hour without a smoke. Much longer though and she'd
be climbing the cages. That's what Wilma's mom said about her own
smoking when she came to visit. That every time she tried to quit she
climbed the walls.

"Hey, Tina?" he said. "How long since you quit smoking?"

"You can still read my mind?" She cuffed him on the shoulder. "It's
been months. But it's still hard, you know. And I'm not sure it's worth it.
What if I die of lung cancer? Big deal. We're all going to die some time and
who wants to get old and ugly anyway?"

"It'd be okay if I smoke then?"

Grabbing his face in both hands, she scrunched his cheeks together,
standing there in the middle of the path, families separating to walk around
them. "Don't even fuckin' think about it! You're supposed to do better
than me." She let her arms drop. "Not that it would take much to win that
contest."

She gave him a shove. "Come on, let's go see the tiger and get it over
with."

There were tiger cubs again. A crowd clustered around the small, caged
area where the babies were tumbling in the sun. While Tina elbowed her
way into the crowd, Corey walked away, circling the larger enclosure. No
sign of the male, but Corey knew he was there, hiding, his stripes blending,
the long blades of grass breaking his outline in perfect camouflage.

Even though he knew them by heart, Corey stopped to read the signs when he'd completed his circuit. The female tiger stretched on the hard-packed earth looking as though she was asleep, except for the twitch of her tail and the flick of her eyes each time one of the cubs came close. Tina was pacing. Corey wished she'd light up and get it over with. He turned to her.

"Did you know the male tiger's a loner? The mother looks after the cubs all by herself."

"Fuckin' cages." She hugged herself and stepped back into a patch of sunlight. "I'd hate this. People staring."

The cubs were done with playing now, and fighting for a place to suck. "They're safe here. At least they're not being hunted. They're endangered, you know." He sounded like a total geek, but he couldn't stop himself. "There are more Siberian tigers in zoos than in the wild."

"Duhhh. Yeah, I do know, Corey. I went to school for a couple of years anyway."

He folded his arms. "Did you know that the Siberian tiger is the rarest of all the tigers? And in Japan they have reserves for Bengal tigers?"

"No shit? What are you? Doctor Baby Biologist? Where'd you pick up all this fascinating information?" She punched him on the arm, and then grabbed at his nose.

He ducked and dodged out of reach. Next she'd come after his ears. He wished she'd cut it out. This was a game they'd played when he was a baby. "I got a book on endangered species for Christmas. From Mark. And I wrote a story about tigers."

"Mark. He's their son, right?" Corey nodded. "Yeah well, maybe you could show me that story some time."

He'd never told Tina that Wilma and Ben had two sons. He still hadn't met Phil, but he'd talked to him on the phone at Christmas time. An awkward conversation, with Corey mostly listening and answering questions. About a week after that phone call, the kid who lived next door had been waiting at the bus stop with Corey and asked him, did he know that Wilma and Ben's oldest son was a fag. And that Ben wasn't his real dad. No, he didn't know either of those things, but Wilma told him later about Phil being adopted by Ben. Trying, Corey was sure, to make him feel better about not having a dad either. Now, when he saw that kid at the bus stop,

Corey walked as slow as he could so he arrived as the bus was pulling up. He could imagine what Tina would say about a fag foster brother.

Tina had taken off down the path to claim the next bench, where she turned sideways, hiked up her knees, and sat hugging them like a kid. He sat at the other end, his arm draped over the back of the bench. A couple of girls were coming toward them, and he felt suddenly stupid. Like he was trying to look like an adult. He hunched forward with his elbows on his thighs.

"So, how's work?" Great, now he sounded like an adult too.

"Same bullshit as usual."

"You still at that parts place?"

The pause was long enough to warn him that a lie was coming. "Sure. Why wouldn't I be?"

Good question. Social workers were always sending Tina to courses and finding jobs for her, but nothing ever lasted. He watched her out of the corner of his eye. Her face was tight. Eyes, lips, jaw, all straight lines. Something was going on with Tina today, something more than smoking and the usual junk. He was tempted to stare her down, but that was another contest he never won. "You should give me the address. Maybe I'll skip school some day and come see you."

"Didn't I tell you to rub a few brain cells together and do better than me? What do you want to see in an auto body dump?"

"Are you still going with that guy who owns the place? What's his name again?"

"Marvin." She shook her head, looked away. "Good riddance."

"I thought you said he was a nice guy. That he knew how to treat a lady. That's what you said, Tina. He knows how to treat a lady."

She flew up off the bench. "Well I was wrong," she shouted. "Okay? It didn't work out." And then she turned and stomped away. He guessed she'd make a beeline for the conservatory. That was her favourite place. Tina really didn't care about the animals at all.

7 BEN FOLDED HIS ARMS OVER HIS CHEST. "SINCE WHEN is Corey an Indian?" he said. This social worker, this Kristel, had looked like she was leaving when he came into the room. She was sitting now, but on the edge of the seat, the chair tilted forward on its rockers as though she was ready for takeoff. "We were told his father's unknown. Correct?"

She rolled her eyes. Honest to God, rolled her eyes at his question. "For the record," she said, "but off record, every social worker who's had this case has the same theory about his father."

She was in a hurry she'd told him, but Ben decided after the eye-rolling moment that she wasn't going anywhere fast. "Are you saying that based on the hunches of Corey's caseworkers you're presuming his paternity?" He wondered how long she'd been here. Wilma had the tip of her finger in her mouth and looked as though she was in pain. He wondered, in fact, how long this kid had been a social worker. She seemed rough around the edges.

Kristel stood up. "I'm looking for any angle I can to give Corey a sense that he belongs somewhere. He's been in seven places in four years."

"And what if we're the last? If it stops here? I'm pretty sure that seven homes in four years isn't a record, Miss . . . " He palmed the card on the coffee table. "Ms. Maclean."

She hesitated. For a few seconds it looked as though she'd sit down again, but there was the watch on her arm, and the ship's clock on the bookcase, and the time display on the VCR in the far corner. Her eyes, huge, black, and unblinking, seemed to sweep the room and gather all those reminders. She stepped away from the chair. "Seven homes don't come anywhere near setting a record. I'm told my brother won that prize, but I won't bore you with the story." She turned toward the door.

"Wait a minute." Ben's fist hit the coffee table, one thump, one quick call to order. "This plan of yours, this camp," he said, "makes as much sense as sending him to Holland for the summer to find his roots. Or are you ignoring the fact that his family is notably Dutch?"

"Oh please." She spun around, her hands on her hips.

Ben turned his palms up. "Okay," he said, "but is that any more ridiculous than you assuming that he's Native and that we're in the same league as a residential school?"

Her sigh was weary beyond her years. Ben felt an unsettling tweak of sympathy. "You know what, Mr. Howard? That's a good parallel. Because really, middle-class foster homes are like present-day residential schools. Look, I'm running late."

He felt Wilma's hand light on his arm, caught the barely perceptible shake of her head. Okay, he'd let the woman go. But he followed her, talking his way across the living room, through the hall, and out the door. "Camp isn't a consideration. We're going salmon fishing with our son out on the west coast in July, and in August Corey's going to Winnipeg to visit his grandmother. That's Wilma's mom. The rest of the time we'll be doing what every other family does in the summer. We'll let you know if we run out of ideas." Kristel kept going down the sidewalk and across the street. So did Ben.

She opened the door, threw her bag across to the passenger seat and then stood beside the car, arms folded, legs braced. "I wasn't going to bring this up. I don't have biases about people's sexual preferences any more than I do about race, but if you're planning to send Corey on a fishing trip with your son, then you'd better reconsider. Have you met Tina Brinkman? She has such a history of . . ."

"Shit disturbing?" Ben interrupted. "Is that what you're trying to say?"

Kristel nodded, just once. "There's a file two inches thick in the Minister's office. Let's not give her more ammunition, okay?"

Ben stood on the street and watched the Honda disappear. For now. Wilma's mom would describe Kristel as the bad answer to a prayer. The other two social workers they'd dealt with since Corey arrived had seemed woefully uninformed, both about the child and about them. Seemed Kristel knew it all. Hell, the fishing trip was a fabrication. So was the trip to Elsie in Winnipeg. He'd pulled all that out of the air to get her to back off.

Wilma was waiting on the front step. She opened her arms. "That was awful. How are we ever going to get along with her?"

"Sweetheart, you ain't heard the half of it." Ben rested his chin on the top of her head. He felt the vibration through her skull when she groaned.

"What else?"

"Nothing we won't be able to deal with if we stay out in the open. How was the zoo? Did you meet Tina?"

"He wouldn't let me. But I saw her."

"And?"

"Young, pretty, what Corey would have looked like if he'd been a girl. Maybe a bit on the tarty side." She tightened her grip around his waist. "I've been kicking myself all afternoon for leaving him. He has a sore throat. He should be in bed, not wandering around the zoo." She leaned back to look at his face. "What's all this about salmon fishing and happy holidays with Grandma in Winnipeg?"

"You heard that, huh? It suddenly came to me that we didn't have any summer plans of our own. You don't approve?"

"Fishing, yes. Grandma, no. She already phones every second day to tell me how to be a mother to Corey. Next Christmas is about right for a visit from Elsie."

"Elsie might be the person to settle Kristel's hash. Can you imagine the look on Elsie's face if she heard that Corey was spending the whole summer at some outdoor endurance camp?"

He'd loved to have seen his mother-in-law at this meeting. At Easter, when the social worker dropped by, Elsie had insisted he sit down with her over a cup of coffee and a hot cross bun. She told him to make sure all of the kids on his caseload were getting enough folic acid. She'd watched a program on television about attention deficit. She told him that her grandson, Philip, had terrible eczema until she convinced his mother—Wilma—to pay more attention to what she was feeding him. It's all related to nutrition, she said. Everything. Ben had wanted to ask her if there was a vitamin, mineral, or amino acid that might have made Phil turn out differently.

"Come on," he said. He opened the door. "We both need a drink. Get the paper and we'll pick a movie, and it had better be comedy." He retrieved the mail from the floor, glanced at the top envelope, and handed it to Wilma.

"I was thinking," she said, "that we should stay home tonight in case Corey calls."

Ben loosened his tie, shook his head. "Willi, he'll be back in the morning. Until then he's in the tender care of his mother."

8 COREY DODGED STROLLERS AND KIDS ALL ALONG THE PATH. When he tried to rush past the monkeys, Tina grabbed his hand, yanked him to a stop. It didn't do any good to tell her for the hundredth time that the monkeys creeped him out, the way they were always swinging and scratching and baring their teeth and screaming. They looked to Corey as though they were making fun of the people, instead of the other way round.

Tina liked them. While she leaned on the fence watching, Corey read the signs. "White-handed gibbons can't swim. I wonder why they put a lake right under them."

"That's life."

Corey narrowed his eyes at a small monkey clinging to the mother's shoulder, glanced sideways at Tina. "I guess it's her job to make sure the baby doesn't fall in the water and drown."

She sniffed. "More like the little twerp has to fall in once so he'll never make the same mistake again."

The gibbon leapt from his mother to a branch, to a hanging rope, then swung through the doorway into the primate house. Corey stuck his hands in his pockets. "No, I don't think so," he said. "Animals are good at protecting their babies." He turned and walked across the road to the glass-walled conservatory.

They waited at the entrance while a bunch of old people in wheelchairs were pushed out the doors. Tina clicked her nails against the bronze statue of two kids, a boy and a girl sharing an ice cream.

"Cute, eh? Looks like you and your girlfriend. Sandi, or whatever."

He hated Tina teasing him about girls. Even more, he hated the way she talked about Shawn, but there was no point in pretending he didn't remember. "Shawn," he said. "And she's not my girlfriend." But she was his best friend. The social worker had let her come along to the zoo with him last year, probably to make sure that Corey didn't run. All afternoon Shawn had plotted how the two of them could take off together. Her wildness had driven Tina crazy.

"Yeah, her. Shawn. What ever happened to her?"

Corey shrugged. He'd meant to ask, but he had a feeling the new social worker wouldn't tell him anything about Shawn. Meanwhile, he really didn't want to talk about her. And he didn't want to look at that statue of the kids—the boy leaning over to take a lick of the girl's ice cream cone. The old people were finally rolling down the sidewalk.

The weight of the air when they entered the building was like the slap of a wet cloth.

While Tina lined up to buy drinks, Corey pushed his way through the crowd at the food concession and down to the garden on the other side. On a bench hidden in the greenery, he closed his eyes. Even the way the plants shimmered and swayed in shafts of sunlight made him feel pukey.

"Hey. Are you okay?" Tina nudged him with her foot.

He nodded, took the plastic cup and held it against his face, glad that the drink was mostly ice. Down here, away from the snack bar, the smell of the indoor forest was so thick and damp he could taste dirt at the back of his throat. Tina sat next to him. Corey squinted at the tops of the trees, the ceiling, the birds flitting past in flashes of light. He used to know the names of the birds in the conservatory, even some of the flowers. When they were still living with Opi, every Sunday—the only day the bakery was closed—they came to the zoo. While they walked around the garden, Opi held Corey's hand, pointing and naming, and crouching beside him to let him put his nose in the flowers. Or lifted Corey to his shoulders to watch the rainbow birds. Then, Opi would nod off on the bench while Corey sat at his feet, sipping at a cup of hot chocolate while he drove two tiny trucks around the cuffs of the old man's brown pants. Tina was never home on those Sundays, not until long after Opi cooked their supper and put Corey to bed.

Corey and Tina had come to the zoo most often in the winter when they had nowhere else to go. Then too, he played quietly beside her while she curled on this same bench, asleep.

His hand slipped involuntarily into his pocket. What had happened to those two little trucks he'd carried everywhere? They were the only toys he remembered from home. He thought they were still with him when he and Tina left Opi's house. He remembered holding them when he went to sleep, the press of the metal against his hand when he snuggled beside Tina in the cold bedroom. They'd lived in a basement suite with plastic tacked over the windows, crackling in the cold wind like ice breaking. Maybe that was where he'd left his toys. At his first foster home, he had a whole case of matchbox cars. But they weren't part of his baggage when he moved.

"Tina?" She'd tilted her head back and closed her eyes. Her throat looked long and white. "Are you awake?"

She sniffed, but didn't move. "Yeah."

Corey pulled the pocket of his shorts inside out, flapping to get rid of bits of lint and crumbs. He waited another minute. "Tina?"

"What?" This time she sounded impatient.

"Do you remember those two toy trucks I had? My tow truck and the tanker?" As soon as he said the words, he was sure she'd laugh. She surprised him.

"Yeah." Her voice was quiet again.

"Do you remember when I lost them?"

She straightened her back and stretched, lifting the hair off her shoulders, lacing her fingers behind her head. When he hadn't seen Tina in a long time, Corey forgot how pretty she was, how even sitting down, she could move as though she was dancing. "You didn't lose them. I kept them for you."

"Where?" Tina didn't save things, not even souvenirs.

"What, why, where, when? Are we playing twenty questions, Cor? Your itty bitty trucks are in my jewellery box." She winked at him. "I figured I'd save them so you can give them to my grandchildren. Better start soon if you're going to keep up the Brinkman tradition of everybody being a grandma before they're thirty."

Never in his whole life had he thought about Tina being anyone's grandma. Even if he'd imagined being someone's dad, he'd never have thought about Tina. How she'd be or what she'd give his kids.

"What else is in your jewellery box?" he asked.

"That's it," she said. "No baby shoes or chunks of hair or dried up belly button."

"Wilma saved her kids' teeth."

"Who the hell is Wilma?"

He wanted to bite back the words. He'd honestly thought he was saying them to himself, in his head.

Tina's lip curled. "Oh yeah. Foster Mommy. Wilma, eh? Wilma Flintstone. And I bet he's Fred, right? Big, fat dope of a guy?"

Why did he start this? He'd been so careful not to say their names, because no matter what they were called, Tina always found a way to turn people into jokes. "Or maybe Wilma the Witch," she went on and on. "Is she a witch, Corey?" She pulled a face. "A foster witch?" Pretty Tina could be so ugly, so angry and tough. "Hey, they're not mean to you are they?" Pinpoints of light, like sparks, flashed in her eyes.

"No, Tina. They're okay. Honest."

She looked at him hard. "Anything weird happens, you tell me, right?" She dug in her purse for a small coil-bound book and a pen. "Write the number in here. I might need to call you." When he hesitated, she grabbed his hand and pressed the pad of paper into his palm. "Just do it. You think I'm going to show up and make trouble? I have all the trouble I need, Cor." He printed his name and the number. Considered doing it sloppy so she couldn't read it, but printed it neat.

"You meet that new social worker yet?"

He nodded. He didn't even want to think about Tina and Kristel together. Tina would arch her back and walk sideways around the social worker like his kitten used to stalk spiders.

"Watch out for her, okay? If she starts bad-mouthing me, I want you to write down every word she says." She shoved the book into her bag, looked suddenly thoughtful. "What do you call the foster witch? Mom?"

Wilma and Ben had never suggested he call them Mom or Dad or even Aunt or Uncle, the way some people did. The first time they met, Ben had stuck out his great big hand. "Hi, Corey. I'm Ben, this is Wilma." Even Wilma's mom, Phil and Mark's grandma, had told him to call her Elsie.

"No," he said. "I call them Wilma and Ben." He figured if Tina ever met Ben, she wouldn't make fun of him. Probably the only thing she'd think of was "Big Ben," and that sounded right. Ben was even bigger than Opi.

Again, she leaned back and closed her eyes. "Aw, what difference does it make? You never called me Mom either. And according to some judge, you're not my kid anymore. You belong to the government, Cor. I wonder how that feels."

The painful breath he'd had been holding in his chest exploded, propelling him off the bench, along the path. He stumbled and caught himself and started to run.

"Corey! Hey, wait!" She caught up with him outside the door, grabbing the back of his shirt. "Aw jeez, Corey, that was dumb. This stuff makes me crazy and mean." People were staring at them. Tina pulled him close. Hugging him for no reason. "It just came out. And it was a shitty thing to say, even if it is true."

But never "I'm sorry." Tina never said "sorry."

He had grown. With Tina's arms around him, for the first time ever he felt as though he was bigger than she was. He squirmed away from the heat of her skin. Even though he'd started shaking as soon as he stepped out the door into the cold wind, his face was burning. "Forget it, Tina. Where I'm living now is okay."

The wind whipped her hair across her face. She pulled an elastic out of her pocket, gathered the crackling hair over her shoulder, fastened it into a ponytail. "Well how am I supposed to know that? They keep moving you around without telling me dick all about where you're going. You could end up adopted and living in California, or locked up with a bunch of losers somewhere."

Any minute she'd tell him that none of this was her fault. Any minute. He sighed. "Nobody's going to adopt me. They already tried that twice and it didn't work, and I'm not crazy enough to be locked up." A couple of kids were chasing a peacock across the lawn. The bird strutted ahead of them as though it really didn't care, but when they were close enough to touch, it flew up and over the fence into the flamingos' cage.

The bottom of Tina's shirt ruffled and lifted. She shivered. "What do

29

you want to do now? I need to get out of here by four. Listen, Corey . . ."

If he didn't get to lie down somewhere he was going to die. "Tina," he said, "can we go home?" He took a deep breath. "Do you think you could find those trucks when we get back to your place? I'd kind of like to have them." His teeth were clattering. Any minute he'd bite off his tongue.

"My place. Right. That's what I was just going to tell you about."

Finally it was coming. The screw-up. Who would she blame it on this time? All around them, mothers and kids were marching by. Dizzy from watching, he dropped down on the grass.

"Are you going to barf again?" Tina knelt beside him, her face next to his. "Cor? What's wrong?"

Another shaky breath. "Just tired. Can we stop in the gift shop on the way out?"

Wobbly-legged, he stood up, Tina holding his arm until he brushed her away.

"What do you want at the gift shop?"

He tried to smile, his dry lip sticking to his top teeth. "Remember those candy sticks we used to eat on the way home?" Candy stick in one hand, little truck in the other, it had seemed such a long walk back to Opi's house, even though it was only two blocks away. He was pleased with himself for remembering the candy sticks. What he wanted from the shop was a birthday present for Tina. He wished he'd brought something with him so he could whip it out of his pocket and say, "Surprise!" He'd like to see the look on her face if he threw a present at her in the middle of her excuses.

"Candy stick. Yeah. Root beer for you, strawberry for me." She tweaked his ear. "It's the least I can do for my kid."

At the door to the gift shop, she stopped. "I'll be back in a minute. I have to pee."

Inside the door, Corey stood behind a rack of postcards, watching through the window. Tina lit a cigarette, then walked in the opposite direction of the bathrooms, toward the main gate.

9 PAST THE TICKET GATE, INTO THE CTRAIN TUNNEL, BY then Tina was running. The exit was crowded with kids and strollers, people already starting home.

Out in the sheltered courtyard leading to the street and main parking lot, she finally found the sun. Since she'd left home, she'd wished she'd worn a warmer shirt, but this one was new and she wanted to look nice for Corey.

She stood on the curb, trying to catch her breath, scanning the parking lot. If Simon would drop off the face of the earth, she could have her kid back. Maybe she could have her life back too. Simon would never stop being jealous of Corey, no matter how many court orders kept the kid away from her, or how many restraining orders kept Simon from them both. The longest Simon had ever stayed away was when she was pregnant. He'd just served three months in Spy Hill, so the kid couldn't be his, he said. Should have known she was jailbait, a slut, didn't appreciate anything he'd done for her. Fortunately, his math was so bad he never did figure out the real possibilities. Tina had chosen to leave that question unanswered. She didn't want to know.

She heard the motorcycle coming from blocks away, the sound as familiar as Simon's heartbeat, stamped out her cigarette, and stepped off the curb. He roared up and slapped the seat behind him. "Let's go!"

He was either too stupid or too stubborn to get the sign language. Finally she screamed. "No! Turn the damn thing off and listen to me!"

He swung his leg over the seat. In one slithery motion he was so close, the new leather smell of his jacket made her eyes sting. "'No,' is not what I want to hear from you, Tina. You said you'd ditch the kid by four o'clock."

"I can't." One good thing about Simon: he told so many lies himself, he never knew whether Tina was lying or telling the truth. "We couldn't get hold of his social worker."

"He's a big boy. He can get himself home. Or not. I don't give a rat's ass what he does." He grinned. "Come on, Tina, you and me have a birthday to celebrate." He lifted her hair, bent his head, ran his tongue down her neck from her ear to the scooped neckline of her shirt. Behind him, two girls about Corey's age gawked at them.

"We can celebrate tomorrow, or all weekend or all month if you want to, but I only have one day with the kid. Then I don't see him until his birthday. Give me a break. I didn't know you were going to be here today."

He was nibbling on her earlobe. "Awwww. You want I should get some special stationery made that says Spy Hill Hotel, so the next time I can send coming-out cards to friends and family?" She knew enough to keep still. If she moved, his teeth would close on that fleshy piece of ear. "Paulette was supposed to give you the message."

"Get yourself a better secretary," Tina said. "Your sister only passes along information she's supposed to keep to herself."

All around them she felt the rush of people leaving. Families and bunches of kids on their own, but no lone kids. No kid like Corey, all by himself. She shoved away the hand that was playing along the bare skin between her shorts and the bottom of her shirt. "Your dickhead brother lost me my job."

"Tina." Simon's face was so close to hers he was a blur. All hair and teeth and eyes that merged into one hard glinting light. "I heard rumours about you and the boss. Gordie kindly offered to play guardian angel, y'know? And now I'm back to pay the rent, you don't need that brain-dead job." He'd spent the afternoon at the bar. His lips would taste of beer and cigarettes, just like his breath. "Fifteen minutes to get rid of the kid, and then I'm coming to find you. Or should I come now and have a talk with Corey?"

Tina walked back through the tunnel, each step jarring another tear from the corners of her eyes. Time was up. Corey would have to go home.

10 COREY WANDERED AROUND THE GIFT SHOP PICKING up coffee mugs, paperweights, napkin rings, checking the prices. Lots of things he could buy with twenty bucks. But why bother if Tina had dumped him? How could she do that? She'd freaked last year when his foster mother was late picking up him and Shawn. She went ballistic at the Stampede when he was about six, and Simon was supposed to take him to the men's toilet but sent him in by himself. She'd stormed in to get him right in front of all of those guys at the urinal. He glanced out the window again. No sign of her. He'd better forget the storming and screaming Tina. Remember that it wouldn't be the first time she'd walked away and left him. Long-gone Tina was nothing new.

His heart thumped in time to the music playing in the gift shop. Drums and screeching birds. Jungle stuff. The girl at the cash desk was watching him while he browsed, like he was going to lift something. He took self-conscious care to return each item to its place. When he looked up, she surprised him by smiling.

"Need some help?" she called. The shaking of his head sent the room whirling around him. Corey reeled and the floor flew up to meet him.

When he dared open his eyes, he was on his back with the girl leaning over him. "Don't try to get up yet!" she said. He shifted onto his side. "Is there someone with you?" She was crouched beside him now.

The spinning had stopped. Corey looked up at her, too tongue-tied with embarrassment to answer. She was a thin, plain-looking girl, someone you'd never look at twice, except that the top three buttons of her shirt were open. He tried to look somewhere, anywhere else, but his eyes kept flicking back to her chest, to the nametag hanging lopsided from her collar. Rochelle.

The bell on the shop door jingled. "Corey?" Tina sounded out of breath. "I'm looking for a kid who came in here a few minutes ago," she said. He scrambled to his feet.

She was beside him in seconds, straightening his T-shirt, turning him around as though she was checking to make sure he wasn't broken. "What the hell were you doing down there?"

Corey wanted to sit on the floor with his head between his legs, but he needed to complete his mission. "I was looking at something on the bottom shelf." He glanced at the boxes of T-shirts. Yeah, right. "Can you wait outside for a minute? I need to get something, a surprise."

"Jeez, Cor!" She tapped her watch. "Whatever! But make it fast."

He stared after her as she wrenched open the door. A man leaned on the other side of the window, smoking. There was something about the way he flicked his hand, blew the plume of smoke straight over his head, held one shoulder higher than the other. But Tina went past without a glance, to sprawl on a bench in the sun.

Corey shook his head. He had to stop this. It couldn't be Simon, because Simon was in jail. Tina had told him so in November. Still, he saw Simon everywhere. The whole city was full of guys who looked like Simon.

He moved carefully down the aisles, his eyes straight ahead, turning his whole body when he wanted to look at something so the room wouldn't start spinning again. He picked up a china tiger with yellow eyes. Fakey looking. Anyway, Tina wasn't good with prissy ornaments. In one of her hissy fits with Opi, she'd smashed a whole herd of glass horses in the china cabinet. He turned toward the cash desk. Rochelle smiled, wriggled her fingers at him, pointed to a rack on the counter.

Earrings—silver elephants with their trunks outstretched. Sparkly, dangly elephants. He flicked them against the card and watched them dance.

"Are they for your sister?" The third button on her shirt was still open. It must be on purpose, but she didn't look like the kind of girl who wanted her bra to show. A bright yellow bra like a flashlight under the zoo shirt.

The nasty glob in the back of his throat made it hard to talk. He shook his head. "My mom." It took a minute before Rochelle figured it out. She glanced startled toward the door.

"That was your mom?" Her own ears were bare, sandy-coloured hair tucked behind them and held with gold barrettes. She took the earrings from him, pursed her lips, and nodded. "Perfect," she said.

Earrings paid for, bag tucked safely into his pocket, Corey stepped outside. The sunlight felt like slivers of glass in his eyes. No Tina. The bench was empty, the courtyard full of moms herding their kids into the bathrooms. No sign of her on the sidewalk between the gift shop and the entrance. He walked in the other direction, toward the bridge. Finally she was there, leaping around and waving on the other side. He trudged across, taking care not to look at the swirling water.

"Here." She shoved a cardboard tray into his hands—a drink, a hot dog wrapped in a napkin, a greasy box of French fries. "Maybe if you eat, you'll quit falling down every ten minutes. Let's go sit. I've gotta talk to you about something."

They climbed down through the rock garden, to the iceberg-shaped building where the polar bears and seals lived. You could watch the seals in their tank from the outside too, from bleachers around the side of the building.

Corey sat on the bottom row with the tray of food on his knees. He looked from the grease-stained cardboard to Tina. "You can have the hot dog and fries. I think I just want a drink." Mistake. She bought it for him, he was supposed to love it.

"You could at least try." She dug through her bag. "You got any coins? I need to make a phone call." He scooped the change from the twenty out of his pocket, handed it to her. "I'll be back in a minute." She walked away, disappearing around the corner of the building.

He did try. Gagged on the first swallow of hot dog, spit the mushy lump into a napkin. By the time she came back, he'd dumped the rest of the food. If he sipped slowly, the drink would last until they got home.

"No friggin' bears left in there. Did you know they're tearing this place down?" She lit a cigarette and picked flecks of tobacco off her tongue while she watched him. Her eyes narrowed behind the curl of smoke. "So what's with the dizzy stuff?"

He crunched a mouthful of ice. "I'm getting a cold or something. It's no big deal."

He liked this spot. It felt safe with the circle of benches on one side, the glass wall of the seal tank on the other. No one else around. "The bears died."

Ben had told him that awhile ago. The last polar bear was sick. Dying. There were going to be new buildings at this end of the park. Corey tipped the cup for another lump of ice, watched a seal cruise by in the tank.

"Cor, about tonight, if you're not feeling good maybe you should go home." She was sucking up to him, making it sound like a favour. "We'll tell your social worker we're, like, postponing our visit. Who says we have to come here every time? I could take you to a movie next week. Maybe out for supper after. Would you like that?"

So pleased with herself, Corey couldn't bear to look at her. He watched the biggest of the seals glide up to the glass, blink long-lashed eyes, flip onto its back.

If he phoned, Wilma would be here in twenty minutes. She'd run up to the gate in her blue sweater, chewing her bottom lip. If it was after five –from the quiet, Corey was sure it was getting late—she might send Ben. They'd have to call his social worker to tell her Tina had screwed up. On Monday, the intercom would come on in Science class: "Please send Corey Brinkman to the guidance office." That Kristel woman would be sitting there, waiting. Corey was scared stiff of Kristel.

He fingered the earrings in his pocket. They were for later, after pizza and ice cream cake, but maybe he should give her the present now. Get the party started.

"I'm not that sick," he said. "I don't want to spoil your birthday."

"This is how it is, Cor." She stubbed out the cigarette. "I ran into a couple of friends while you were in the gift shop. I told them it was my birthday and they kinda want to take me out to this club."

When he didn't answer, she kept on babbling. "Say we put off the birthday party till next weekend, when you're feeling better? It'd be a lot more fun."

His chest was pounding, hammer beats echoing in his skull.

"Say something! You know this silent treatment drives me nuts, Corey. You're being selfish."

Eyes on the murky water in the seal tank, he ran his tongue over his cracked lips. "Okay." Deep breath. "After our party, you go to the club with your friends. I'm twelve. It doesn't matter anymore if you leave me home alone."

"Thanks!" He felt the spray of her spit on his cheek. "You're a real little shit for bringing that up, you know. You think I didn't try to be a good Mommy? It was never good enough. Now you're sick, and I'm trying to make the best of this day, and it's still my fault. What exactly do you want?"

He could look up into Tina's face, mumble his "sorry." The purple splotches would fade, she'd unclench her fists. He'd phone, go home with Wilma and Ben. Tina would go out with her friends.

"Sorry" wouldn't come. There was a lump the size of a shoe blocking his throat.

Tina lit another cigarette. She sat down hard on the bench, puffing smoke through her nostrils like she was breathing fire. "So what are we gonna do?"

Dumb seal must have gone around twenty times by now. Always the same flip in the same place, the same wink. Nowhere else to go. "Please let me come, Tina. I don't care if you go out. Honest. I won't tell the social worker." He was pleading so hard he was panting.

She threw the cigarette at her feet and stomped on it, rising beside him, shaking her fist. "Stop it! I know where this is going, Cor. You get all worked up and then you run! Don't you ever run away again, you hear me?" Her fingers dug into his arm. "One of these times you curl up under a bridge or behind a bush, the wrong person is going to find you, Corey Brinkman!" When he flinched, she let go. With a shaky hand, she patted his cheek. "Aw, come on. Let's try again next week. You're sick."

Corey pulled away from her hand, her eyes, her voice. "You're my mom,

Tina. You're supposed to look after me if I'm sick. That's what moms do."

She sagged. All the air seemed to leak out of her. He was sure she was going to give in, until they both turned to the sound of footsteps approaching from the other side of the building. Two seconds, and Simon swaggered into view.

"Hey, Corey! Long time no see."

He'd dreaded the time when Simon would step out of his nightmare and back into his life for so long that there was almost no fear left for the moment. Just a horrible sense of betrayal. He'd given her the money for a phone call, and she'd called Simon.

11 THE OLD MAN HAD IGNORED THE RINGING, sliding lower and lower in the recliner until he could no longer see the kitchen wall where the phone hung. He was expecting no calls. Inez was with her daughter in Edmonton, and there was no one else to whom he'd care to give the time of day. Probably someone wanting money, whatever he could afford to help find missing children. That was a good one. That was yesterday's plea. "I have three missing children of my own," he'd shouted. "I gave to that charity already."

When the ringing didn't stop at five, six, ten times, he knew it was Tina. He could imagine her with the phone mashed against her ear, cursing him for not answering. "Brinkman, get an unlisted number," Inez told him with a face like she'd sucked a lemon. She'd only had to meet Tina once. "Get an unlisted number."

"Yes, yes," he'd waved her words away. "Someday." But how could he? Corey was out there somewhere. For two years he'd bounced back and forth between Tina and Social Services, and then she'd let him go. Signed him away, except for a few hours of visiting each year. But still, Corey was out there somewhere. What would he think if he tried to phone and the number was unlisted?

He hoisted himself out of sleep and looked at the clock. Four thirty. No wonder his brain felt clotted and cold like cottage cheese, the back of his throat bitter with heartburn. He'd meant to close his eyes for a short nap after the bowl of stew, but he'd been asleep for two hours. Would still be asleep if not for the phone.

A sour belch erupted from his burning gut. Christ, if Inez would only believe him when he told her he wasn't born to eat food so hot it caused mortal pain on the way in and the way out.

For another minute, he let his shoulders fall against the back of the chair and closed his eyes. He'd been dreaming about home. So often now his sleep took him back. Was it any wonder he'd awoken, yearning for the porridge and vegetable soup of his childhood? During the war there was only bread as thin as his mother's lace curtains, sparrows snared on the kitchen windowsill, and, at the worst of times, rats. He could still hear his mother when she set the covered dish on the table with tight lips. *Het is maar vlees.* Just meat, and they quietly ate whatever the pot scraped up. But that was a long time ago, far away from this kitchen and the woman who cared enough to bring him a pot of stew.

He eased himself out of the chair and stood at the window. The wind had picked up; behind the fancy copper towers that all but obliterated his view of the sky, a bank of cloud was forming. Not likely to rain though. He should water the seeds he'd planted yesterday.

He looked for his old cardigan at the back door, but instead there was a different sweater on the hook. Dark brown, with a pattern like blue and yellow lightning bolts in bands around the sleeves. He shook his head. Inez. *Brinkman, you old fool, this will teach you for letting a woman into your house after all these years.* After Bepp died, there'd been women—he was, after all, a healthy man—but he never brought them home because of Anna, and then Tina. He rubbed his face with his hands. Afraid of teaching them bad morals. What a joke that turned out to be.

He unlatched the screen door, stepped into the backyard. A flock of starlings quarrelled in the branches of the Mayday tree, black shadows against the lacy flowers. From a sack on the back step, he scattered sunflower seeds across the rows of freshly sown beans and peas. Give the sparrows something to pick at besides his garden. A mangy-faced squirrel clambered the top rail of the fence on scratchy nails, stopped a few feet away, waiting.

"Yes, yes, you lazy old pirate, but only a few. Go fend for yourself." He reached into a second bag and dusted a handful of peanuts onto the grass, cracked one for himself, chewed slowly. He'd get rid of the fiery stew and make a potato soup tomorrow.

He was a good cook. He'd fed Anna after Bepp died, then Tina and the boy. Had he been dreaming about Corey too, that the child felt so close today? As though he was still on the stool at the kitchen sink, the tip of his tongue poking through his lips, watching the curls of vegetable parings drop off the peeler. Brinkman wiped a bit of moisture from the corner of his eye with the cuff of his sweater. Leave it be, he repeated to himself once more. For four years he had made that his litany. Leave it be, let them go. What a feeble old man he was today.

Sometimes for weeks, he could forget about them all. Pretend it had been only Bepp and him, and spread the loneliness back to when she died. Imagine his life if, when Bepp was gone, he'd packed his bags and moved on. Maybe to Africa, where his brother had run. But he couldn't leave Anna behind, and to take her to Bepp's mother in Rotterdam when she was already eight years old would have been too much for a child who could hardly keep up in school in English, never mind learning another language.

He was glad for the heavy sweater. The sunshine on his window was a tease. Outside, a cold wind from the mountains tore at the new leaves. But a good day for the zoo, if they were dressed warmly. Somewhere he had a trunk full of wool that Bepp's mother had sent from the old country. Skeins and skeins of wool that was never knit into the sweaters she must have imagined for her grandchild. One tiny sweater Bepp had finished, finally, but by then Anna was too big. He'd unwrapped it from the tissue the day Tina was born and carried it to the hospital. Then, against everyone's protests, with Anna leaning on his arm, he carried Tina home, and carried her for six months while she cried from colic. It seemed he would carry her forever.

Today he had vowed he would not answer the phone. No matter how many times she rang, he would sit in his chair and pretend he was deaf. He'd wished her a happy birthday. That was enough.

A week ago she'd called. "Opi they're going to cut off my phone."

"I'm not paying for a phone for your boyfriend's business."

"It's not for Simon! I don't even know where Simon is. But I get to see Corey on my birthday and I need to have a phone."

"If you don't know where he is, he's in jail." He'd hung up without a promise, but he slipped the money into an envelope the next day with a birthday card and walked to where she lived to put it in her mailbox.

As always, when he thought of Corey his ears were tuned to the zoo.

41

Each year the road got busier and the sound of the traffic louder. Soon, no zoo sounds would reach this house, not even the roar of the tiger that long ago had drawn the child to the window with eyes as big as soup bowls. Such a strange and beautiful boy. Brinkman wondered what it was now that called to his great grandson.

12

SIMON WAS SO CLOSE, COREY COULD SMELL THE familiar hot metal scent of him. "Get up, and get moving. I'm taking you to Mommy's house."

"Go away." Corey felt his words creep small as mice from behind his fingers. He had his hands over his face, eyes squeezed tight to shut out the black boots that were toe to toe with his running shoes.

And then Tina's voice, all puffed up again, "You wanted a sleepover, we're having a sleepover." He peeked at her, standing there blazing at both of them with her hands on her hips. "You heard Simon. He's taking us home and then he's leaving. Get up, Cor."

He tried to curl into himself, to make the two of them disappear.

"Sure, Corey. I'll give you a ride. You'd like that, eh?"

Corey let his hands drop. He looked straight into Simon's eyes. "I don't want to ride on your stinkin' bike."

Simon's fist came down like a hammer on his shoulder. Corey swung his legs over the back of the bench, scrambled to his feet.

"Simon!" Tina's voice like a whip. "I told you to keep your mouth shut, and keep your hands off my kid."

"It's not my mouth that's the problem here, Tina." He put one big boot up on the bench and leaned forward, his face inches from Corey's. "Still don't know how to share, little man? I thought by now you'd have learned."

Behind Simon, beyond the screen of bushes that separated this enclosed space from the main path, Corey saw a uniform separate itself out from the stream of people. A security guard strode to the corner of the building, arms folded, watching.

With a flicker of his eyelids, Simon followed Corey's gaze to the man. "You've got three minutes, Tina. I'll wait for you at the gate." Two long strides and then he stopped, lit a cigarette, and strolled away, head back, sliding through the crowd with a snaky skill Corey had once practised.

"You lied!" Corey turned to Tina's stark white face. "You said you wanted to go out with some friends. You told me on the phone you didn't even know where he was. If anyone—anyone!—knew he was with you, I'd never get to visit you again!"

"I didn't know he was around till he showed up this morning. You weren't supposed to even see him. I had it all worked out." She clenched his shoulders, her nails biting into his skin. "But it never works out, you know?" For once, real tears shone from her eyes. Not the sparkly diamonds she could squeeze out whenever she needed them. These were big messy tears that would smear the makeup around her eyes. "Corey, you don't understand about me and Simon. About why I have to be with him. It's just the way it is." She dug in her bag for coins, his coins. "Here. Go phone your foster mother and tell her you're sick, you need to come home."

He snatched the money, and ran to the deserted polar bear house. At the payphone, he pretended to call. With his back screening the phone, he randomly pressed number pads while the thumb on his other hand held the coins hard against his palm. Knowing Tina was watching from the entrance, he moved his lips, nodded, and cradled the phone. Money still clenched in his fist, he stomped back to her, every footstep reverberating in his head.

"You can go."

She hesitated. "You talked to her?"

He stared mutely back, not daring to open his mouth, his stomach heaving.

"Should I wait with you?"

When he shook his head, his ears buzzed with the movement.

Tina's lips moved, forming sounds he couldn't hear. She looked as though she'd try to hug him, but instead she let her fingertips trail his bare arm from the edge of his sleeve to his clenched fist. "Okay." Fading in and out. "She's coming, and she's going to look after you. Right?" The words tangled with the static in his ears.

He hesitated, glanced away to a smoking figure beyond the bridge. Not Simon. Some other man.

Tina leaned close enough to brush her cool cheek against his. She turned and walked away. Her brown legs flashed in the sunlight, and then she melted into the crowd and was gone.

Corey leaned against the wall with his eyes closed. That same hammer was at work inside his skull. The coins burned into the palm of his hand. Faking the call was a stupid thing to do. He needed to go back to the phone, call Wilma, and wait at the gate. Easy. But his feet were moving in another direction, and they were going to get him in trouble. Again.

13

TINA KNEW SHE SHOULD HAVE WALKED BACK to the tigers with Corey, waited until Wilma Wonderful showed up. Instead, she tried to catch up with Simon, and got to the parking lot in time to see him flip her the bird and roar away.

"Asshole!" She screamed after him. "You're a double-A Asshole, Simon!"

She stamped her foot and cursed the old man. If only he'd answered the phone, her plan would have worked perfectly. "Opi," she was going to say, "you have to keep Corey overnight."

Opi wanted to see Corey so badly it was making him crazy, she knew it was. But he was so damn stubborn he'd probably die before that happened. Every visit she had with Corey, she made sure her grandfather knew. Once, she'd seen him shadowing along behind them. He had no use for Social Services—who did?—and swore he'd never try to get Corey back. The one thing that might crack through his thick skull was the chance of Corey running into Simon. That was what she'd planned to tell him. "He has to stay here until morning, because Simon's at my place."

She paced, keeping one eye on the road for Simon in case this was another one of his cute games. She'd give him ten minutes.

So fucking bloody stupid! She shouldn't have phoned. She should have walked over there with the kid, said "Here you go. See you tomorrow." The old man was always home. Nowhere for him to go. The only hitch would be if Inez was there. Tina had no idea where the hell this woman had come from. Younger than Opi, with a crazy accent as thick as the old man's, but from some place in South America. Listening to the two of them made Tina's head hurt. It was a fucking miracle they could understand each other. But Tina didn't need a translator to figure out what Inez thought of her.

A gust of wind ruffled a stack of newspaper on the bench a few feet away, lifted the top sheet, and skimmed it across the cement to wrap around Tina's ankles. She kicked free and shivered, wishing she had a sweater.

She sat on the bench and stretched her legs in front of her. Not bad. She'd been sunning on her balcony for two months to get this tan. Even before the snow was gone she'd wrapped up in a blanket and sat there smoking for ten minutes every day with her legs on the railing. They were smooth and brown and slim. Nothing like the pasty stumps on the woman dragging her two kids toward the parking lot. Tina had no respect for women who let themselves go as soon as they had kids.

She dug in her bag for her smokes, but the crumpled package was empty. After promising herself that she wouldn't smoke in front of Corey, she'd sucked her way through the whole damn pack. She slumped on the bench.

She wanted to kill Simon, but when they'd tangled on her bed a few hours ago, the world had felt sweet again. A couple of months ago Simon's sister, Paulette, had dragged her along to a psychic. The woman said Tina and Simon had lost each other in another life and, no matter what happened, she had to hang onto him in this one. But then what about Corey? Madame Olga had also said she felt a deep sadness in Tina, unresolved grief over a lost child. She told her to never stop hoping, that the kid would find her. Then she'd gone off in left field and said "she," a daughter, would find her. So did that mean, in her next life, she was going to hook up with the baby she'd aborted right after they took Corey away from her?

"Hey, Tina!"

She put her face in her hands and groaned. The real psychic experience— think about Paulette and *poof!* There she came, clumping across the pavement on four-inch platform sandals. She was dragging a snotty-nosed kid about two years old with her right hand, and a red plastic purse as big as a suitcase on her left. If her jeans had been any tighter, her stretch marks would have shown. The black T-shirt had been washed so many times it was turning green. "Jesus, Paulette. What are you doing here?"

Paulette flopped onto the bench, kicked off her shoes. She dragged the kid up between the two of them. "I've been walking my damn feet off looking for you. Simon showed me your birthday present this morning, so I figured you'd be down here with Corey." She folded her arms, and stuck out her feet, wriggling the ugliest set of twisted, blistered toes Tina had ever seen. "Pretty good I remembered that, eh?"

"Yeah, that's real bright. What do you want?" Tina glanced sideways at the little boy who was now leaning on her, his face wet against her arm. Grabbing her purse, she wrenched away, and shoved a wad of Kleenex at Paulette. "Aw fuck, Paulette! Wipe his nose!" She swiped at the mucousy smear on her arm, squinted at the kid. "Who is this?"

Paulette hauled the child's head back so that he was arched across her knees, kicking, trying to squirm away from her heavy hand. She clamped the tissue around his nose. "Blow!" she commanded. "This is Sheldon. My little sister Genevieve's kid. She's in detox, so I got him for two months. Foster care."

"Oh that's rich. While your kids are in somebody else's foster home."

"Nah, my kids are with my mom in Saskatoon."

The boy stretched listlessly across Paulette's bulging thighs. Tina reached with one finger to touch his forehead. "He's burning up. The kid's sick, Paulette. Take him home and put him to bed."

"It's just a cold. He's had it for a couple of weeks. He's tired from walking around the zoo." Paulette shook the kid's cheek between two of her fingers. "We had fun, eh Shel? Tell Aunty Tina what the monkey says." Sheldon looked back at her with dull eyes. "Kid does an imitation of a monkey that'll split your gut."

"It's not just a cold," Tina said. "He's got green snot pouring out of his nose. Didn't anyone ever tell you that when it's green there's an infection?"

"Fuck off, Tina. I got my kids back. Where's yours?"

Paulette dug a package of cigarettes out of the big red purse, pulled one out, and tossed the pack at Tina. "Didn't see you for a long time," she said. "Your name came up when I was at Social Services picking up my cheque for him." She looked down at Sheldon, blowing a cloud of smoke over his sleeping face. "Today I figured it would be kinda nice to see Corey. I thought him and Sheldon could play."

Tina snorted. "Corey's twelve. He doesn't play anymore." She could imagine the look on Corey's face if she'd been dragging Paulette and Sheldon with her.

"So where is he? Isn't he supposed to stay overnight with you?"

Tina stared at her. "Who told you that?"

The big, brown cow eyes blinked. "I dunno. Isn't that what you always do on your birthday?"

"No, it's not. I always meet Corey here, then I go home and so does he."

Paulette shrugged. "I guess I heard wrong. I figured if Corey was staying with you I could leave Sheldon at your place and go out with you guys tonight." Her chin began to jiggle, and for a minute Tina thought she was going to cry. "Fuck, Tina. I haven't been anywhere since I got this kid. The one time I leave him sleeping to go to the store for smokes, the social worker shows up. He's pounding on the door, the kid's inside screaming his head off. I wasn't even gone fifteen minutes." She sniffed. "And now I got a cousin working at Social Services. She's the one told me you had Corey staying overnight."

Oh wait a minute. This was too rich to be true. "Your cousin? Kristel is your cousin?"

"Yeah. All those Macleans are my Aunty's people. Second, third, fourth cousins, I don't know. Hey, she asked me if Corey was Simon's kid."

Which also meant that Kristel was Simon's cousin. Second, third, fourth, or whatever, it was all in the family. Tina threw the cigarette butt into the street and folded her arms. "And you said?"

"I told her the kid don't look like Simon."

Tina felt numb. Cold. Like someone had opened a window behind her and let winter pour across this bench in the spring sunshine. She let Paulette babble. Corey had finally stopped asking about his father a couple of years ago. "Get over it," she'd told him. "I don't know. Even if I did, I wouldn't tell you. You're in the same boat as I am, Cor. I've never gone looking for my daddy, because I'm sure what I found wouldn't be a thrill."

In that big, fat document in her dresser drawer, sheets of paper pressed with a fancy seal, and those lousy words: In the matter of the child, Cor David Brinkman. There was a form that was blank except for the typing in the section that said Father: unknown. One of the only smart things she'd ever done for Corey.

Paulette stood up, draping Sheldon over her shoulder like a sack of rice. He whimpered, but barely stirred. "You taking the train?"

Tina nodded. "That's it? You came all the way down here to see if you could dump the kid at my place?"

As they walked together toward the CTrain entrance, it dawned on her. Not for an evening. Not just to have Corey look after him while Paulette dragged her fat ass along to Tina's birthday party. She would have disappeared sometime during the night. Tina would have been stuck with Sheldon for days.

"Nah, like I told you, I wanted to see Corey. No shit, Tina. I always liked that kid. Did I tell you I seen him at the Stampede last year? He looked like some rich little faggot. He could've walked right by and pretended he didn't know me, but not Corey. Gave me a hug."

Tina knew Paulette had a soft spot for Corey. Everyone did. He was smart, and cute, and well behaved. She'd made sure of that. Big-hearted Paulette had tried to convince Simon that Corey was his kid. That way, she'd told Tina, Simon wouldn't be jealous. Wouldn't ever hurt Corey. She might have told Kristel that Corey didn't look like Simon, but for years she'd claimed that he had Simon's eyes, Simon's hair, Simon's build.

Paulette was patting Sheldon as she walked, thumping in time to her footsteps, but the kid was out cold. She paused to shift his weight. "Tina, that Kristel's got a spur up her arse, you know. When she was no bigger than Sheldon here, her mom left her and the other five kids in a car outside the King Eddie one night in winter. They damn near froze to death. They gave the three biggest ones back, but Kristel and her little brother ended up like Corey, living in a whole bunch of foster homes." Paulette stopped patting, and held the kid's bum tight to her chest. "She had a kid when she was sixteen, but she made Social Services pay for everything so she could haul her skinny butt to school for about ten years. Now she's looking down her nose at the rest of us. Figures if we weren't lazy and stupid, we'd do the same."

They stood on the platform now, waiting for the train, Paulette puffing with the effort of carrying Sheldon up the stairs and talking non-stop. Her forehead and upper lip were beaded with sweat, her breath got wheezier with each step. "Reach in the side of my bag would ya, and find my puffer."

Tina handed her the inhaler, hesitated, then held her arms out for Sheldon. She felt a wave of revulsion when his nose connected with her shoulder, and a surge of sadness as the hot cheek nestled into the hollow under her chin.

Paulette drew three deep breaths from the inhaler. "If I had her brains, you think I'd waste them on being a friggin' social worker? She could have been a lawyer. You gotta give her credit for raising shit to get what she wanted, but why'd she have to turn into such a hard little bitch? You watch out for her, Tina."

"Why didn't you tell Simon to watch out for her. To stay out of the way. I've been dodging bullets all day because of him."

Paulette opened her arms to take Sheldon back. "Jesus, Tina, you still don't get it do you? Fourteen years you've had a ring in Simon's nose. What I'd give for a guy who's that crazy about me."

Oh shit, not this line again. "Save it," Tina snapped. "I don't need you telling me what a lucky girl I am." In Paulette's world, finding a guy who only pushed you around when he was drunk was true love.

So Kristel was from that world too. But with the guts to get out of it. It looked like the best way to watch out for Kristel would be to stay away from her. By the time Corey's birthday rolled around, and it was time for the next visit, there'd be a new social worker.

The door slid open, and Tina followed Paulette onto the train. Maybe things had worked out in the end. But only if someone remembered to tell Kristel that Corey was home, that she didn't need to come to Tina's in the morning. That was Foster Mama's job, and Tina hoped to hell she'd do it.

14

WILMA STOOD IN THE DOORWAY TO COREY'S ROOM. The walls were still bare, no adolescent signature scrawled there in posters or banners, but at least the room was beginning to look lived in.

For the first two months, Corey had behaved like the perfect guest, barely rumpling the bed when he slept, hanging the towels with corners matched, carrying his toothbrush and shampoo back to his room and stowing them in a plastic bag in the open suitcase. No matter how many times she'd laundered and folded clothes, deposited them in the dresser drawers, hung his jeans in the closet, everything found its way back to the suitcase.

He'd made his bed this morning, the comforter trailing long across one side, heaving over the width of the bed in hills and gullies. Wilma peeked under a corner at a wad of socks, T-shirts, and shorts jammed against the foot of the bed. She picked up his clarinet from the floor and perched at the head of the bed, smoothing first the pillowcase, then the cool line of the instrument.

"Corey has a good ear," the band teacher told them at the last interview. Especially for someone who'd never had a music lesson, and had missed the first month of school. Someone who'd changed schools so often he couldn't remember where he'd been, Wilma wanted to add.

The French teacher, too, had praised his ear. Corey seemed, she said, to have a smattering of another language in his head as well. German, maybe? Dutch? It slipped into his French. The first Wilma and Ben ever heard of his grandfather was when they asked him where the words were coming from. "My Opi," he said, and left the kitchen table, closing his bedroom door behind him.

Wilma pulled the clarinet case out from under the bed, and carefully stowed the instrument. The room smelled faintly of young male, that same musky scent of the room when Mark and Phil shared it long ago. Before Phil claimed the basement bedroom for his den. Wilma felt a rush of loneliness for her boys. She lifted the pillow, held it to her face. She wasn't allowed to hold this child long enough to learn his scent.

In the foster parents' class, they'd been told that they should never even sit on the child's bed for fear of allegations. Wilma's hand had shot up. "You mean we're not to touch a foster child in any sort of affectionate or reassuring way? Not ever?"

The social worker had looked sympathetic, but shook her head. "Not unless you're very careful about the appropriateness and, even then, you leave yourself open to misinterpretation. Unfortunately, kids in care become savvy pretty quickly, and abuse allegations are something they can use against you."

"Against us?" Wilma had whispered to Ben after she sat down. "I thought we were all on the same side."

How many times had she come to this room in the night when there were bunk beds against the wall? Philip, peacefully asleep in the bottom bed, his blond hair fanned across the pillow. Mark, the one with night terrors, wide-eyed in the top bunk. Wilma, on tiptoes, brushing the dark curls off his forehead, hoisting herself into the warm bed, curling around his sturdy body until he closed his eyes and his breathing became slow and deep.

When Corey cried out in his sleep, Wilma was always instantly awake, her feet twitching to take the short trip down the hall, put her head on the pillow beside his, and pull this slim brown-haired boy into the safety of her arms. To chase away the nighttime monsters, because there were already too many daytime demons that he had to learn to defeat on his own.

"I'm afraid to ask what you're thinking, sitting in here."

Wilma looked up, startled. Ben was leaning in the doorway.

"I was thinking that I don't know Corey's scent."

"Jesus, Wilma, don't say anything like that when this new social worker is lurking. She'll think you're kinky. She's already warned me that Corey had better not have any contact with Phil."

Wilma pulled the pillow tight across her knees and leaned on her elbows. She was going to have to hate Kristel Maclean instead of just disliking her intensely. Phil hadn't been home in almost five years, and here was more fuel for Ben's pig-headed stand. Compliments of Kristel.

"It's not an issue," Wilma said. "We've been through this with every single social worker and it's not an issue." So many questions, and what she'd wanted to shout at them all was, "Stop worrying! He's gone. Won't come back until we meet him halfway and we're cemented into place. No chance of movement here."

The card that had come in today's mail was leaning on the sugar bowl, strategically aligned with Ben's place at the table. A Mother's Day card, ten days early. Sweetly floral, with a gooey verse that she knew Phil had chosen with a lopsided grin. The familiar script sloping across the inside of the card was almost identical to her own.

A hug and twenty-four kisses from your favourite son. Got a ride to Calgary next week (via Winnipeg—won't Elsie be surprised? Hoping she'll put us up for the night). Job interview. I'm staying with friends, will phone when I get there. Make a reservation somewhere nice for the Monday after Mom's Day and I'll take you for lunch? Bring Corey. And Dad if he has time. Love ya Mama Willi!

Wilma didn't give a damn what Kristel had to say about it, Corey was coming along to lunch, and he was finally going to meet Phil. The invitation to Ben was a mere formality. Until Ben was willing to visit Phil in his own home, Phil wasn't coming back to theirs. And while Phil was living with another man, Ben wasn't crossing that threshold. And if Phil was in town but wouldn't come home, Ben wouldn't meet him anywhere else either. Around and around and around, with Wilma trying to soften Ben, and Mark reminding his older brother that their dad could be as thick as a stone wall, but was still their dad.

"Looks like everything is an issue with Kristel," Ben said. He sat down on the bed beside her and patted the lumpy quilt. "Finally looks like there's a boy living here. Did you find anything interesting in the bed?"

She shook her head. "I'm afraid to look too closely."

The day Wilma uncovered the dirty pictures in Mark's room, Ben had found her red-faced, too choked to speak. "What have you got there?" She'd thrust the stack of glossy magazine pages into his hand, and rubbed her own hands against her sides feeling as though they were covered in slime.

"Wow!" Ben whistled long and low. "Where'd you find these?"

"There." She'd pointed to the bed where a brown envelope protruded from between the box spring and mattress. "I was going to flip the mattress. Right there." This time she kicked at the bed with her stockinged foot. "Right there in Mark's bed."

"I wonder where he got them." He sat on the edge of the bed and began to sift through the pages.

"I don't care where he got them. Probably from some other kid. I want to know why!"

"Oh come on, Willi, he's thirteen." He'd picked up the envelope, stuffed the pictures inside, dropped it onto the bed, stood up, and pulled her close. He kissed her with soft, kind lips, slid his warm hands under her sweater, and then tilted her chin up so that he was looking into her eyes. "This is how you want him to think about girls, right? Sweet, tender stuff?"

"Yes," she said. "That's it."

"Someday he will. I've talked ad nauseum with him and Phil about respect and relationships, but when you're thirteen it's all about animal instinct—lust. Don't say anything, okay? I'll talk to him."

She'd never asked what he'd said to Mark. Probably told him to find a better hiding place. But now she was curious. "Ben, what did you do with that brown envelope from under the mattress?"

"I added the pictures to my own collection. His were way better than mine." He tweaked her chin. "I can't remember. Probably slipped them in the paper recycling bin with great reluctance. Kidding aside, Willi, you'd better brace yourself for more of the same with Corey." He looked away. "I'll be relieved when you find the dirty pictures. Never happened with Phil did it? I don't want to think about what was hiding under his mattress. Maybe I should have given him a subscription to Hustler instead of all that crap about respect and feelings."

She stood up. No point in screaming at Ben that maybe he should accept that Phil's being gay had nothing to do with him, or anything he did or didn't do while the boys were growing up. They'd been over that ground so many times, Wilma had worn out her shoes.

Ben stretched out on Corey's bed and closed his eyes. "I'm beat. Wake me up in half an hour would you?" And then he turned onto his side with his face to the wall.

Wilma closed the bedroom door behind her, intending to wander outside and check the petunias in the garage window, but got only as far as the kitchen table. She picked up the Mother's Day card. A hug and twenty-four kisses. Since he was six years old, Philip had penned progressions of this line. Seven kisses, eight kisses, nineteen kisses later. When she was ninety years old, the seventy-two kisses would send tears tracking through the wrinkles and pooling in the folds of her double chins.

If they were going to a movie, they should eat soon. But Ben was tired, and Corey wasn't feeling well. He might need to come home, and if they weren't here when he called ... How stupid. Wasn't his mother's house 'home'? Wasn't she capable of giving him orange juice and Tylenol? He was probably in bed already.

15

COREY KICKED AT THE SHALE, HIS EYES ON THE ground as he walked the few steps to the seal tank. He pressed his wet cheek to the glass and watched a grey, speckled torpedo cruise past. On the next circuit, the seal glided to a stop with its nose to the wall of the aquarium. Corey tugged his shirt from the waistband of his shorts, scrubbed his face.

"What you are staring at? You're in as much trouble as I am, locked up in a stupid tank of water. If I could let you out, you'd be in even worse trouble."

He tapped a finger at the tip of the seal's nose. His own eyes were reflected in the shine of the chocolatey pools behind the glass. From where Corey stood, the surface of the water above the seal looked as unbreakable as the glass walls of the tank.

Out of the corner of his eye, he caught a flash of pant leg coming around the corner.

"Zoo's closing, son. You should be on your way out." The security guard loomed over him. "Folks around somewhere?"

Corey raised his arm and pointed to the farthest corner of the building. "My mom's over there."

"By the lions?" The guard folded his arms across his chest. *Always,* Corey thought, *always people in uniforms stand that way when they talk to kids. But never to adults. If Ben and Wilma were beside him, the man's arms would be at his sides. And with Tina beside him? Then what? Men struck a different pose in front of Tina.*

"Yeah. At the lions. Guess I'd better go find her."

He ignored the lions on the grassy hillside, slipping instead behind the monolith of rock beside their enclosure. A stroller hung with diaper bag and jackets was parked next to a cavern, carved deep into the man-made stone. A woman knelt beside the lions' fence, doling out juice boxes to a gang of kids. Corey climbed into the cave, onto a recessed ledge, feet up, legs pulled to his chest. With his forehead resting on his knees, he waited for the pounding in his head to stop so that he could come up with a plan.

"What are you doin' in there?" He lifted his head. The kid, silhouetted against the light at the opening, sniffed and rubbed a streak of snot across her cheek with the back of her hand. Coarse, black pigtails sprouted from a perfectly round head. He'd ignore her. Sometimes that worked.

"I said, what are you doin'?"

Not this time. He glared at her, turned his face to the inside wall. A larger shadow moved across the stone.

"Come on, Breanna. Time to go."

"There's a boy in here. I think it's Corey."

He bolted upright on the clammy bench.

"Corey?" The woman's voice was too familiar. No wonder the face, the voices made him shudder. Breanna, Brendan, Tyler and whoever else was living at Carmen's house.

"Corey Brinkman? Is that you?"

Nowhere to hide. He unfolded himself from the bench, nodding, slipping back into the light.

"Well for heaven's sake!" Carmen beamed at him. Jeans, baggy grey sweatshirt, wisps of hair twisting every which way around her face, trying to escape from the messy braid. She clapped a hand onto his shoulder. "Hey guys, look! It's Corey."

He felt as though he'd been caught halfway out his bedroom window in Carmen's house. Even though she had no reason to suspect that he was guilty of anything, his brain was spinning excuses. Flushed cheeks, a tongue that wanted to stumble all over itself, not a chance he could look Carmen in the eye.

He would probably still be living with Carmen and her pack of kids if he hadn't run that last time. Only two strikes allowed in Carmen's house. She'd picked him up from the police station with a face wiped clean of smiles.

"I can't do this, Corey. There are too many other people in my house who need me. I can't be lying awake worrying that you've been picked up by some lunatic and you're on your way to Vancouver in the trunk of a car."

But the thing was, he knew that. He knew that Carmen never took older kids or teenagers and had only taken him because there was nowhere else for him to go. He'd been kicked out of another foster home, the one where he'd lived with Shawn. Carmen's was supposed to be temporary. After a couple of weeks, Carmen said it was fine, he could stay, but that she wouldn't put up with runaways. But knowing that he'd have to move again if he ran from Carmen's had made no difference to his feet. None at all.

He couldn't remember what had happened at school that day, but he did remember the relief he felt when he turned down a different street instead of going home to Carmen's. He hopped on the first bus that came along. It was a day just like this one, with brassy sunshine scorching his arm through the bus window. He'd ridden all the way to the edge of the city, where there was suddenly nothing beyond the houses except fields and, off in the distance, the blue shadow of mountains. Then he'd followed the last of the passengers to the door. Same as today, the cold wind had dried his sweat to goose bumps. Skeleton houses circled around a lake that had been hacked out of raw earth. He'd spent the night in one of those half-finished houses. He could still remember the smell of new wood against his cheek. Early in the morning, one of the construction guys had found him and called the cops.

Carmen had given him another chance after the first run. She said it was because she liked him. The other kids were attached to him, and everyone's entitled to one bad choice. But when she took him home from the police station the next time, his suitcase was waiting at the front door. As usual, the house was a mess and the little kids climbed all over him, but he hadn't really wanted to leave, he hadn't meant for things to work out that way.

And here she was again, smiling. Looking as though she'd just asked a question and was waiting for the answer. "Fine," he said. He swallowed, freshly surprised at how much it hurt. Like he'd swallowed a sock full of needles.

"Carmen, do you have any Tylenol with you?" He knew she would. Carmen never left home without her bottomless bag of wet washcloths, baggies of pretzels and dried fruit, frozen juice boxes, and a change of clothes for the kid who'd be sure to pee his pants or throw up.

She nodded as though that were a perfectly normal question coming from someone you hadn't seen since you kicked them out of your house about a year ago. She patted the bulging plaid bag on the stroller and was reaching into it when she stopped herself, a suspicious question mark sliding across her wide eyes, her smooth forehead.

"What for? Are you alone, Corey? What are you doing here?" She raised a hand to his forehead. Quick and cool.

"You're burning up! You should be home in bed."

"I will be. Soon. I'm waiting for my foster mother. She's picking me up in, like, half an hour. She said to wait by the lions."

"She left you down here by yourself?"

For sure, tonight she'd be on the phone to one of the other foster mothers she hung out with. "Who'd leave a kid, a runner like Corey, alone at the zoo? What kind of a foster mother is that?" she'd ask.

"No," he said, shaking his head. "I was here with Tina. But she had to go at four o'clock. She had a doctor's appointment." He was getting very good at this. Looking right into her face and lying.

Carmen's lips pulled tight over her teeth, her nostrils flared. "Oh right. Tina."

Tina had come to Carmen's once, in a cab, to pick up Corey for their visit. It was the first time she'd ever been allowed to come to one of his foster homes. And the last time. She'd curled her lip at the clothes Corey was wearing, made him throw away his shirt when they got to the zoo.

"That place is a pigsty. They took you away because of where we lived, and they put you in a bloody pigsty." He'd almost corrected her. Why they took him away had nothing to do with their house. It was Simon. But when she was like that, ranting and blaming someone else, you couldn't talk to Tina. "How much attention is she giving you with a dozen snotty noses running around? Look at your shoes. What's she doing with all the money she's getting paid is what I want to know."

It had never seemed to Corey as though Carmen had much money. She looked as poor as ever.

"So your foster mom will be here any minute?"

"Uh huh. Only I have a sore throat and I was supposed to take another pill while I was here, but I forget my jacket and I had the bottle in the pocket."

She looked at him with one eye closed. "I'm not sure what's going on, Corey, but if you have a sore throat I guess Tylenol isn't going to hurt you." Kneeling beside the stroller, she fished a plastic tube out of the diaper bag. "You don't look too good, pal." She shook a tablet into his outstretched palm. "I think I'd better wait with you."

He stared calmly back at her, the Tylenol crumbling with the sudden heat and moisture of his hand, the heat of all that lying. Clapping his palm to his mouth, he licked up the bitter powder, gagged when he tried to swallow.

Carmen snatched the juice box from Breanna's hand. "Wash it down. I'm going to phone to make sure your foster mom's on her way. Not that I don't trust you, Corey, but I'd hate to see you screw up again." She dug a rumpled grocery receipt out of her bag. "Here. Write the phone number on this."

How many times was this going to happen today? If he gave her a fake number, she'd know as soon as she called. He scribbled Wilma and Ben's phone number on the scrap of paper. Crossed his fingers. Hoping for what? That Wilma would answer and be able to read his mind from halfway across town, and come down here without asking any questions. And then they'd live happily ever after. No, he'd better hope that Wilma was outside in the garden, that Ben wasn't home yet. Or that Carmen would trip over something on her way to the phone and break her arm.

Carmen's train of whining kids straggled up the hill, across the bridge, with Corey tagging along, fretting, looking every which way for an escape route. The gift shop was closed now. Carmen lined up the four kids on a bench. "Sit! Corey's going to mind you while I phone."

They watched her stride away, the big diaper bag swinging against her hip. Now what? Run? Leave the little kids alone? When he looked down, all four were staring at him, inching farther toward the ends of bench to make room in the middle. Corey groaned. As soon as he sat, Breanna crawled onto his lap, laid her cheek against his chest and, with a sigh, stuck her thumb in her mouth and closed her eyes. He felt like he was sliding backward. In a minute Carmen would be back. He'd end up pushing the stroller out the gate. They'd belt the kids into her van. By the time they pulled up at her house, all four would be asleep. He'd help her carry the droopy bodies into the house, and line them up on the couch in front of the television. Within an hour she'd have them fed, washed, and in bed. Compare that picture to the picture of Ben and Wilma's quiet house; he was a moron for getting this far into trouble.

The little boy on the other side of him was leaning heavily by the time Carmen stomped back. "The phone's busy."

"That's probably Ben. He makes a lot of calls when he gets home from work. I bet Wilma's waiting for me at the other gate. I remembered while you were gone that she said to meet her at the gate. The one by Dinny." He waved his hand at the river, at the splash of bright green poplar trees along the path that would take him back to the tigers, and the gate where he'd met Tina. The path he had no intention of following. "I'll walk back. I'm sure she's there."

"I guess I'll take your word for it. I'm parked on this side. It's late and I have to get these guys home. You have money for the phone if she's not there?"

"Yeah. No problem."

She gathered the kids off the bench, lifting a whining Breanna from his arms. "You're okay, Corey?"

"Sure. She'll be there." He felt chilly with the loss of Breanna's warm weight.

"No, I mean where you're living now." She worked for a minute on her hair, tucking wisps here and there, before she picked up the smallest child—her own kid, Corey thought, but he really couldn't remember—and strapped her into the stroller. "We think about you often, Corey. I'm sorry it didn't work out at our place."

The taste of the Tylenol and warm apple juice clung to his tongue like fur. He looked longingly at the fountain outside the washrooms. "It's okay. They're nice people."

"Yeah? Well, you make sure you don't mess up this time." She knelt with her back to him, zipping up the line of jackets. In the minute she was occupied, Corey reached down, picked up her diaper bag, and jiggled it against his leg, working his hand down the inside. He slid the tube of Tylenol out with his palm, then a quick transfer to his pocket. Just borrowing, his friend Shawn would have said.

When Carmen was finally organized, Corey watched her straggly parade weave its way to the door of the CTrain tunnel.

The wind had died, at least in this sheltered spot. He raced to the water fountain, gulped until the swallowing hurt more than it helped, then sat down on a bench with the late day sun warm on his arms. Two girls passed by, both with small gold rings pierced through their nostrils. Like Shawn. Funny how she'd popped into his head like she was telling him to steal the pills. He pulled the plastic bag out of his pocket. Too bad for Tina. The next time he saw Shawn, he was going to give her the elephant earrings. She had so many holes punched in her face, so many rings, she'd probably wear these in her nose. No present for Tina, and he wouldn't tell her any of the stuff he'd been saving either. Like how he was playing in a band, and learning French, and how they had this Grandma, Elsie, and she was so much like Opi but so different too. On second thought, Tina wouldn't want to hear about Elsie. It would be like telling her about Wilma saving teeth.

Corey had found that box on the top shelf of his closet with a bunch of other stuff. Inside there was a heap of yellowy-white kernels. When he took the box to her, she'd looked embarrassed. "Oh. Just teeth," she said.

Wilma had saved her kids' teeth. Phil's and Mark's. He liked that about Wilma—that she was the sort of mom who saved things.

The courtyard was almost empty now. If he followed the path Carmen had taken, he'd come out through the train tunnel, into the parking lot. Up and over the hill was Memorial Drive. He was sure he still knew the way, but a heaviness in his legs anchored him, weighted him to the curved back of the seat. On his left was a wilderness of paths he didn't know. 'Aspen Woodlands', the sign said. On his right, the Prehistoric Park.

Corey closed his eyes and felt his face relax as though the skin was melting against the bone. The tight knot in his stomach loosened. The confusion, the muddle in his head shifted and was still. He was at the zoo. There wasn't another place in the whole world that he knew better than the Calgary Zoo. For right now, he could stop thinking about where to go. He'd already arrived.

16

BRINKMAN SAT ON HIS FRONT STEP WATCHING the rush hour traffic on Memorial Drive, throwing peanuts to a mangy squirrel. The wind felt bitter, even through the heavy sweater. Coffee was what he needed. Good strong coffee with four spoons of sugar and, a little later, a slice of bread.

All the while he sat, he had one ear cocked for the phone, not because he intended to answer it, but he liked to know when Tina called. To prepare himself for the next time.

Finally he stood, clapped his hands at the squirrel, and went in to boil coffee. While he waited for the dark smell to fill the kitchen, he sat at the table, running his hands over the worn Arborite as though he was dusting it with flour. Two years since he'd closed the bakery, and still he awoke at four every morning. His hands never stopped fashioning loaves of bread while he ran through his list of regrets.

His saddest failure was that he'd lost the boy. If only he'd held his tongue through the filthy accusations and kept his temper. Tina was so desperate at that point, she'd argued with the social workers that even if they wouldn't give Corey back to her, at least they could let him go to his Opi.

He went to their office that winter morning as they asked, walked in circles downtown looking for the right building. He'd arrived five minutes late, then waited forty-five minutes more to be ushered into a cubicle by a social worker who looked scarcely older than Tina. All the way there, Brinkman had practised his speech, a carefully worded plea to have Corey returned. The man interrupted his first sentence.

"How old was your daughter," he wanted to know, "when your wife died?"

"I thought," Brinkman answered, "I came here to talk about Corey, not about my wife."

"We don't have much social history for Corey." The man went on scribbling on his page, not looking up. "Tina's only given us a few sketchy details."

Sketchy, Brinkman thought, *was a good way to describe the child's history.* Somehow, though, even without Tina's help—he could imagine Tina with her hands on her hips and her lip curled, and for a moment he was proud of her—somehow they snooped out the details of his family. He leaned forward so that his large hands were on the edge of the desk, so the young man could not avoid looking at him. "I can take care of my grandson. He does not need to be locked up in a home."

"Mr. Brinkman, Corey is not locked up anywhere. He's staying with a family very capable of looking after children who've had traumatic experiences."

"What traumatic experience?"

Now the man's bug-eyes behind round glasses stared at him. "You didn't know Corey was assaulted by your granddaughter's boyfriend?"

"Of course I know that, and I know also the boyfriend is walking around free while the boy is locked up. Does that make sense?"

Mr. Social Worker lifted his pen from the page and, behind the glasses, his eyes were like slate. "Apparently the other thing you don't know is that Tina is denying Simon Miller had anything to do with Corey's injuries. She says he fell off the back step."

Cornelius Brinkman stared back at the challenging eyes. "What does Corey say?"

"Exactly what his mother told him to say. That he ran out the back door onto the slippery step and went flying through the air and broke his arm when he landed against the tree." He tapped the file folder in front of him. "There's a report from six months ago when he fell off his chair and broke his front teeth. Your grandson isn't a particularly clumsy boy is he, Mr. Brinkman?"

"No! He's a good boy." *En goede jongen, such a good boy,* he thought. "He would do what his mother asked."

So now she'd taught Corey to lie. Corey, who couldn't even look you in the eye when he broke a corner off the cinnamon buns while they were cooling. The old man sighed and looked away. The walls of the cubicle were padded and upholstered, with splotches at regular intervals, as though greasy heads had rested while they waited. The air felt old, stale. He was finding it difficult to breathe.

"I can look after my grandson. What else do you want from me?"

"How old was your daughter? Anna, is it? How old was she when she had Tina?"

"Sixteen." He slid the words out from between heavy lips.

"And the baby's father?"

"She wouldn't say."

"And how old was Tina when she had Corey?"

"Fourteen."

"Corey's father also unknown?"

He shifted in his chair, his eyes on the young man.

"Mr. Brinkman, when your wife died, and you and Anna were left on your own, did you contact any social service agencies? Didn't you think, didn't anyone suggest, that a young girl might need a mother, or at least someone to talk to? When she was pregnant, didn't anyone tell you there were options available? Counselling, at least. That she was too young to care for a child?"

"No!" He pushed himself out of the chair to tower over the desk, gratified to see the social worker press back in his chair and glance toward the doorway. There was an audible clearing of a throat from behind the partition, the sound of someone rising. "Nobody suggested. What are you suggesting? That I wasn't a good father to the girls? That I'm not fit to look after Corey?"

"I'm suggesting there are a lot of questions, Mr. Brinkman. Two very young girls pregnant, two unknown fathers. No one in the family willing to give any information."

So. This was why they had called him here. The pieces of the filthy picture they were painting slid into place. Brinkman reached across, seized the social worker by the front of his turtleneck shirt, and dragged him forward so that he sprawled on desk. Instantly, a pair of strong arms seized him from behind.

They never charged him with anything, but they never talked to him again about looking after Corey either. Only once, a woman had called and said she wanted a meeting. He'd hung up on her. He'd had enough of meetings with social workers. He would leave it to others to keep the boy safe.

17

COREY WATCHED A LITTLE KID IN A STROLLER licking a fistful of ice cream cone. He could taste ice cream, the way it would melt down the back of his throat, cool and sweet. *Don't think about food.*

Wilma and Ben would be eating supper soon. He dreaded meals when he first moved in with them—the only kid sitting at the table with two adults. Worried that he'd make a mistake, forget his manners. Tina had been strict about things like, 'chew with your mouth closed' and, 'keep your elbows in' and, 'don't lift up your cereal bowl to slurp the milk'. Opi slurped and smacked, his arms on the table, grease on his chin. Corey wondered how Tina knew all the things moms are supposed to bug you about. Her mom ran away years ago.

The kid had bitten the end of the cone now and was sucking on the bottom, ice cream trickling from his hand to his elbow. Tina would have grabbed that cone, licked the edges clean. When she handed it back, there'd be about a spoonful of ice cream left. She didn't carry a wet washcloth around in her bag, like Carmen, but she could snatch something away from you like a snake swallowing a mouse. The only time Corey had ever seen that was here, in the reptile house at the zoo. It was gruesome. He'd screamed so hard, Tina had to take him outside. And Simon. Simon always reminded him of snakes.

When he saw the security guard coming across the bridge, Corey stood and walked slowly up the hill. As soon as he knew he was out of sight, he made a quick left turn into the men's toilet. The place stunk. He stood at the urinal and tried to pee. For hours he'd had to pee, but now all he could manage was a dribble. There were voices outside the door, then fading into the girls' toilet next door. He washed his hands, soaped, rinsed, splashed his face with water. Took his time doing all the things a kid should do, as though someone was watching. On the other side of the wall, pipes creaked. More voices, footsteps. He peeked out.

A mess of wagons and strollers were parked outside the gift shop. There was a pile of junk in one of the wagons. Papers, a water bottle. A jacket? He shivered. Someone was moving around in the gift shop, a shadow at the window. What would Rochelle do if she saw him steal somebody's stuff from the wagon? Probably come out with that dopey smile to ask him how his mom liked the earrings. Probably still had the buttons undone on her shirt.

Corey stood up tall and walked out of the washroom without looking toward the shop window. Straight to the wagon. He scooped up a red sweater, a pile of newspaper, started to pick up the water bottle. Half full. He imagined some kid sucking on that bottle while his mom pulled him around the zoo. A kid with a runny nose, slobbering into the water. No thanks. He leaned against the wall for a minute while he got his bearings.

One last glance around, then he darted across the road. On the left side of the path into the prehistoric park, Ankylosaurus was roped off like Dinny. On the right side there was an amphitheatre built into the hill. Only a shell of a building, but it would be warmer than sleeping in the open. If he curled up under the last row of benches, no one would see him from the doorway. All he wanted was to put his head down on the woolly ball of sweater. To sleep. Maybe all night.

When he rounded the side of the building, he saw a padlock on the wooden gate. His throat tightened. He stuck his fist in mouth, bit down hard on his knuckles. Okay, so the Tylenol hadn't cured him and the door was locked, but there were lots of other places to hide. There always were.

He was tempted to run deep into the prehistoric park, then leap behind a pile of rock. Or slip into the bushes bordering the path, creep toward the top of the hill where he'd be able to see if he was alone. Yeah, right. Like no one would notice a kid pretending he was in a chase scene in a dumb movie. He trudged slowly up the middle of the path, hands in his pockets, the sweater and newspapers tucked under his arm. Gawked around, but kept moving. If anyone asked, he was walking through the park, across the bridge, back to the same gate he'd come in. *Don't do anything weird.* He'd learned a long time ago that the best way to be invisible was to look like you knew where you were going.

At the top of the hill, he stopped to stare at T. Rex rearing up over the waterfall with a jagged yellow grin. What if he came back to Wilma with one of those teeth in his hand? 'If you guess what this is,' he'd say, 'I'll never run away again.' Except how many times could you promise? Every time he ran away, he'd sworn to someone that he'd never do it again. And to himself. He lied to himself as much as to anyone else. When Ben and Wilma found out that he wasn't with Tina, they'd know for sure that they couldn't trust him. Who wanted a kid you couldn't trust, sleeping in your son's bedroom?

On the lake below, not a ripple disturbed the reflection of Tyrannosaurus on his hillside. Corey felt himself drawn down the path toward the glassy surface, imagining a hiding spot at the bottom of the lake where the liquid sun would wrap around him like a blanket.

Still moving deliberately, trying not to look like a lost kid, he stood beside the water, scanning the routes that intersected here from all directions through the park. When he glanced down, he saw a boy in the water—a skinny, sick-looking kid who suddenly dropped to his knees. He dipped his hand into the lake, trickled cool water over his cheeks, waited for the bits of mirror to collect back into a watery image. Did he look like a boy who knew where he was going? No. He looked lost. But he had an idea. Just part of a plan, and if he could find somewhere to hide, he'd think it through.

He stood and checked out the possibilities. The best slopes were pounded with signs—pictures of feet with big Xs across them. Once, when he was little and came here with Opi, he'd decided to play a trick, to hide. He'd scooted behind one of the jutting ledges of rock. Bits of falling gravel had given him away, and the old man's voice boomed through the park. *Kom hier! Ondeugende jongen!* Corey froze, stunned that his Opi would call him a "bad boy."

When he'd skidded down the gritty slope on his bum, landing at Opi's feet, a big hand grabbed him by the collar. Opi hauled him over to the sign.

"You see that? It's written so even idiots who can't read know what it means. We obey the rules. Do you understand?" Maybe it was a good thing he never saw his grandpa any more. This way he didn't know about all the rules Corey had broken.

He stepped over a 'no climbing' sign, wedged himself into a crevice where there was barely enough room to hide from view, leaned back, and let the rock hold him.

18

IF TINA HADN'T PULLED OUT TWENTY BUCKS after they got on the train, Paulette would have followed her all the way home.

"Here." She reached across Sheldon's limp body to tuck the bill into the pocket on Paulette's T-shirt. "It's all I've got. Take the kid home and put him to bed. Pay one of your cousins to babysit, and you can come out with us for a while. I'll phone you when I find out where we're going."

"Aw Tina, I don' wanna take your last bill."

"Don't worry about it. Simon'll spring for rent and buy the groceries. He likes playing house, especially after he's been locked up for a while."

Paulette blinked at her, face all wrinkled up like she was trying really hard not to say what was on her mind.

"What?" Tina rolled her eyes, crossed her arms. "Same old shit? I don't appreciate your brother?"

"Yeah, that. But mostly you don't have to be sarcastic about everything, Tina. Maybe tonight you could act like you're having a good time? You spoil everybody else's fun when you sit there with your nose in the air."

"Many gracious thanks, Miss Manners. I'll keep that in mind."

No goddamn way was she going to let Paulette tag along, and she'd make sure Simon didn't phone either, but at least she wouldn't feel guilty after giving her the twenty. In spite of her big mouth, Paulette was a good shit. She'd done Tina a few favours when nobody else would even talk to her.

"Here's your stop." She swung her feet to the side, to let Paulette pass. "Put that kid to bed as soon as you get home!" She watched Paulette step out onto the platform and trudge away. Two blocks to the bus stop, and another twenty minute ride before she was home.

Three more stops for Tina. She kept her feet in the aisle, hoping the good-looking suit who'd just climbed on would take Paulette's seat. But he stepped aside to let an old lady sit down instead. Muttering, and dragging her shopping bag across Tina's lap, she started in on a rant about parking and transit and why the hell she had to pay for a bus pass. Tina ignored her, watched Mr. Perfect Gentleman instead. He was standing, hanging onto a post across the aisle from her. Caught her looking at him. Winked.

She ran her fingers up the back of her neck so that her hair rippled across her shoulders. Crossed her tanned legs, stretched her neck so the skinny shirt rode up below her bra. God, if only someone like him was taking her out tonight. She'd put her hair up so that curls wisped around her face. She'd wear the strapless black dress Marvin had given her for Christmas, and skimpy shoes with three-inch heels. 'Fuck me' shoes. They'd go someplace where there was candlelight and white tablecloths, and waiters in white jackets, and no bouncer at the door. She could imagine the way this guy's skin would smell. Like expensive men's cologne, and starched shirts and good food. No stale cigarettes, or tongue that tasted like it lived in a beer can. Even though Marvin took her nice places and knew how to act like a civilized human being, he still had stubby, callused hands, and the metal and grease smells of the shop clung, no matter how much aftershave he doused on himself.

The train slid to a stop again, and more people packed into the aisle. All day long she'd been beating her way through a crowd. The only quiet had been the few minutes in the conservatory, those yellow birds flitting through the palm leaves like sunshine. Then she'd blown it by telling Corey he belonged to Social Services. Like he was nothing but a picture and a bunch of lies in a file somewhere. She'd make it up to him. Not next weekend like she'd promised, because Simon was back, and he wouldn't let her out of his sight for at least a month. Maybe she could talk him into a trip to Vancouver. Through the mountains on the bike, just the two of them. When it was just the two of them, they were like some old married couple. That's what she'd tell him—they needed a second honeymoon. Or was it the third, or fourth, or fifth? When they finally came back, Simon would be restless. He'd take off with Gordie and the guys. That's when she'd call Social Services, that holier-than-thou-cow, Cousin Kristel. She'd take Corey out for supper, somewhere special. Wear the black dress for him. When he was about six, she'd let him choose what she should wear when she was going out. Pretty was what he wanted. Wear something pretty, Tina. She looked down at her shorts.

Funny how they always seemed to show up wearing the same clothes. She'd remind him about that next time, make him laugh. Not one lousy laugh out of him today. Next time would be different. Maybe she'd even try to explain a few things to him, now that he was older. Like why she went away and left him at exactly the wrong time, and about Simon, and maybe about why she needed to smoke. Instinctively, her hand slid into her bag. Paulette had her last twenty, and all that was left was the handful of change from Corey's pocket. Poor little bugger. One lousy hot dog to remember her by today. But there was no point in buying him presents. The stuff she used to bring along—a cool shirt, a baseball cap, CDs—all disappeared from one visit to the next. When she asked about it, he'd say, "I don't know what happened to that hat. I guess I didn't take it with me when I moved."

Her stop was next. Before Tina could stand, the old lady jumped up and pushed her way into the aisle. Stood directly between Tina and the guy. He smiled, let granny barge through, then waited for Tina to step out the door in front of him. She was tempted to turn the wrong way, to walk beside him, pretend she was with him. There was a high-rise across the street, probably where he was going. Up on the twenty-third floor, his wife was likely already home. She'd have kicked off her three hundred dollar shoes, poured a glass of wine, and would be waiting for him. No kids. That was another thing she needed to tell Corey. Make sure you marry someone who doesn't want babies. She wanted Corey to turn out like this guy who was walking away. On his way home to dinner.

19

"I SHOULD HAVE OFFERED TO PICK HIM UP IN the morning." Ben leaned on the counter, watching Wilma peel garlic for the salad.

She smashed the clove against the bottom of the bowl. "We're not supposed to have any contact with Tina, remember?"

"That whole secrecy thing is ridiculous." He began tearing up chunks of romaine. "If you'd been the least bit inclined, you could have met her at the zoo." As a matter of fact he was surprised that Wilma hadn't seized the opportunity. He'd have gone in with Corey and offered to buy lunch. If he was ever going to get close to this kid, he needed to get a handle on where he'd come from.

"No," she said, "I wouldn't do that, but I shouldn't have taken him in the first place. I have such a bad feeling about this." She drizzled olive oil and vinegar over the salad, slamming the bottles on the counter, tossing with two forks with such fury that lettuce and dressing sprayed across the counter.

"Slow down." Ben snatched the bowl away. "By now he's in front of her TV, pigging out on all the junk she bought to make up for not seeing him for six months. I'm sure he's fine, Willi." He licked his fingers, and wished that he'd been awake to make the salad dressing. Hers was always too light on the oil, heavy on the vinegar.

"No, he's not. He's not fine. And even if this visit goes okay, there's Kristel. She's so aggressive, I know she's going to provoke Corey into running again."

Any benefit from the half hour sleep was gone. Kristel might as well have been standing in the kitchen with them, her presence was so strong. "Let's not talk about social workers for one whole evening, okay?" he said. "I've had my fill today." He picked up the barbecue seasoning from the counter and shook it over the plate of chicken. "What's new at the zoo? They should be breaking ground for the new buildings soon."

She grabbed the shaker from his hand and shoved the chicken out of reach. "I have no idea. I didn't go in." She put her hands on her hips. "And where do you think Corey will be when those gorillas move into their new home?"

"Hopefully we'll be dragging him down there for the ribbon-cutting. But for God's sake don't tell Elsie about it or she'll take the bus out here to be first in line."

A year ago, Ben had made the mistake of suggesting a visit to the zoo when Elsie was in town. They'd been watching the gorillas, a lactating young female sprawled in the hay in a corner of the enclosure. When the gorilla began idly tweaking her nipple and licking the drops of milk from long black fingers, Elsie had burst into applause. "Oh to be able to do that in public!" she'd exclaimed. And then she clipped Ben with an elbow to his ribs and a sly smile. "The sweet taste of mother's milk, eh Ben? You must remember that?" Wilma had rolled her eyes and headed for the door.

Now she shook her head, looking as though she hadn't a clue what he was talking about. She wouldn't remember that day. Wilma found the gorillas unsettling and always walked away long before he was tired of watching.

"Sending Corey to Winnipeg for a week might not be a bad idea after all," she said. "Elsie's totally in love with him. If we convince him of how much we care about him, maybe he'll stop running."

Back to this paranoia again. Ben tried to stifle the exasperation. "Look, you have to quit worrying about whether he's going to take off again. We're doing the best we can, Willi." He reached in front of her for the plate of chicken. "Did you light the barbecue?" Without waiting for an answer, he opened the patio door and stepped outside.

After he'd slapped two chicken breasts onto the grill, Ben leaned on the deck. Tulips lined the path to the back gate, their heads tightly closed against evening. On the other side of the screen, Wilma was slamming cupboard doors.

A basketball hoop hung on the side of the garage, the net tattered and barely there. He'd spent hours, years, shooting baskets with Phil and Mark. Try to coax Corey into throwing a ball, or even watching a game on television, and the kid looked around all panicky as if he was trying to figure out who Ben was talking to. When Ben had suggested to Wilma about a week ago that Corey wasn't a great fit in their house, she'd gone ballistic. Who said Ben got to decide what a child should or shouldn't be interested in, she wanted to know? And had it occurred to him that Corey didn't know how to do any of those things, and might be too self-conscious to try?

Had it occurred to Wilma that he was the one feeling inadequate? Scoutmaster, coach, buddy to the boy's pals, Ben had never met a kid he couldn't connect with. But it was going to take more than a few chummy outings to the ball diamond to feel like he and Corey were even the same species. Giving up was out of the question, especially since this had been his idea and was born out of his anger at Frank Marshall for being so goddamn blasé about giving Corey back. As though he was a pair of shoes that didn't fit, or a puppy they couldn't house-train. At the time, Wilma was casting around for a new project. She'd closed the bookstore, squeezed by the big chain stores until there was nothing left. He knew she'd fall for a needy child, and she had. What he hadn't figured on was the frustration on Wilma's face whenever she pulled back a hand or an arm that was reaching instinctively to greet or comfort Corey.

Telling Wilma not to touch a child was like telling her not to breathe. She communicated with Phil and Mark through their skin. Even now that they were grown, she was like her mother. She never walked past, or let them pass, without touching. Ben's memories were like snapshots. Wilma sitting beside one or the other of the boys at the kitchen table to help with homework, one arm around their shoulders, her cheek against theirs, the other hand moving across the page, explaining. Wilma at the door before they left for school, pulling toques over their eyes, collars up, rubbing noses. Mornings when he woke to the alarm, reached across the bed, and found cool sheet where her warm body should have been. He knew if he walked down the hall he'd find her in one bed or the other, too tired to come back after she'd been called by a whimper or a cough, or a small boy sniffling beside their bed.

He could hear Wilma inside, rattling dishes and probably chewing on her lip until it was scored white from the edges of her teeth. He'd remind her again that, even though Tina was a poor specimen of a mother, she cared enough to come back regularly and raise shit on Corey's behalf. How many young mothers would have the guts to keep kicking at the fence Social Services had thrown up around the boy? Pregnant when she was fourteen, if you did the math. Imagine dealing with that if you were her father. In spite of the trouble with Phil, Ben was glad they'd had sons.

20

THE OLD MAN CUT A THICK SLICE OF BREAD, FILLED a heavy white mug with coffee, spooned in sugar. He sat at the table stirring and stirring, his eyes wandering now into the next room. The polished surface of the china cabinet gleamed in the late sun. Even the frame around the wedding picture had been polished. Inez again. What would Bepp have thought of some other woman wiping the dust from her image?

"What did she die of, your pretty young wife?" Inez had asked.

"Liver problems," he'd said curtly.

Inez, as always, knew not to ask any more. Such a smart woman, she'd figured him out long ago. For at least ten years, Inez and Jorges had cleaned the office building next door to his shop, stepping into the bakery late every afternoon before they started work, for something sweet to have with their coffee. Then Jorges died two years ago—collapsed behind the big polisher that kept right on going down the hall past the office where Inez was dusting. She looked up and knew instantly, she said, that she would find him crumpled, dead, in the shiny corridor. She'd disappeared for six months, her nephew taking over the job. And then, one day, the bell over the bakery door jingled. Brinkman peered out of the back room where he'd been stealing a catnap, and she was standing there alone. He'd never seen her without Jorges at her side, holding her elbow.

"Are you back then, to clean?" he'd asked.

She shook her head. "In this whole city, I can't find sweet rolls like yours." She was lonely, she said, and in her grief the only person she could think of who seemed to be carrying a weight of sadness equal to her own was him—the tall, slope-shouldered baker with the pale blue eyes.

Slowly, she'd pulled from him the details of his life, but never asked again about Bepp or how she died. Wherever she was, no doubt his Anna was suffering liver problems, if she wasn't already dead. Tina? Maybe the curse had passed her by. He hadn't seen her drunk since she was a teenager. She smoked like a chimney, but she swore to him after Corey was born—for all that her swearing was worth—that she stayed away from drink and from drugs, and that she would keep Corey from them too.

Corey, Corey. Good little boy. Brinkman spread a thick layer of butter on the bread, sprinkled it with sugar. He bit through the gritty crust, followed with a slurp of coffee, and chewed. The only other sound in the room was the hum of the clock on the wall. Past six o'clock. The zoo was closed. If this time she'd told the truth, if the boy really was spending the night, they would be on their way to Tina's apartment.

21

COREY PRESSED HIMSELF TIGHT TO THE ROCK, listening. No voices, no scuffling feet on the path. All he could hear was his own heartbeat pounding in his ears. Cheek brushing the rough wall, he peeked out. No one. Not a ripple on the lake, or even a bird in the trees. Big old T. Rex leering down at him as though they were all alone, not only in the zoo, or in Calgary, but in the whole world. He shifted to the other side of his cave, scanned the path that led higher into the dinosaur world. Nothing there either.

He wished he'd worn his watch, but it was on the bedside table where he'd left it this morning, knowing better than to turn up for a visit with Tina with something new. For all the bitching she did about how people took him so they could make money, and how nobody spent anything on him, it made her mean and jealous if she thought someone else was buying him presents.

He was so thirsty, even his eyes felt gritty. No place to drink in this part of the zoo. Nothing but swampy water and rocks and dinosaurs. He tried to remember the places where Opi had held him to drink from water fountains, but instead of travelling in his mind in the direction of the animals, toward the monkey house where there was a fountain on the outside wall, he turned toward the sound of the traffic. Out there, over the high wire fence, was Opi's house.

Only once had he made it all the way back to Opi. When he got to the house there was no one there, so he'd walked to the bakery. He didn't have any trouble finding his way, but it was winter. So cold by the time he stood looking at the sign that said, 'back in ten minutes', he couldn't feel his feet inside his running shoes. He'd planned to wait in the alcove of the door until Opi came back, but a police car pulled up. As soon as the woman cop hopped out and walked across the sidewalk toward him, he knew he'd been stupid, really stupid. When he didn't come home, they knew exactly where to look for him. He was only gone four hours. He never ran to Opi again.

Right now he was so close, he was sure that if he stood on tiptoes and peeked over that pile of rock, he'd see the kitchen window. Opi standing at the sink, scrubbing a potato for his supper. He would see the door at the side of the house and the alley, and the short walk to the bakery. Tina told him once that Opi had always wanted a son so that he could change the sign on the bakery to 'C. Brinkman and Sons, Bakers', just like the sign back in Rotterdam. Imagine living in a place called Rotterdam, she'd said. No wonder he packed up Bepp and ran away to Canada. Corey thought they came because it was even colder in Rotterdam than it was in Calgary. Opi had told him so, and he'd told him that Bepp missed the sea. The Bow River wasn't enough.

The wind had found Corey now, licking away the last bit of the sun's heat from the rock. He shook open the crumpled ball of wool. It was a kid's sweater, cherry red, with bunches of yellow flowers knit onto the front. Trust him to find a girl's sweater. He was tempted to leave it there, spread on the rocks like it had been washed and left, the way Opi hung clothes outside to dry, but already he could feel the rising damp from the river. He turned the sweater inside out, flowers hidden except for lumps of colour on the back. When the wool settled over his knees, it was only seconds before his skin responded with itchy heat, and the memory of mothball stink.

Tina dragging a blue sweater knit by his great grandma from an old suitcase. Shoving his arms into tight sleeves. 'Wait until Opi sees you!' But he was clawing at the picky wool within minutes. Then Opi coming through the door. 'Look! I found that sweater I used to wear! The one grandma knit for Anna.' The old man's eyes misting over. Corey dragged forward to stand in front of his grandfather, embarrassed before he even knew what she was up to. 'It's too small, can't you see? He needs a new one, and maybe some pants and socks. I don't have any money, Opi.' And then the mist froze over, his grandfather's eyes sparked icy blue.

On top of the china cabinet in the living room, a picture of both of them—Opi and the grandma who made the sweater. Opi's collar lifting his chin high above the stiff front of his shirt, hair slicked straight back, wire-rimmed glasses, not even a hint of a smile. The woman beside him was a ghost. White dress, pinched white face. Bepp.

Bepp, Bepp, Bepp. After the shouting, Corey wandered around the house repeating her name. Adding a burp, and another and another. The big hand on his shoulder, propelling him to the door, to where Tina sat on the step smoking.

"Opi's mad cause I burped Bepp's name."

"Well what did you do that for?" She moved over on the step to make room for him. "It's funny, but she was a drunk, and that's why it makes Opi mad. And so's my mom, Anna. She's a drunk too. Only don't tell the old man you know that. It's a deep, dark secret."

"Where's your mom, Tina?"

"Who knows?" She stubbed out the cigarette, kicked the butt off the step. "Who cares? Let's walk down to the store and get a coke."

Corey rested his flushed cheek against the rock and closed his eyes, Tina's voice singing him to sleep.

22

WILMA STOWED THE LEFTOVER SALAD in the fridge, put her coffee cup in the dishwasher. She whisked away the placemats. Propped Phil's card against the salt shaker again. In front of Ben.

"It's Mother's Day next Sunday. I should have kept Corey home today and she could have seen him then, instead of her birthday. Wouldn't that have been more appropriate? Can you imagine how she must feel on Mother's Day?"

Ben grunted. He gave the paper three quick shakes, that irritating little *ripple, ripple, ripple* thing he did every time he turned the page. When she tapped on the paper with her fingertips, he finally lowered it, peering over his reading glasses. "What?"

"Have you talked with Corey about Mother's Day? I don't want you taking him shopping for something for me unless it's his idea."

"For crying out loud, Wilma, I don't need anything extra to think about tonight. We'll make breakfast for you. He can scramble eggs, can't he?" He narrowed his eyes. "If you're wondering if I noticed the card, the answer is yes. What do you want me to say about it?"

"That we shouldn't have to meet our son at a restaurant? That he should come here on Mother's Day?"

"Fine with me. Pass that message along to Philip."

Over and over the same terrain. She was so tired of stepping on rocks. "Ben, he won't. You know that. Not until we agree to have dinner at his place, with his friend."

"Right. And you know that I'm not ready to do that. But don't let me hold you back. Go to Toronto. Sleep on their couch. And tell him for the fortieth time that he's always welcome at home."

Wilma sat down hard in the chair across from him. "It's not me he's waiting for. It's you."

"Well, he's going to have to wait a while longer. Wilma please, let it go."

She reached across the table, grabbed his hands. "This isn't going to change, you know. It's . . . genetic maybe. So if it's anyone's fault it's mine, not yours at all."

He pulled his hands free, took off his glasses and rubbed his eyes. "You still don't get that part, do you? I can't absolve myself because I'm not Phil's father. If anything, that makes me more responsible for him, not less. When I asked you to marry me, I promised you I'd be the best damn dad in the world for your baby. This wasn't what I had in mind. Not at all. Please. I don't want to talk about it. Not now."

Not now, not last week, or last month, or during the year after Philip came home late from school one winter night, and laid two copies of the school newspaper on the kitchen table where they were eating their supper. "Here," he said. "You both need to read this. I have an article." When Wilma's lips parted to congratulate him, he'd shoved his hands in his pockets and shook his head. "No, Mom. This isn't something that's going to make you happy. Let's talk about it later. I'm going over to Pete's to work on some physics problems." And he was gone, leaving behind the cold air that had been clinging to his sheepskin jacket.

Mark had been quiet during dinner, barely picked at the small servings on his plate. When the door closed behind his brother, he stood up, carried his plate to the sink, and turned to Ben and Wilma. "I'm glad he's finally going to tell you," he said. "I just want you to know, before you get upset, that the hardest part for Phil is telling you."

Even then, when Mark ran out of the kitchen and slammed his bedroom door, they'd looked at each other in bewilderment. Finally, they opened their personal copies of the paper. They sat there, eyes criss-crossing the page in unison, lips moving in a mute duet.

Ben had groaned, rolled up the paper and thrown it across the kitchen.

Wilma stared at the black print. She imagined Phil in his room, the desk lamp laying a soft patina on his blond hair, his narrow shoulders hunched over the keyboard, long fingers *tap-tapping* in frantic bursts. Then pausing when he threw back his head to stare at the ceiling. Book reports, essays, science projects. Ever since he was old enough to organize thoughts on paper, she'd marvelled at the intensity of his concentration, the maturity of word and thought. But this piece of writing? This article on what it was like to be gay in high school. How long had it taken to find the words, and the courage to pour them onto the page?

"Did you know this?" Ben sat rigid in his chair, hands gripping the edge of the table. "Tell me the truth, Wilma. Did you have any clue? Or is this an experiment or provocation he's dreamed up to test the reaction?"

She shook her head so vigorously she could hear banging in her ears. "No, no, no! Phil would never do that to us. Not something so big as this. Oh God, Ben, think of what he's been struggling with."

"I don't want to think about it. Not any part of it. It makes me sick to think about it!"

Ben's anger had burned down to cold, grey ash by the time Phil came home late that night. They sat in the living room listening to what he had to say—almost exactly what he'd written in the school paper—and they'd assured him that their love could not be compromised by anything he did, or was. Not ever. But the next morning, Wilma awoke feeling as though someone had died the day before, and that she would give anything to go back to sleep. Ben had come home from work that night to say that he was going to give it time. Somewhere he'd found a shred of doubt to cling to. Maybe, he suggested, Phil was wrong, and this was a phase and that it would soon pass. He was, after all, a high-strung, sensitive kid who was forever getting wrapped up in causes. Meanwhile, Ben needed time to work through his own feelings, and he would prefer that the subject stayed closed. And so it had, for five years, except about three times a week, when she couldn't help herself.

She glanced at Ben. He'd returned to his paper, to the Entertainment section. "Have you looked at the movies?" he asked.

She stared at the card until the basket of ivy and violets on the glossy front blurred. Tomorrow she'd remind Corey that, even though he'd just seen his mom, a Mother's Day card arriving in the mail would warm her heart. Didn't all mothers, even the ones with missing pieces, still have those oversized hearts when the card said, 'from your favourite son'? She'd get the box out of the closet, show him all her cards with the wonky crayon printing.

"Wilma." Ben spread the movie section in front of her. "What do you want to see?"

She pushed the paper away. Corey, is what she wanted to say. I want to see Corey asleep in the room down the hall. And if I'm allowed to be extravagant about what I want to see, I also want to see Philip take the front steps two at a time, suitcase in his hand. And even though she drives me crazy, I need her, so I'll be downright greedy and claim a third wish. I would like to see Ma pull up in a cab, leaning in to give the driver some advice about what herbal teas he should drink to reduce his stress in traffic, before she hustles up the sidewalk with her apron in her pocket. But it's not Christmas.

Wilma was suddenly so tired, the thought of leaving the house felt like more weight than she could shoulder. The ache at the back of her throat—the warning that things would get worse before they got better—would not go away until Corey was home. And there was still a long, long night ahead of them.

"Let's go downtown to Eau Claire and take a chance on the shortest lineup. I really don't care what we see."

23

COREY JOLTED AWAKE, HIS HEAD BOUNCING against the rock. He rubbed the back of his skull. Hot, so hot his hair was damp, his cheeks burning. But his arms shivered and his legs shook.

The voices, the shouting that woke him, had come from inside his head. He'd been dreaming about Shawn. He tried not to think back. Tina had taught him that. Don't worry about who your dad is, don't ask where your grandma is, forget about the last school, the last place you lived, and where you're living now. Think about when you're old enough that Social Services doesn't get to tell us what to do anymore. But thinking ahead wasn't working today, never really worked. So instead, he'd closed his eyes in this cave and thought about Shawn. Shawn creeping into his room, his first night in that foster home they shared. Into his bed. "I heard you crying," she whispered.

Next morning, she pulled him aside when no one was listening. 'Shhh. It's okay. At home, I always sleep with my little brother when he cries in the night and our mom's too drunk to hear. I'll be your big sister! It's safe, because I only stay until you're sleeping. No one knows.' He'd been dreaming of Shawn, her warm skin, the night Shawn made the mistake of falling asleep. Their foster mother coming in to wake Corey and finding him all tangled in Shawn's arms and legs. That was what woke him—their foster mom screaming at him. He knew the end of the dream anyway. Two hours later, both he and Shawn were out the door, moving in different directions, calling back to one another that they'd keep in touch. He wondered if Shawn still talked about home and her little brother, as though she was going there any minute.

Corey unfolded a section of the *Herald*, layering it between his shoulder and the rock. His shirt was damp with sweat. Shawn would laugh if she saw him now. 'Sweet!' she'd say. 'We can hide in here for days and days. Come out and steal food and pretend we're looking at the animals in the daytime, and sleep up here at night.' It would be warmer if there were two of them. But what would he do with Shawn in the morning? You couldn't be invisible when Shawn was with you.

He picked up another chunk of the paper. Maybe if he read he could forget about being cold, forget about Kristel, who was probably looking for him already. Ben and Wilma smiled at each other when he came into the living room to watch the news. Like they thought it was cute. He used to sneak out of bed after Opi was asleep and turn on the television. No cable, so he'd watch the news with the sound turned way down, waiting for Tina. He liked watching things that were happening far away, so far away that they didn't matter. Finally, he'd get tired of waiting and creep back to bed.

Wilma had started leaving the paper beside his cereal at breakfast. He read the City section first. Imagined that someday Tina really would win the lottery. There she'd be, grinning, holding the cheque by the corners. 'See, Corey, our dream came true. You can come home now.' Except there was no home if Simon was there.

Okay, that was enough. If he was going to get out of here, he had to stop seeing Simon around every corner. Stop feeling sorry for himself, too. He was acting like some little orphan kid. He had a home. As a matter of fact, he had two homes, because Elsie had told him he was welcome to stay with her any time. If he got tired of Wilma and Ben, she'd teased him, he could hop on a bus to Winnipeg and live with her. He actually believed she meant it. So what was he worried about? About Kristel for starters. Corey didn't get to decide where home was, and neither did Elsie.

Tired of leaning, he slid down the wall, sat on the gritty floor, tried to ignore the rank smell. Someone, or something, had used this hiding spot before him. It stunk like the last place he'd lived with Tina. He went to sleep in that house with his face buried in the pillow. Better to smell his own sweat than the pissy smell that hung around, no matter how much air freshener Tina sprayed. She said a bunch of guys had lived there before, and guys were pigs and couldn't pee straight. 'But get used to it,' she said, 'because there are plenty worse places than this one.'

Yeah, this cave smelled like some kid had climbed in here to piss. Maybe some other kid who was hiding. One thing about living in foster homes, he knew that he wasn't the only pathetic kid in the world.

All he wanted was to go back to sleep, but he couldn't. This muddle in his head was sure to turn into dreams again, and from dreams he always woke up screaming. He couldn't risk that. Someone would hear him for sure, and no way his screams would be mistaken for those of the animals. There was so much pounding in his head, he couldn't hear anything else. Hands clasped over his ears, he took a long, slow breath. Then another, and another. Fought to keep his eyes open. He was awake. Alone in a freakin' dinosaur park, but awake.

He only had to get through one night. If he worked things out, tomorrow he'd be back at Ben and Wilma's, where he hardly ever had bad dreams anymore.

'Nothing to be scared of. Have a drink of water, and go back to sleep now, son.' Ben's voice the first night in their house. He was there so quickly, Corey awake without even remembering the nightmare. Son. The word had circled in his brain after Ben left the room. With the window blind closed tight, the door ajar, a single light in the kitchen flickering, he felt safe and snug. Son. He decided it was only a leftover from the times Ben must have come into Mark's room in the night.

Later, the door had opened and Wilma slipped in, sat down on the edge of the bed so quietly he wouldn't have known she was there if she hadn't pulled the blanket up over his shoulders. Her hand hovered over his forehead without ever touching, but so close he could feel warmth.

There had been other times since, when he woke up from a dream and, within minutes, she'd be standing beside the bed. He always pretended to be asleep, because he was afraid she'd stop coming. They must have taken the training course. They must know the rules. Shawn loved the rules. She said they gave her power, knowing that foster parents were afraid she might make allegations against them. Corey had never heard the word until he met Shawn. Biggest word she knew, for sure.

A teenage foster kid had made allegations against Carmen's husband, which was why they only took little kids. At Carmen's, Breanna cried herself back to sleep from nightmares every time Carmen was out, because her husband wouldn't even go into the girls' bedrooms. When he read bedtime stories—his own little girl snuggled on his lap in the rocking chair—the kids sat lined up on the couch. Breanna would be hugging a stuffed rabbit so hard her eyes bulged as much as the glass beads on the toy's face.

Corey wished he had something to hug. His body was ice, his face was on fire, his ears throbbed. Right this minute, he'd be happy to be back at Carmen's too. Carmen, Tina would've said if Corey hadn't been living there and she'd met her somewhere else, was a good shit.

Kneeling now, he poked his head out of the safety of his cave and blinked, then blinked again. Sunset was staining the prehistoric landscape a rosy pink. T. Rex had come alive, seemed to be quivering, getting ready to pounce. The sky behind him was darkening so fast that soon all that would be visible would be his teeth. Corey's own teeth rattled together, and there was no way he could stop them. Now, even awake, he was dreaming a stone dinosaur was about to swallow him up.

And then, as though he was calling to Corey, telling him to snap out of it and plan his escape, the tiger screamed. The hair on the back of Corey's neck bristled. Scuttling backward, he pressed against the rock. Finally, he did let his eyes fall shut, imagined himself in the long grass, in a trampled nest still warm from the weight of the big cat. And the tiger, not threatening him, but crouched beside him, snarling to anyone, everyone on the other side of the fence that this was his boy.

Long after the roaring faded, the air still rippled. The stink had wafted away. A fresher breeze settled over Corey like a damp blanket. With a shaky hand, he pulled another section of paper free, fanned it over the gritty ground, and curled into a ball, the red sweater stretched tight and barely covering his legs.

If only he'd been smart enough to wear the jeans and a sweatshirt, instead of changing into these summer clothes. He'd dressed this morning, looked in the mirror, and the boy in the Levi's and brand new hoodie was someone he hardly recognized. He wanted Tina to know him, so he'd changed into this T-shirt she'd given him two years ago. That day, Tina had made him peel off the one he was wearing and throw it in the garbage so he could put on her present. Extra large, dark blue with a Nike logo. The kind of shirt the 'in' kids wore. But after a few washes, Carmen had accidentally thrown it into hot water with the baby clothes. It came out of the dryer more grey than blue, and the swoosh had eventually peeled until there was nothing left but the outline and a few flakes. Still, he'd hoped Tina would remember.

From that far end of the park, the tiger called again, this time in low, raspy-throated growls, reminding Corey that he wasn't alone. Pulling his knees tight to his chest, he hunched into the sweater and looked down at the City section. Always stories about robberies and drug busts. Stories that he read, looking for Simon's name, hoping he'd been arrested for something so bad they'd lock him up forever. Every time he saw one of those 'Wanted' pictures, he was sure it was one of Simon's friends, one of the pack of men in leather jackets and mirrored glasses who followed him around.

Corey didn't remember their names, or their faces, but still they turned up in his dreams. Yipping and whistling, giggling outside the door, pounding fists, chanting Tina's name. Tina all red in the face, screaming at them to take their party somewhere else. Her kid was sleeping. Except he was never sleeping. How could you sleep with wild animals outside the door? And even though the voices went away eventually, Simon always came back, and then Corey would wake up on a blanket on the living room floor, the bedroom door locked.

He felt like there was a snake in his stomach, slithering and biting. Hungry. And it would be a long time till breakfast. If he'd made it to Tina's, he'd have had leftover pizza in the morning, while she drank coffee and smoked. Or maybe he could have talked her into letting him make porridge the way Opi taught him. Sprinkled with so much brown sugar there was no white showing until he poured on a river of cream. Like Tina would have oatmeal, even the instant kind. Or brown sugar. Or real cream. He had no idea what she kept in her fridge or her kitchen cupboards. The only place he ever saw her was at the zoo. Their safe place. But today it seemed like his nightmares had climbed over the fence and followed him here.

24

"I'M TIRED OF YOUR FRIENDS, SIMON. I HAVEN'T seen any of them in six months, but I'm still tired. I don't want to spend my birthday with them." Tina knew she sounded like a kid, standing in front of Simon with her arms folded, her lip trembling. Like Corey when he'd tried to convince her to let him come home today.

Simon was there when she got back, the way she'd expected, with a brown paper bag full of Chinese food, and a bottle of cheap white wine. He was on his third beer. She could tell to the half-bottle how much he'd drunk, and when it was time for her to get out of his way. He'd taught her that himself. She was only fifteen when he told her, "Tina, I won't ever hurt you, but stay out of my sight when I'm drunk."

He served her wine in their finest plastic—an orange Tupperware glass that used to have a lid with a spout that Corey had learned to drink from. She thought it was a joke when she saw him pouring the warm wine into the cup, but Simon didn't have that much of a sense of humour. He'd just dumped her toothbrush out of the glass and brought it from the bathroom.

Not bothering with plates or forks, he'd pried the lid off four containers and lined them up in front of her. "Happy birthday, babe. Now eat this shit before it gets cold. It's still your favourite, right? Gordie said go to Tony Roma's for ribs, but I told him my Tina likes chicken balls. Hey, Gordie didn't know chickens had balls."

Ha ha. That was when she'd told him the first time that she was tired of his friends.

With one sweep of his arm, he sent the cardboard containers flying onto the beige carpet. "You know what I'm tired of, Tina? I'm tired of you looking at me and my friends like we're six kinds of crap."

She reached down to pick up the carton of noodles, sliding her fingers under the wormy strands. Wiping her hand on the hem of her shirt, she leaned back. "Do you ever wonder if there's a classier way, Simon? If we could maybe figure things out and live like normal people."

"What the hell are you talking about? Same as always, eh? Nothing's good enough for Tina."

"I want my kid back." She shook her head, startled at her own words. God, was that what was chewing her up today?

He snorted and draped his arm over her shoulder, palm sliding until her breast was cupped in his hand. "Well Mommy darling, don't let me hold you back." Then he drew her close, and covered her mouth with his. The tenderness of that kiss was like an old memory. When he released her, she folded her arms and stared at him. He shrugged. "Okay, so you really miss the little fucker. I get it, you know? What do you want me to do?"

"Don't mess with me, Simon. If you mean that . . ."

"Yeah, I mean it." He traced her lips with his fingertip. "I've fuckin' had enough of all this bullshit too. If you want the kid back, I'll get him back for you."

She shuddered. "Jesus, that's not what I want! You sound like you're gonna kidnap him!"

"Why not? Who's gonna notice if one more kid nobody wants disappears? We pick him up after school one day, hop on the bike, and head for Mexico. You're his mother, right? You got a birth certificate somewhere? Before anyone notices he's gone, we're across the border."

A cheap motel in some Mexican border town. Corey curled up on the floor while she and Simon shared the bed. She knew that motel. But the last time they were there, Corey wasn't part of the picture. She'd signed the papers giving him up, and told Simon to take her as far away as possible. Somewhere she had a real picture of her and Simon outside a motel with pink stucco walls. She'd thought about cutting Simon out of the photo and sending it to Corey. She flashed, now, to another picture that had been in her mind all day—a bright snapshot of the lady in the blue sweater who'd brought him to the zoo. There was a man who matched that woman, and a pretty house, and a bedroom that Corey told her was full of books.

"Thanks for the offer, but I was thinking more of living here, where the kid could maybe go to school and grow up."

"So what am I supposed to do about that?"

Tina held her breath and looked at the floor. Sauce from the tub of ginger beef was leaking onto the rug, mottling, blending with all the other stains from takeout suppers. "Maybe you could think about taking that anger management thing they talked about when I was trying to get him back. If you did that, maybe they'd let Corey come home. Nobody else seems to want him anymore."

He shoved the table halfway across the room with the heel of his boot, and jumped to his feet. "This isn't my problem, Tina. How many fuckin' times do I have to tell you, it's up to you to keep the kid from makin' me mad."

"Like the cat?" she said. "Like I was supposed to keep that pussy cat from bugging you." She felt her mouth pull down at the corners. That picture was supposed to be gone by now, the one of Simon holding the limp, black body in the palm of his hand.

He'd come back a few hours later with a marmalade-coloured kitten. "They didn't have none the same colour at the shelter. But a cat's a cat, I figure."

She'd told him to take it back, but found out later that he'd given the orange kitten to Paulette's kids. Paulette, when Tina told her about Smoky, had rubbed her eyes, then looked across the room to where Simon was lolling in the reclining chair, giving her kids rides on his bucking bronco foot. The kids squealing, fighting to be next. It wouldn't last. Uncle Simon got bored long before the kids. He'd be yelling at them to leave him alone any minute. But they always came back the next time. Maybe they had shorter memories than Corey. Corey never knew that it was Simon's idea to get the cat in the first place. He wasn't home when Simon went ballistic because he caught the cat on the table, licking the butter. Tina told him Smoky had sneaked outside and onto the road.

Paulette finally spoke. "I always figured it's too bad you didn't have a girl."

"What the hell difference would that make?"

She shrugged. "Just would've worked better."

Now, half a dozen years later, Tina tried to imagine a twelve-year-old girl, sitting on the couch beside Simon, sharing sweet and sour chicken balls and shanghai noodles. A twelve-year-old girl telling him she didn't want a ride on his stinkin' bike. Maybe Paulette was right. She could hear Simon laughing if a girl told him that. But if it was Tina's girl, would it be any different than it was with her boy?

"I'll be back in half an hour," he said, "and don't you ever mention that cat again." The door slammed, then opened again. "Hey, wear something sexy. I've been thinking about you in that leather skirt for six goddamn months."

Tina knelt on the grungy carpet, and began to scrape up the congealing bits of food.

25

WILMA WAS HALFWAY TO THE CAR, BEN BEHIND her locking the house, when he called to her. "Phone's ringing," he said, and ducked back inside. She waited, contemplating the tulips. She'd been so busy closing down the bookstore last fall that she'd let Ben plant the bulbs. Instead of using her roughly-drawn map, creating a splash of red at the top of the sidewalk close to the back door, another of yellow in the sunniest spot near the garage, he'd alternated colours along the length of the walk. The tulips marched single file—red, yellow, red, yellow, all the way to the back gate. The buds were closed tight on themselves tonight. Spring in Calgary. She could taste frost in the deep breath she inhaled. Good thing the petunias were still inside. She was planting those when Ben was at work.

Finally he reappeared, locked the door again, and loped down the sidewalk, jingling his keys. "Too late. Do we know someone named Carmen? All she left was a number."

"You didn't call back?"

"If it was that important, she would have left a message, right?"

Wilma unlocked the passenger door and threw the car keys over the roof to Ben. She picked up the wrapper from a throat lozenge Corey had sucked on the way to the zoo. Ben was going through the usual routine of adjusting the seat, tilting the rear-view mirror, fiddling with the seat belt. She should have insisted they take his car. No. She should have insisted on driving, but he was incapable of sitting beside her without shifting back and forth between his imaginary accelerator and brake. Extra irritation she didn't need tonight.

She twisted the piece of cellophane into a bow, like she was twisting that name in her mind. She didn't know a Carmen, but the name felt familiar. Everything in this evening felt dangerously familiar, including the night air against her skin like a cold hand. The night was reminiscent of another when she and Ben had driven circles around the city looking for Corey.

Carmen? Wilma shook her head, let it drop back against the headrest, and closed her eyes, her hands curved around the edges of the seat. Since she'd stepped outside, the world felt tilted, as though she'd been drinking, smoking maybe, even though it had been years. If she relaxed, she'd float out the car window toward the river, and follow the silvery current to the zoo.

During the fifteen minute drive downtown, they barely spoke. Ben parked a block away from the Eau Claire market. As they walked, Wilma felt her balance restored, her feet finally connecting with the sidewalk. The trees on Prince's Island were daubed with sunlight the colour of butterscotch, and the river smell rushed toward them with a cold, salty edge. Except for Ben's hand on her elbow, grounding her, Wilma could have convinced herself that she'd slipped back twenty-five years onto a sandy path in Beacon Hill Park.

Ben linked his arm through hers, and she settled heavily against him, pulling him to a stop. She stood in front of him, tilted her head. "Do I look different?"

Squinting, he swivelled her chin side to side. "Nope. Am I missing something important?"

"Ever since we left the house, I've felt like I've been drugged. Everything's moving at three quarter speed. A minute ago, I swear if I'd closed my eyes I would have been eighteen years old when I opened them again."

Ben whistled. "Before or after we met?"

"Before. Wandering around Victoria in the night. The smell of this night reminds me of Victoria. And by the time I met you, I was nineteen."

By the time Wilma met Ben, she'd been back from Victoria for six months, and was mostly hiding in her bedroom. She and a friend had hitchhiked to Jasper to work at the Lodge that summer, after their first year of university. Before they went back to Winnipeg, they'd detoured to the west coast, to hang out with a bunch of kids they'd worked with in

Jasper. Although Wilma couldn't be sure, she pinned Philip's conception to a night in a sleeping bag in Beacon Hill Park with a lanky, blue-eyed boy from Kentucky. His name was Steve, and he'd said he'd look her up in Winnipeg. He was going to stay in Vancouver for a month or two, and then hitch his way east. If he'd shown up back home, who knew how things would have turned out?

As things did turn out, Elsie had marched into Wilma's bedroom one day and said it was time for the moping to stop. Wilma was coming to her cousin's wedding whether she wanted to or not, because Elsie was tired of people talking behind her back. If she could look all her snooty in-laws in the eye, then so could Wilma, even with her big belly and bare left hand. Ben was the cousin's best man, had been his roommate for three years of university. He was the only one who asked Wilma to dance at the reception, apart from Uncle Eddy who kept patting her shoulder and telling her everything would work out fine. Uncle Eddy and the rest of the family were still under the impression that she was giving up her baby when it was born, and couldn't understand why Elsie hadn't sent her to live with her aunt in Vancouver. Some time soon, Wilma would remember to thank Ma once again for standing beside her.

She looked up at the sky, an arch of cloud in the west, just waiting for the sun to light that dark underbelly. "There's going to be a fantastic sunset," she said. "Let's skip the movie and walk instead. I don't think I can sit still for two hours."

Ben stroked her forehead. "Maybe you've got what's ailing Corey? Feels like a fever to me."

For twenty minutes, they followed the bike path east along the river, Ben's arm hooked through Wilma's, keeping her to the side, out of the steady stream of bike traffic.

She was surprised that he hadn't steered west instead of letting her choose this course. They were at Fort Calgary now, across the river from St. George's Island. Getting closer and closer to the zoo.

Two boys about Corey's age whizzed by on bikes, one with a sweep of blond hair flattened to his cheek by his helmet.

"Remember how Phil always took his helmet off as soon as he was out of sight of the house?" The boy rode with the same long-legged grace as Philip.

Ben snorted. "How could I forget? He said he didn't want to ruin his hair." His arm had become heavier as they walked, cranking her left shoulder to an uncomfortable height. She pulled free and picked up the pace.

"I should get Corey out biking," Ben said. He rubbed his hands and jammed them into his pockets. "You're sure you're not cold? Ready to turn back?"

Wilma shook her head. "I don't think Corey knows how to ride a bike. When Ma was here she asked him to ride over to the grocery store and get a couple of things for her, and he came up with a lame excuse for walking instead."

"What else can't he do? Do we know if he can swim? How many other rites of passage has he missed?" Ben sounded out of breath. When she glanced at him, his face had a glassy sheen of sweat. He'd been away all week. He must be exhausted. She should have insisted they stay home tonight. "The kid's been in foster homes for almost four years, Willi. Someone along the way could have taught him to ride a bike."

"Carmen!" Wilma shouted. "One of Corey's stops along the way! Ben, you're brilliant. Carmen was Corey's foster mother before he went to Frank and Judy's. She's the woman with a pack of little kids. Why on earth would she be calling us?" She pumped his arm for an answer. "Maybe Corey's with her."

A guy in spandex biking shorts veered, yelled at her to wake up. Ben pulled her onto the grass. "Let's either get off the road or watch for traffic." He took the cell phone out of his pocket. "Probably another Carmen. If it was foster mother Carmen and she had Corey, she'd have left more than a phone number. Call home, get the number from the machine, and you can put your worries to rest. I'll bet you get Carmen's Carpet Cleaning."

What she got instead was a child who could barely talk, who chirped a cheerful "Okey!" when Wilma asked her to get her mommy, then hung up. The cell was already warning her that the battery was waning, so she let the connection go.

Hunched into her sweater, shivering in spite of the thick wool, she tapped the phone against her palm and tried to dredge up every single thing Corey'd ever said about Carmen, but there was little. He was as guarded in his comments about his previous foster homes as he was in talking about his mom. They'd stopped asking about his grandfather because his face pinched up in such a look of pain when he said that name, Opi. My Opi. 'I don't remember my Opi very well,' he'd say, then in the next breath, paint a picture so fresh, Wilma was sure she'd be able to pick the man out of a crowd.

She glanced at her watch. They'd been walking for half an hour. A bit further, and then they could turn back for coffee, and then they could go home. To wait. For what?

They were across from the zoo now. Through the trees, she could see that the parking lot on the other side of the river was empty. Dinny had only the traffic for company.

"Want to see if the gates are still open? Tiptoe through the tulips? I caught a glimpse from the fence when I dropped Corey off and the gardens looked glorious." *And maybe you could learn something about design,* she thought.

"Wilma . . ."

"Forget it. I know it's way past closing time. I was making conversation."

"He's at Tina's by now, or at McDonald's, or some pizza joint. If he's not feeling well she'll give him Tylenol and he'll fall asleep by nine o'clock. If he's not any better in the morning, we'll take him to the clinic as soon as Kristel brings him home, and get a prescription. He's not a baby. Nothing will happen tonight that we won't be able to take care of in the morning."

"What if he's not there in the morning?"

With a heavy sigh, Ben sat down on a bench at the side of the path. A plaque screwed to the wooden slats told them this place of rest was dedicated to the memory of a beloved grandfather. Wilma sat down beside Ben and took off her shoe, shaking out a stone that she'd been trying to ignore for blocks. The river reflected the turquoise tinge of the darkening sky. She watched a flock of Canada geese cruise in, slicing their landing across the water with such perfection she felt like applauding.

Ben finally spoke. "Then I guess we won't sleep tomorrow night, but I think you're wrong."

She slouched, her fingertips sinking into a tuft of grass beside the bench and ripping it out by the roots. He didn't need to remind her of the other sleepless nights when Corey had been missing. The first time after only a week in their house. The social worker had picked him up at school and taken him out for lunch. Corey went back into the building through the front door, exited through the back. Nobody missed him, until Wilma called the school at four-thirty to find out if there was a reason he was late. That night she'd paced the driveway, watching a frosty full moon, waiting for word from the social worker. He'd call the police, he'd said, but Corey didn't have any predictable haunts. Once, he'd snuck into an exercise club downtown just before closing and hidden in a locker. When it was safe, he curled up on a bench where an early morning lap swimmer found him at six o'clock. Another time, he'd spent a sultry summer night in a nest of bushes in a residential playground. A couple of teenagers cutting across the park spotted his foot protruding from the shrubbery. Another night he'd spent in a half-finished house. 'He goes,' the man had said, 'wherever his feet take him. And then he sits down and waits.'

So they'd worried and paced, drinking gallons of coffee and napping in shifts for one more whole day, and part of the next night. At two in the morning, Wilma was slumped in the rocking chair in Ben's bathrobe. Ben had finally agreed to go to bed; he was supposed to be flying to Denver the next morning. When the headlights fanned through the dark at the bend in their street, she ran out in her bare feet. If she closed her eyes, she could still feel the icy ripples of the concrete, the cold wind lifting her hair, and Corey trembling inside the circle of her arms.

She'd swept him through the open door, past Ben standing grey-faced and stern in the hallway, turned her back on the policewoman who followed her into the living room, and led Corey straight through to his bedroom and closed the door. Pushing him to sit on the bed, she'd opened a dresser drawer, took out a pair of pyjamas that were still creased from the package, and laid them across his lap.

"I'll run a bath for you, and make hot chocolate. Have a quick soak, come to the kitchen and drink the chocolate, and then you can go to sleep. We'll talk in the morning." With a shaky hand, she cupped his chin, turned those huge, frightened eyes toward hers, and put a finger on his lips when he tried to speak. "Tomorrow, Corey. Tonight we all need to sleep." When she turned, Ben had been standing behind her rubbing his eyes.

Closing the gap between them on the bench, she put her hand on Ben's thigh and spread her fingers to draw some warmth from the solid muscle. He was looking across the river to the lot on the other side where she and Corey had parked.

Wilma shivered. A chill had suddenly risen from the river. "It's going to be so cold tonight."

"Stop worrying. He's with his mom." When they stood, she huddled against Ben for a moment, turning up the collar of her sweater to keep the wind off her face. "And bear in mind that we didn't commit to a lifetime of sleepless nights when we applied to look after Corey. I have no intention of keeping the porch light on indefinitely for a child whose picture ends up on the back of milk cartons."

Without responding, Wilma turned her back on Ben and the zoo, and began the walk toward the silhouetted towers of downtown.

26 IF COREY CLOSED HIS EYES, HIS HEAD FILLED with voices and flashing pictures. If he opened them, the stone walls began to wobble and close in. He took a deep breath, and climbed out of his hiding place.

The sun was gone, the sky lit with a colour he'd never seen, except in a crayon box, or in pictures of the water around those tropical islands Tina was going to visit when she won the lottery. While he stood there, trying to balance on legs that felt like they were Jell-O instead of bone, the last bit of turquoise faded away, and the shapes of rocks and trees seemed to flatten. It was like a painting.

Darker and darker. Finally, he felt his feet moving, taking him to a fork in the path. It would be even colder down in the trees, darker. He plodded toward the orange light at the top of the park. Now he could hear the rumble of traffic. If he could scramble up that last huge wall of rock, he'd be looking down on Memorial Drive. And if he had his bearings right, from here he should be able to see Opi's corner. The problem was, he didn't have much sense of direction. Not much sense at all, when that big wind started rushing through his body, pushing his feet.

When they caught up with him—and he was so lame at this, it never took more than a day—the social workers always asked him where he was going, as though he was running toward something. And whenever Tina found out he'd run, she tried to blame someone, as though Corey was running away from something. Ben was the first person who'd ever seemed to understand. "I get it, Corey," he'd said. "But could you try to stop yourself the next time? Really try."

Great job, Cor. All you had to do was make a phone call. Ben was going to be some impressed.

Keeping to the edge of the path, trying to keep his mouth closed so the wheezy sound of his breath wouldn't give him away, Corey trudged toward the long ridge of rock that separated the zoo from the traffic. This spot would be safe. He had a clear view in every direction, and there was no one in sight. Just him and a geeky-looking, striped dinosaur. Good old Corythosaurus with his tufted head, shiny eyes, and long neck was craning up from the swamp below, as though he'd been waiting all evening for the boy with the same name. Tina had thought it was hilarious when Corey was barely old enough to read and found his own name in the dinosaur's. 'Yeah, right,' she'd said. 'I named you after that stupid-looking dinosaur. Corysaurus David Brinkman. Says so right on the birth certificate.'

For a while now, he'd been thinking about changing his name to Dave. No one would ask him to repeat that or spell it. He'd be Dave Brinkman. Easy. The kind of name a popular kid would have. Maybe Dave would have a gang of friends who'd hang around his locker joking with the popular girls. The ones in tight shirts who were always giggling and bumping up against you if you were one of the guys. The ones who ignored a kid named Cor, looked right through him as though he was part of the junk falling out of his locker.

Dave. Shawn would like that too. She was always picking new names for herself, but so far Shawn was the only one that stuck. Really, her name was Siobhan, which was the strangest name Corey had ever heard. He didn't think even Shawn-Siobhan knew how to spell it. She said she hated that name. It sounded exactly like her old man's pyjama pants whistling against his legs when he came down the hall and into her room at night.

Wilma didn't think much of his plan. She said Cor was a great name, strong and original. David was okay, but Daves were a dime a dozen. Chances were pretty good that by the time he turned into Dave he'd have moved anyway.

When Corey narrowed his eyes, the outline of the dinosaur blurred. He could have sworn the head was nodding. As though the streetlights were deliberately placed to floodlight the park, as well as the traffic on the other side, the swamp toward which Corey had been moving was as bright as a movie set. But below Corythosaurus, the trail twisted through trees and tall grass and swarmed with shadows. Corey sat down on a bench and peered into the dark.

It must have been at least half an hour since he'd heard the tiger call. The only noise now was from the traffic on the street, and the planes overhead. Opi said there was a flight path over his house, over the zoo, and downtown. The shadows were beginning to close around him. Corey stretched out on the bench, his arms folded over his eyes. Not here, but Opi's garden. Lying on the cool grass watching the jet streams.

Opi's pant leg brushing his arm as he stomped past. "More and more noise. Can't they fly their planes over someone else's house?"

Tina, smoking on the back step. "I wish I was on one of them," she said, "instead of stuck in this shitbox place."

Opi holding up his hand. "*Houde uw bec!* There's a child here. We don't need to hear such language."

Hoodjabec! Corey liked the sound of that one. Funny how he could still remember so many of Opi's Dutch words. Sometimes in French class he mixed up the two languages and everyone looked at him like he was crazy. He hated being called on in class. He'd learned that the trick was to never put your hand up, but to be sure you were looking at the teacher with just enough attention so that her eyes skidded past you instead of zooming in.

Houde uw bec. Corey whispered it under his breath whenever Tina mouthed off at him. Not a good idea, really, because she was the only person he knew who'd understand what he was saying.

He lurched upright on the bench, clutching his knees. He swore he could smell Tina's cigarette. But the cold air held not a trace. He rubbed his eyes, tilted his head back to watch another plane on its descent. From here it looked as though it was dangerously close to the ground already. He imagined Shawn on that plane. Social Services flew her back from Vancouver once when she ran away, and she'd been talking about it ever since. Flying, she'd told him, was better than nail polish remover, or beer, or her mom's sleeping pills.

"But I thought you wanted to go home, Shawn," he'd said. "You're always talking about going home tomorrow. Hitching to Vancouver is, like, the wrong direction."

She'd planted her hands on her hips and rolled her eyes. "There are a lot of different ways to get home, Cor."

Shawn would love this place at night. The orange light, the way everything seemed touched with fire. She'd be dancing to keep warm. So many times, she'd grabbed his hands and pulled him to his feet and made him dance with her. 'I can't dance,' he'd tell her, but she'd keep twirling and shaking. 'Everyone can dance, Corey.'

If only his head would stop spinning, he'd find an open building and get out of the cold. Even the straw in the stinky elephant house would be better than this. Only there was a baby elephant, and he knew that mother animals were even more dangerous when they were protecting their babies.

So were human mothers, one of his social workers had told him a long time ago. He searched the puffs of cloud for her name. Maggie. He hadn't thought about her in ages, but now he realized that Wilma reminded him of Maggie. Maggie sitting on the couch beside him after that one time he'd tried to run to Opi's house. Back in a few hours and there was Maggie waiting at the foster home. "Did you see your grandpa, Corey?"

Too embarrassed to look her in the eye, he stared at the carpet between his feet.

"Did you know I tried to arrange for you to visit your grandfather, but he wouldn't talk to me?"

No, he didn't know that. He didn't want to know. Caught by surprise when she lifted his chin with her thumb and looked straight into his eyes.

"You were looking for your mom, weren't you?"

"I need to tell her about the court." Whispering as though it was a secret. And then Maggie surprised him even more by putting her arms around him and giving him a big hug. "She knows," she said softly. "She knows about court. She signed the papers saying she agrees to the guardianship order. I guess she thinks it's the best thing for you, Corey. You know she loves you."

He didn't know that either. Not then and not now. And he'd never bothered to tell Tina he knew about her signing the papers that gave him away. She'd have an excuse, and he was tired of her snarling and pretending to fight to get him back. He was so tired.

27

TINA SHOULD HAVE GUESSED THAT THERE'D BE nothing surprising about the birthday surprise Simon had promised. Just him and his friends and another stinkin' bar. They were all half pissed and it was only nine o'clock.

She pushed away from the table, sending a minor earthquake through the litter of glasses and ashtrays. "I gotta use the phone. I'll be back in a minute."

"Aw no, don't leave me, babe." Simon stood up, snaked his arm around her waist, held her so tight to his side she couldn't move. "Who needs to hear from you in the middle of your party?" His other hand clasped her wrist and squeezed, pulling her around to face him. His breath on her face was rank with smoke and beer. "What's the matter? Cat got your tongue?"

She wrenched away from him. "Some celebration. You fucked up my visit with Corey for this?"

"Awwww." Simon's brother, Gordie, leered at her. He was like an unwashed clone of Simon. The spoiled one, Paulette called Gordie. Born after their dad left, so there was no one to whip him into shape. A bandana flattened his hair into a greasy fringe, low on his neck. "She'd rather be playing patty cake with her kid." Tina had never met the other two guys at the table, hadn't been able to hear the names Simon shouted in her ear over the din in the bar. Couldn't care less.

"Damn right I'd rather be with my kid."

Simon's fingers clenched her arm. "Who are you phoning, Tina?"

"The foster home." She winced, tried to pull away. "Corey's sick and I want to find out how he is. That okay with you?"

His nails dug deeper into her bare skin. It was time to take his advice and get away from him. He was drunk. "You know, I'd be a happy man if you worried about me like you worry about that kid."

She stared back at the shadowed face, startled to notice that there were lines around Simon's eyes, deep channels that ran from the sides of his nose to his chin, and a heavy, fleshy look to his throat. He'd put on weight in jail. The sly, teasing Simon—the one Paulette said could charm the pants off a dead nun—was losing it, losing his looks.

"For fuck's sake, Tina, it's your birthday. Have a drink and loosen up. Then we'll go home and have our own private party." He nuzzled her ear. "I can make you forget the kid."

She braced both hands on his leather-covered chest, shoved as hard as she could. "Not this time, you can't." He reeled backward, and before he could regain his balance, Tina threaded her way through the tables, pushed past the bouncer, was out the door and running.

A half block away from the bar, she stopped to look back. He hadn't followed her. She hoped he'd pout, spend the night at Gordie's or Paulette's. She shivered. It was dark now. Her silk shirt felt like ice on her skin. She stepped into a phone booth, pulled the notebook from her pocket, and punched in the number Corey had printed there.

Goddamn answering machine. Nice voice though. Mr. Foster Father sounded like a lawyer or a doctor. But where the hell were they? Corey was sick. Those flushed cheeks and the way he couldn't swallow. He'd had dozens of ear and throat infections when he was little, and she knew the signs. The machine beeped, she cleared her throat.

"Yeah, this is Tina Brinkman. I wanted to make sure Corey's okay. He didn't look so hot this afternoon and he gets these throat infections. So maybe it would be a good idea to take him to the doctor and get some antibiotics. And tell him I'm sorry today didn't work out, okay? Oh yeah, and he's allergic to penicillin."

Another beep and she was cut off. Shit, she'd sounded like an idiot. So now what? Maybe they'd at least tell him she called so he'd know she was worried. She felt bad about the visit. The last two had been so perfect, she'd managed to talk the social worker into letting Corey stay overnight for the first time in all these years. The last one, the one before Kristel, she could wrap around her pinky. A cute guy. Wore his hair in a mullet, and actually listened to her, instead of reading her the rule book like that little witch this morning. So she was Simon's cousin. Must be a rule against having a kid on your caseload if you were related to the mother's friend. Time for a phone call to Social Services. You like rules, Kristel?

She hung up the phone. Where was Corey? If she'd had the guts to stand up to Simon earlier, Corey'd be asleep on her couch. Didn't she have the right to tuck her kid into a bed for one night and to watch him sleep? She used to lie awake beside him and stare at his face.

So where was he? She kicked at the wall of the phone booth. After he'd called, he said they were on the way. But had he called? She'd been so wound up in trying to hold Simon off, so relieved when she finally convinced Corey to let her go, that she'd hardly paid attention to the look on his face. She could always tell when he was lying by the look on his face. The kid was such a lousy liar. She'd keep phoning until they answered. Her phone was disconnected because she forgot to pay the bill. The neighbours in the apartments around her were all so scared of Simon after the last time he tried to kick her door in, nobody would open up to let her use a phone.

She crossed her arms and rubbed the sleek silk until her palms were hot from the friction. Her leather jacket was hanging on her chair back at the bar, but she could count on Simon to bring it home. He'd bought it for her.

He'd be back. If not tonight, then tomorrow. And to keep anyone from calling the cops, she'd let him in. God, who was she trying to kid? She'd let him in because she was lonely and there was nobody else. Nobody who cared about her the way Simon did. Paulette was right; why else would he stick around for fourteen years? "You and me, Tina, we're meant for each other. I don't want nobody but you." He said it over and over, and she'd never stopped believing him. Simon could no more let go of her than she could let go of him. Fourteen years was half her fucking lifetime.

That was why she'd had to turn her back on Corey today. Corey had somewhere to go, someone to look after him. What else could she do? Her only option had been Opi, but she knew the old man sat there and ignored the phone. At least she was spared listening to him. If she'd shown up with Corey, he'd have known that Simon was back. As always the screaming would be in Dutch, but she'd heard the words for 'slut' before. Like he didn't know there was such a thing as sex. The old hypocrite. She knew what he did in the back room at the bakery, but that was one thing she'd never had the guts to throw in his face.

She was in grade four that day she went to the bakery after school instead of straight home. She'd wanted to show Opi her report card— a sucky little geek back then. The 'back in ten minutes' sign was on the door, but she knew he always left the rear door unlocked when he went to the post office, or the bank, so she went around to the alley. There wasn't anywhere she'd rather sit and wait than Opi's bakery with the glass case full of ginger cookies and butterhorns and cinnamon buns and that spongy smell of fresh bread.

Usually, the radio was on and she thought, at first, that the moaning sounds were coming from the radio, and the excited yips were the dog. Trudi, the woman who sometimes worked in the front of the shop, had a mean little dog that she locked in the bathroom. But Trudi couldn't be there. If she was, why would the shop be closed? Tina was halfway into the shadowy back room before she realized the heaving white shape on the cot was Opi's bare bum, and the yipping was coming from under him, from Trudi. When the chihuahua came flying out from under the bed, Tina ran out of the room, slamming the door, and ran out the back, down the alley and all the way home. If Opi even heard the sound of someone intruding, he never guessed it was her. When he asked her where she'd gone after school, she told him she was at a friend's house. That was the first time she lied to him about where she'd been or where she was going. It got easier and easier once she met Simon.

It was Opi's fault that Corey had to go back to that lousy foster home this afternoon instead of being with his family where he belonged. When she finally talked to him again, she was going to tell him he'd screwed up, missed the visit he'd been waiting for.

A car cruised up to the curb with the passenger window down. "Looking for some fun?"

Tina ignored the asshole and started to walk, but he drove slowly along side. When she heard the sound of a bus behind her, she ran for the stop and scrambled on. From the welcome warmth inside, she watched the car pull into the centre lane and peel away. She settled into a seat in the middle of the bus, with the driver tracking her in his mirror and a guy in coveralls, lunch kit on his lap, watching from across the aisle as though he could see right through her clothes. She tugged at the short leather skirt, turned her face to the window. Her hair falling across her cheek had soaked up the stink of the bar.

Two more people climbed onto the bus, but the driver unfolded a newspaper and poured a cup of coffee from a thermos. Terrific. He was going to sit here and make up time. Tina leaned into the aisle and waved. "Hey! Is this a bus or what?"

He looked up at her in his mirror. "Yeah, in about five minutes it's a bus. I'm running early."

"Yeah? Well I'm running late."

He lifted the paper and ignored her.

She turned to the window. A bunch of kids were huddled outside a video store and, from the back, one of them looked like Corey. But when he turned, his face was darker, heavier, and of course the clothes were wrong. Corey had been wearing shorts. She knew better than to expect to see him in a gang of teenagers. The kid was a loner. The only friend she ever heard him talk about was that weird chick he'd dragged along to the zoo one time. The one who climbed into bed with him, and freaked out the foster parents. Tina had freaked too when they acted like Corey was some kind of junior rapist.

How could she have a kid old enough to be accused of that kind of shit?

She was twenty-six years old today. Big grown-up birthday, her own apartment, no job at the moment but she'd find another one. She always did.

The sky was streaked with bands of pink, mauve, and navy blue, scudded with puffs of silver cloud. Happy birthday, Tina Brinkman, here's a sunset just for you.

28

THE OLD MAN PLODDED FROM ROOM TO ROOM, window to window, in the dark cage of his house. How strange that he could still feel the imprint of a small body against his chest. And yet why wouldn't he, on this night that was teeming with the memory of his children, all of them beyond his reach? Hadn't he carried them all just so, room to room?

Anna, so docile, he'd come home from the shop to find her in her crib rubbing the satin hem of the blanket on her cheek, her mother snoring on the bed a few feet away. He would feel such guilt at having left the two of them alone all day, that he carried Anna against his shoulder from the time he came in the door until she was fed, bathed, and so deep in sleep she scarcely stirred when he returned her to the crib. Such guilt at dragging Bepp across the ocean, away from her mother and her sisters who would surely have kept her afloat, that he cooked an evening meal, tended the baby, tidied the house, and then nudged Bepp to her own side of the bed when he crawled in. When the alarm woke him at four, it was time to start the day over again. Often he would find Bepp in the kitchen, rubbing her eyes, holding her head in her hands, working so hard to pretend she was fine.

"I'm going to make *gehaktballen* for supper, Cor. Leave me money for the meat, please. I'll put Anna in the buggy and walk to the store." Then she'd press her fingertips to her temples where the skin was like skim milk, a blue vein pulsing. "But I have such a headache." There would be no meatballs when he came home, and Anna would be playing quietly in her crib.

Shadowy little Anna, so agreeable that after Bepp died and Anna turned into a teenager, he never guessed she was taking off her pantics for every boy who looked her way. He thought she was with her friends after school. It turned out she had no friends. She has poor judgment,

Mr. Brinkman, they told him. Back then they didn't know that his baby daughter had been poisoned by the alcohol her mother drank. They knew only that she was incapable of making the right choices.

Anna had stayed until Tina was three years old, but only because he'd bullied and threatened, and paid a woman to look after the both of them while he worked. A babysitter for the baby and the mother. Finally, one night she'd climbed out her bedroom window after he'd fallen asleep rocking Tina. She'd never come back. Once, the police phoned to say they'd found her in Toronto, but by then she was a week away from her eighteenth birthday and what was the point, they asked, of sending her home? If Anna was still alive, she was forty-three years old. She didn't know she had a twelve-year-old grandson. Another brown-eyed child. The first time he held Tina, Cornelius Brinkman had felt compelled to check the wristband and the placard on the plastic bassinet. Baby Girl Brinkman bore no resemblance to any other Brinkman female he'd ever seen, nor to the fair, soft bodied, blue-eyed women in Bepp's family. When Corey was born, the gold-flecked eyes were no longer a surprise. The child was as familiar as a fingerprint.

He drained the syrupy dregs of coffee and stood to heat the pot for one more cup. He wouldn't sleep anyway. When Inez came back, he'd tell her it was the stew. That her spicy food had awakened his ghosts. No sleep for him when the boy was in his thoughts. So many nights he'd lain awake, listening for Corey's barking cough. Then he would bundle the baby in his quilt, and take him outside into the night air until he could catch his breath again. Colic, croup, earache. He knew as well as any mother what to do in the night.

Tina was not like Anna. Until she started playing hooky from school and hanging around with a wild crowd, she was bright and happy and he had hopes for her. A sunny child skipping back and forth between the bakery and home after school, and following him around chirping constantly. That at least hadn't changed. Even now, she was never quiet. On the phone or at the door, she was always needing and wanting.

But Tina loved her son and she was a good mother. Except for Simon, that slime, she would never have lost Corey. Men were attracted to Tina like bees to a tulip, but each time she even looked in another direction, Simon crooked his finger and she ran to him.

He'd only spoken to Simon once. The first time Tina brought Simon to the house—no, he wasn't fool enough to believe that it was the first time, but it was the first that Brinkman was home—she'd introduced him as though he was a gentleman caller, and she a young lady. Simon stood on the living room rug in his big, black boots, his arm around Tina's waist as though he owned her. "Hey, Mr. Brinkman, how's it goin'?"

He'd ignored the question, looking pointedly at the dirty snow melting off the man's feet. That it was a man, not a boy, who'd claimed his granddaughter should have warned him, but he'd tried to be civil. He sat at the table and drank the weak coffee Tina poured. "What line of work are you in?" he'd finally asked, after they all stared silently at their own spots on the kitchen wall.

Simon shrugged inside the cracked leather jacket and scratched the back of his neck. "I guess you could say I'm in sales. Buying and selling." Then he smirked at Tina, and the room seemed to fill with a bad smell.

Brinkman heaved up on the sash of the window and stuck his head into the night. Anna, Tina, Corey, all out there somewhere.

29 COREY MADE HIS WAY TO THE FAR END OF THE prehistoric park, creeping along the edges of the path, pulling into shadows when he thought he heard a crunching footstep ahead of him, but so far he was still alone with the dinosaurs.

Alone, and hungry, and thinking about the ice cream cake that would've cooled his throat. Tina had promised to buy ice cream cake for his birthday. Not likely she'd remembered to buy it ahead of time. They would have stopped at the Dairy Queen on the way home. The more he thought about it, the more it seemed she'd never intended to have him stay overnight. She'd decided even before she came to the zoo that she'd rather be with her friends. Or it could be Simon's fault, Simon wanting her all to himself. Tina might be the one person in the world who wasn't afraid of Simon, but she couldn't say no to him. When that social worker long ago tried to tell Corey that Tina loved him, he wanted to scream, "That's not it, Maggie! That's not how she loves me. That's how she loves Simon." Instead, he'd blubbered like a baby.

"How do you feel about Simon," Maggie had asked.

"I hate him!" That was true. As long as Corey could remember, he'd hated Simon. Even when Simon tried to be nice to him, Corey could tell it was fake. All for Tina.

He stopped, put his hands over his ears, and shook his head. He had to get them out of his brain, stop remembering, and think of a way to get out of this mess. He wasn't lost. He knew his way around the zoo. He was safe here. Just him and the animals, and probably a couple of guards at each entrance. By morning, though, he had to get home without anyone knowing where he'd spent the night. The north gate led to the CTrain station and traffic and light. The other darker side of the zoo was his best chance. The way he and Wilma had come in.

He leaned against the flat face of a boulder and looked back over the fiery swamp. Big Daddy T. Rex back at the other end of the park, and here on her own hill, Mama T. Rex rearing up with her baby at her feet. Tina and him? No. In the blink of his eye, before he turned and began to creep forward again, that mother dinosaur looked more like Elsie.

At the suspension bridge that would take him across the river and onto the main island of the zoo, he heard voices coming closer, getting louder. He swung himself around the back of the rock. On his left, the path wound down into bushes and tall ferns where he could lie hidden, but the thought of stretching on the cold earth made his skin prickle. This was supposed to be a swamp. The rock was fake, but the things creeping around in the mud were real. He'd stay here, flattened against the stone, hoping that whoever was coming would walk right by without looking back.

Then, to his surprise, the voices seemed to be fading instead of coming closer. A minute later, another shout, laughter, the jangle of a bicycle bell. Not people in the zoo, but bikes going by on the path that ran along the river. Bikes.

Elsie had tried to get him to ride one of the bikes in the garage to the grocery store. If he had wheels he could be on his way to Winnipeg by now. If he knew how to ride.

Below him, the bushes rustled. Maybe a mouse or a bird. Not a snake, because this was fake rock. He knew that from standing on the other side of the fence long ago with his Opi, and watching them build the park. Snakes were too smart to hang out in a man-made desert. Still, his trembling caused a spasm in his feet that skidded loose gravel onto the path below.

He swallowed hard, bit his lip to keep from crying. His throat felt as though it was peeled raw, the back of his T-shirt wet with sweat. On the other side of the bridge, there were washrooms next to the monkey house where he'd be out of the wind. If he was lucky, the monkeys would be inside, but he wasn't counting on it. All the whooping and chattering and swinging, the way they looked at him, they reminded him of Paulette's kids. He'd run into Paulette at the Stampede last summer when he was living with Judy and Frank—the second people who were supposed to be adopting him. Corey would never forget the look on Judy's face. They'd been rushing through the grounds to get to the grandstand, because Frank's company had fancy seats and they were having supper in the restaurant before the chuck wagon races and show. When Paulette came puffing up beside them, he'd almost pretended he didn't know her, but then she'd turned to the guy who was with her and said, "Hey, this is Tina Brinkman's kid." Frank and Judy jumped back as though someone had hit them with a board. A grungy, smelly, ugly, old board.

Corey'd wished he wasn't wearing the stupid plaid shirt and new jeans they'd bought him for Stampede. He'd wished he was wearing Tina's Nike shirt and his old ripped jeans. He walked right up to Paulette, right into her big fat hug, knowing it would drive Judy nuts. Maybe that was when Judy and Frank changed their minds about wanting him to be their son. Then Ben heard they were throwing him out, and everything worked out from there.

Oh yeah. Everything had worked out great. He was just having a holiday at the zoo. Sweet place to spend the night, Cor. A crescent moon hung over the towering statue of the angry mother dinosaur. From behind her, the roar of traffic, sirens screaming past. And every ten minutes or so, the tiger called again.

30

BEN SLID INTO THE BOOTH AND PICKED UP A menu. At least there was dessert to consider. Across from him, Wilma was chewing on her lip. Chewing over his declaration by the river, he was sure. "Deep dish apple pie sounds good, don't you think?" he said.

"I'm not hungry. Just cold."

"Look, Willi." He leaned toward her. "I know you're worried. I'm sorry I came on so heavy out there."

"There is nowhere else for him to go, Ben. Kristel said today that she thinks he has as much of a chance at surviving as a dog who chases cars." She stared out at the street. "His mom hugged him this afternoon. Grabbed him as soon as she saw him and held him tight. I could have cried, because I realized she's the only one who gets to do that. Every six months. For four years, Ben! Four years of being untouchable, except for two hugs a year. If he leaves us and goes to live in a group home the way they say he will, because that's all that's left, then what?"

He tried to catch the server's attention; the place was bustling on this chilly night. He had a feeling time was running out, but not only for Corey. Wilma was not in any mood to sit in a coffee shop and munch her way through a wedge of cheesecake. "Don't you think you might be taking those cautions about touching to the extreme?"

"Me?" She turned finally and looked at him with red-rimmed eyes, a face bleak with concern. "You're the one who told me to be careful I didn't say anything kinky. Is it kinky to want to touch a child so that he knows he's alive? But you don't have to worry about this." She shook her head, wisps of wheat-coloured hair clinging to her collar. "No. It's okay for you to throw a manly arm around his shoulder, or clap him on the back. Do that when Kristel's around, and she'll put the two of you on the next foster care poster."

From a couple of tables away, the waiter nodded at Ben, held up two fingers.

"Kristel, Kristel. I thought we agreed to leave her at home. Her own home, wherever that is. Suddenly, she's having coffee with us, jerking your chain. Let's order shall we? So you can warm up, and then we'll go home."

"We should phone from here and check the messages," she said. "We should try Carmen again."

Ben filed the menu behind the napkin dispenser, pulled the phone from his jacket pocket, and handed it to her. She jabbed at the buttons, then shoved the phone across the table. "Your battery's dead. I noticed a pay phone outside when we came in," she said. "I'll order for you while you're gone." From a pocket on the side of her purse, she pulled out a neatly folded piece of paper and handed it to him.

"What's this?"

"Tina's number. It's written on the back of the picture on Corey's dresser. Just the number, but I checked in the phone book and it's her."

"And you want me to call and confirm that he's there."

"No, I want you to confirm that he's not there. I can't do it. I don't want to talk to Tina."

"Apple pie," he said, and stomped toward the door.

She was right about the cold. It would dip close to freezing tonight. Ben rang the number on Wilma's note, listened to an out-of-service message, and flipped open the phone book. A short list of Brinkmans. The obvious one, C. Brinkman, at an address in Bridgeland probably a stone's throw from the zoo, answered on the first ring. He hung up as soon as Ben told him he was looking for Tina.

He was tempted to leave it at that, but he knew Wilma would never settle for a simple "wrong number." She'd call back herself, tell the old man Corey was lost, and before the evening was over, they'd be picking up Grandpa Brinkman and dragging him along on the search.

So he tried one more time, choosing his words carefully. "I'm sorry to bother you so late in the evening," he said, "and I apologize if I have the wrong person. I'm trying to reach Tina Brinkman and I wondered if you might be her father, Corey's grandfather?"

There was silence, then a voice that sounded raspy from lack of use. "Tina is my granddaughter, not my daughter. What do you want from her?"

"My wife and I look after Corey," he began, "and he's supposed to be with Tina tonight. We need to reach her to be sure that worked out, but the phone number we have is out of service."

"I can't help you with that."

From there, Ben felt as though he was pulling answers out of the old man, like a hammer working on a bent nail.

"Would any of the other Brinkmans in the directory know how to reach her, do you think?" he finally asked, speaking slowly, wanting to keep this man from hanging up again.

"No," he growled. "There's only Anna, Tina's mother, and she's gone. Ran away. No other Brinkman knows us. Leave me alone, please."

Before Ben could apologize for troubling him, he heard the unmistakable racking sound of a sob. Then a click.

He hung up the phone, and took a deep breath. Anna? Tina's mother ran away? He was sure they'd been told that Corey's grandmother was dead. C. Brinkman sounded like an old man. Maybe seventy-five? A twelve-year-old grandson. A twenty-six-year-old granddaughter. Yeah, there was room for another generation, but just barely. Someone named Anna? Or maybe Ben was the only one who was confused, and Wilma knew all of this already.

Wilma was waiting for some other answers. This time he dialed home to check the answering machine, his eyes on a couple of kids panhandling on the corner while he listened. Older than Corey, but still he shuddered to think of where they'd end up before the night was over. Sitting on the bench beside the river with Wilma, he'd imagined the night's activity in the park on the other side. A park well-furnished with needle drop-bins. He tried to forget that the zoo parking lot had been listed in the *Herald* as one of the notorious pickup spots for gays in the city. Tried to put all of that out of his mind, and did the same thing now as he went back inside to Wilma.

She'd taken off her jacket, and was leaning chin in hands over a steaming cup of coffee. At his place, coffee and a bran muffin.

She sat up straight when she saw him. "Ben, what's wrong? Where's Corey? Who did you talk to?"

He cupped his face with both hands, rubbed his eyebrows with his fingertips, blew out a long breath before he spoke.

"That number for Tina is out of service. Directory assistance doesn't have a new listing. So I looked for other Brinkmans in the book. I talked to an old man. The grandpa. He doesn't know where anyone is."

"Did you call home to check the messages?"

He nodded. "Elsie," he said, "and Phil. And Tina."

"What did Tina say?" When he hesitated, she grabbed his hand. "She doesn't have him. I was right, wasn't I? Ben, what did she say?"

He waved at the server. "Could we get the bill, please." He picked up her jacket and held it open. "I'll tell you on the way home."

"Home? If Corey's not with Tina, we're not going home." Her voice had risen an octave. People at the next table turned to listen. "Tell me right now what she said."

"She wanted to know how he was. She said he was sick this afternoon and she also says he's allergic to penicillin." He frowned. "Did we know that?"

"Yes, of course. Corey told me that long ago. It's on the medical report." She stood up, yanked the jacket out of his hands, and rammed her arms into the sleeves. "You go pay. Give me that phone number. I'm going to call Corey's grandpa back."

"Why? Do think he lied to me?"

Wilma shrugged and raised her palms. "Maybe you didn't ask the right questions. Or maybe too many questions."

All around them now, people were watching and listening. Ben lowered his voice, took her elbow, steered her toward the entrance. "This isn't straightforward, Wilma. I don't think he's Tina's father. He's her grandfather."

"Then what happened to her parents?"

"There's someone named Anna. He said she's Tina's mother, but it sounds like she's long gone." He was on the verge of telling her about the grandfather's tears, but that would make her all the more determined to talk with the old man. To reassure him, to convince him they were good people and that Corey belonged with them. He'd spare C. Brinkman that attention. For tonight anyway.

Wilma wriggled her shoulders snug into the jacket, and began buttoning in a businesslike manner. "Never mind," she said. "We'll figure it out later. But we still need to give him our number. If Corey didn't go home from the zoo with Tina, and his grandpa lives near the zoo—he told us his Opi lives near the zoo—isn't that the obvious place for him to be headed?" She plucked the bill out of his hand, dug through her bag, and then hustled over to elbow her way through the cluster of people at the cashier's desk. "Excuse me," she said cheerfully to the lineup, slapping down a twenty-dollar bill. "Emergency. We have to run." She'd gone from totally dejected to full of purpose, in the space of about three minutes.

Ben caught her arm. "Leave him alone, Wilma. I've caused him enough grief tonight." She shook her head and pulled away, but he held tight. "That man has lost his grandson." And then he corrected himself. "His great-grandson. If he wanted to see Corey, he would have made the effort. Don't meddle."

She glared at him. "Maybe he regrets never making the effort. Maybe he's too stubborn or too proud, or too something else to admit that."

Ben released his hold on her sleeve. "Maybe he is, and maybe he does regret it. But it's not up to you to fix that."

She stalked out the door ahead of him. Ben caught up with her at the corner. "We need to go home and sort this out. Make some phone calls. Maybe that woman, Carmen, does have Corey. That seems the most logical answer. Or maybe he tried to call us, and when he didn't get an answer he headed home. He might be waiting for us already, or at least on the way."

Wilma threw up her arms. "Oh, logical! You can be logical, but when I say something's the logical route you do a quick turn down some other street. He's alone. Out here somewhere in the cold. He's wearing shorts and the oldest, thinnest shirt he owns—God, I wish I knew why he dressed that way today—and he's sick." She was wringing her hands. Ben knew that it was going to take some fast talking to convince her to get in the car and go home.

31

CORNELIUS BRINKMAN HUNG UP ON THE FIRST phone call. Not able to understand what the voice was asking of him, barely able to hear the caller, he simply said, "Wrong number," and hung up. Then, while he was closing the window on the roaring of the tiger which had begun at the same time as the ringing of the phone, the man's words coalesced in his mind and he realized that he'd been talking about Tina, and about Corey.

So strong was the jolt of memory that Brinkman slumped against the counter with his arms folded across his chest, as though he was holding a child, a tiny boy with matchstick arms and legs. Like an armful of kindling, except when he was asleep and then he pressed warm and damp into the shoulder, the moist face, the small open mouth leaving a print on the shirt front after he was eased carefully onto his bed.

When the phone rang a second time he picked it up and listened again. Polite, cautious, the man on the other end sounded hesitant, but definite about who he wanted.

"I'm sorry to bother you," he said, "but I wondered if you might be Tina Brinkman's father. Corey's grandfather?"

Cornelius would have hung up again except for the mention of Corey.

The man said he looked after Corey, and then questions and questions that Brinkman answered with a yes, and a no, and I don't know, giving away nothing. No, he lied, he hadn't talked with Tina in months. He didn't have an address and if the phone was out of order it was out of order. Finally, that feeling that he was holding the child in his arms at the same time that he was slipping away was too much. When the man asked about family, Brinkman had choked out Anna's name and then Corey's and then he'd hung up.

He poured another cup of coffee, and sat in the darkening kitchen with his eyes on the phone. It wouldn't ring again tonight. Of that he was sure. He was also sure, from the sound of the man's voice, that Corey was lost.

The man who called had assumed he was Tina's father. For a moment the old rage rose in him and he'd almost shouted into the phone. But then he realized that this was not an accusation like the one twisted into the social worker's sly questions. It was simply that the man didn't know Anna had even existed. Sometimes he himself had trouble remembering. He had no image of Anna as a mother or a woman, just as *een klein meisje*, a little girl in a yellow frock with a sash tied into a big bow. Bepp had sewn the dress in one of her short dry periods.

It was dark in the kitchen now, the streetlight pouring through the window onto the tile floor like a film of thin grey dust. Brinkman rose with a wince at the stiffness in his legs, lifted the coffee off the heat. The scorched smell when he ran water into the thick coating on the bottom of the pot brought bile to his throat again. The piece of bread lay on the table, one bite out of the thick crust. If he didn't eat properly his blood sugar would fly as wild as those old crows in the Mayday tree. Inez would find him two days from now on the floor. Not fair for a woman to live through such a gruesome discovery twice.

In the dark of the kitchen he chewed, trying to form a picture of Corey in his mind. Always he went back to the tiny boy, but Corey was twelve years old, almost a man. Though Brinkman had long since given up on his mother's Jesus Christ and Holy Mary, he prayed fiercely to an unknown power that the boy, Cor David Brinkman, would bear no resemblance to Simon Miller. None. And please, whoever was listening, let the man, the one who called, find Corey and protect him from all things evil.

32

COREY'S EARS ACHED. PLANES OVERHEAD, TRAFFIC
and sirens outside the park, and over and over again the
voice of the tiger. He wondered if something was wrong,
something or someone upsetting the big cats.

He was stiff from crouching in the bushes, his feet numb. Just when
he'd convinced himself that the security guards would have no reason to
walk through the dinosaur park, he'd heard off-key whistling, and then
the scuffling sound of someone approaching. He'd run down a branch of
the path that dipped into trees and thick plants. There'd been just enough
time to dive into the darkest shadows behind a garbage bin.

He counted while he waited, trying to figure out how many footsteps
it would take to get the man across the river, or far enough in the other
direction, if that was the circuit he was making, that it would be safe for
Corey to move again. Twenty-seven, twenty-eight ... he kept his eyes
closed, trying to ignore the tickle of grass on his legs, the rustling and
slithering around him. He pressed his burning face against the cold metal
of the garbage container. After being invisible for so long, he couldn't
believe that now, when he needed that power the most, it wasn't working.

On the way to every new foster home, every new school, in every new
social worker's car, Corey had learned to slide inside himself and pretend
he was blind, deaf, and invisible. He never remembered later how he got
to those new places.

Meeting Ben and Wilma for the first time, crawling into his corner
in the social worker's car, his head shaking. I can't. I can't get out. Jim was
his social worker before Kristel—a guy with an earring and an old beater
of a car, and papers everywhere. Once, when Jim had left Corey alone for
five minutes in his office, Corey had snooped through an address file and
found Tina's phone number. 'We'll sit here until you're ready,' Jim had said,

when they were parked outside Ben and Wilma's house that first day. And he started telling Corey about the Howards and how their boys weren't at home anymore and how they'd never been foster parents but they'd heard about Corey. 'Yeah, Cor, you're right to be scared. I haven't met them either. For all we know they could be trolls.' Corey laughing then, even though he was still shaking inside. Finally his legs started to work again and they were at the door. Wilma standing there. 'Hi, Corey.' A soft, pretty voice. She sounded almost as nervous as he was. Ben, as big as a bear, with the kind of voice that made you hope he was on your side. He could remember all this. Why? Was that when he lost it? The magic invisibility? For the first two weeks, Ben and Wilma watching him leave the house every time as though they were going crazy. Corey was sure Jim had told them he was a runner. And when people expect something, you may as well get it over with. So he ran. Thinking that when the cop brought him back, Wilma and Ben would give him the usual countdown on his chances and tell him how he'd now used one of them, but no. A bath and hot chocolate and bed. That bed that he wanted so badly right now he was ready to run back up the hill and jump the fence onto Memorial Drive.

He opened his eyes, poked his head out from behind the trashcan. Not a sound or sign of anyone. Nothing but the trickle of water. Funny how he'd never noticed the sound of water in this park until tonight. Around the two lakes, a gentle slapping of waves, and from some of the deeper gouges in the rock, the gurgle of underground streams. He licked his lips, but couldn't find enough spit to wet them. His tongue felt hot and raspy, like the tongue of a kitten he'd had long ago. Smoky, Tina had called him, when Corey couldn't think of a name. Not quite right, because Smoky was jet black, but he'd liked it anyway. When Smoky died, Corey ran away. Walked right out the door while Tina was on the phone. Opi found him sitting beside the river a block from his house. Tina never told any of the social workers that he'd run away when he was six years old. She couldn't blame the foster homes if anyone knew that he'd started running a long time ago.

He should get up now, start moving toward the bridge, but if he closed his eyes he could imagine himself in bed with that puffy blanket pulled under his chin, the light from the kitchen throwing a pale yellow block onto the bedroom wall.

The second time Corey ran from Wilma and Ben, their youngest son was home for Christmas. Big, handsome Mark whose bedroom Corey was borrowing. All of that first day, Mark being super friendly and promising to take him to the mall to buy presents for Ben and Wilma. Corey watching the way Wilma reached out to touch Mark every time he came into the room, and realizing suddenly that Ben and Wilma didn't need another kid. They had this perfect son, and they had Philip, even though they didn't talk as much about him. Why did they want Corey? Sooner or later they'd get tired of him. The longer he was there, the more it would hurt to leave. He'd learned that a long time ago, and here he was making the old mistake of liking a place. So the next day at the mall when he and Mark split up to buy presents, Corey went right out the door and hopped on a bus.

Two nights later, after the police had hauled him back again, Mark tapping on the bedroom door. Corey in bed with the kitchen light shining on the wall, branches whispering against the window.

"Jeez, dude, you had everybody worried sick. Mom can't handle this kind of stuff, you know." Corey trying to mumble that he was sorry. Mark shaking his head. "You don't have to be sorry. You didn't ask for any of this shit." Sitting now on the edge of the bed. "But can you tell me one thing?"

Corey pulled himself up on the pillows, his eyes on Mark.

"Do you want to live here?"

Corey nodded.

"Why?" Mark asked.

Corey bit his lip and looked at the tall, smart son who belonged to Wilma and Ben. Then he looked around the bedroom that was really Mark's. Whatever he answered, he was sure it would be wrong. He shrugged and turned away.

Mark reached across the blanket to put a hand on his shoulder. "Is it because there's nowhere else for you to go?"

With his head down, he nodded again. Mark's hand grew heavier and his voice sounded thick, like the words were stuck in his throat. "Aw, Corey, that really sucks, man." After a minute, he lifted Corey's chin so that he was looking into his face. "Why don't you stick around? I think it'll be okay."

Corey rested heavily against the side of the garbage can. He'd hold Mark's voice in his mind. All night if he could. And then there'd be no room for Simon to close in on his dreams.

33 IN THE TINY BACHELOR LIVING ROOM, TINA shifted a pile of Simon's clothes from the futon to the floor, and stretched out in the dark. The room reeked of takeout food and the eggs Simon had fried in the morning before he took her to the zoo.

The walls were striped with the shadows of Venetian blinds that would neither fully open, nor close. If Simon parked out back, he'd look up at the window and see slivers of fluorescent white from the stove light that was also permanently on.

Tina's hand slid into the crevice of the lumpy mattress and snagged a package of matches. She'd shoved them there this morning. They were from an Irish pub Marvin took her to on St. Patrick's Day. Souvenirs of Marvin wouldn't go over well with Simon.

Matches from the bar date with Marvin, smokes from tonight's party with Simon. She shook so violently that she burned the tip of her finger striking the match. Now the glow of the cigarette would give her away, like the flicker of the television the last time he stood out there in the dark, watching.

"That's creepy," Paulette had muttered, when Simon bragged about sneaking up on Tina. She'd turned to Tina. "That woulda scared the shit out of me." And then to Simon, "Aren't you ever gonna grow up?"

Tina sniffed. "I'm used to it. Except who wants to play with a thirty-year-old kid?" Maybe he'd give up the game if she could learn to ignore her heart flying into her throat when the door crashed open against the heel of his boot, or his hand snaked out to grab her arm when she rounded the corner of the building. Always after they'd had a fight. An excuse to pull her so close they'd melt into that one complete and deadly hybrid that she would never be able to abandon for anyone else. Not even for Corey, who was changing so fast she had a hard time conjuring up the memory of his baby weight in her arms. The smell, the taste, and the feel of Simon would never change.

You can go. That's what Corey had said, but he'd never answered her question and he hadn't looked her in the eye. Tina blew a plume of smoke and watched it drift toward the ceiling. The little bugger had lied to her about phoning, and she hadn't bothered to notice, hadn't wanted to know, because that would only have complicated her escape.

She sat up, scooped up Simon's black sweater, and pulled it over her head, the stench of stale smoke and smell of his body so locked into the wool they settled like a mantle over her. She crossed her arms, let the sweater hold her tight. Shivered. Her feet were damn near frozen too.

When she opened a drawer to look for socks, light glinted off the black leather jewellery case on top of the dresser. She picked it up and carried it back to the futon. A birthday present from Simon the year she met him.

"I'm gonna fill this sucker with pretty things for you, Tina. Every goddamn birthday for the rest of your life, you can expect something special from me."

She shook the box gently. He'd done it too. The case was crammed with earrings and bracelets and rings. And two matchbox trucks. She lifted them out and held them in the palm of her hand. The tow truck was chipped to the grey undercoat, with a few dull flakes of yellow paint clinging to the hoist. The other was a tanker, but only the cab remained. Somewhere along the way, the white gas tank with "Shell" in bold red letters had been lost. Tina hooked the nail of her little finger under the door. It popped open and she held the truck to her eye and peered in at a tiny, plastic figure. Still staring straight ahead, miniature plastic hat on his head after all these years.

Corey was two years old when Simon showed up drunk one night with a Kleenex box full of toys. He'd been living with his mom then. They'd had a fight and old lady Miller had thrown all of his junk into the snow.

"Three lousy cartons full of stuff," he whined, "and she says it's taking up space." Corey was playing on the kitchen floor with a stack of plastic cups and lids. "This'll keep the kid quiet while you and me have some fun." When Simon turned the box over and shook it, plastic Smurfs and matchbox toys tumbled out of the oval opening. Corey reached for a rusty tow truck.

"What are you trying to do?" Tina snatched the toy from his hand and threw it back in the box. "That thing has sharp edges, and if he puts it in his mouth he could choke on it, and it's dirty!"

"That's sweet, Tina. Your kid's too good for my stuff, right? Any present I give him is shit?" Simon swept up a handful of cars and flung them across the room. She'd had to lie to the old man and tell him the glass in the china cabinet was shattered because Corey had banged a toy against it.

Later, she'd tried to make it up to Simon by letting Corey play with the stuff—after she sneaked it out to the kitchen and washed it all—and Corey'd grabbed these two trucks and wouldn't let go of them for anything. She'd hid them when he went to sleep that night. Simon got pissed off about something else and took the rest of his toys with him when he left.

When Opi kicked them out, she'd thrown all the stuff from her dresser drawers into a box, and Corey had jumped on the trucks like they were buried treasure. Almost as though he could remember them, three years later. He'd carried them everywhere; she was forever crawling around on the floor looking for lost wheels. The night after they took Corey away, she'd held the trucks in her own hands when she went to sleep.

34

COREY STRUGGLED TO OPEN HIS EYES. IT WOULD be dark now, but at least this darkness was thin and icy cold, nothing like the suffocating blackness of his nightmares. Mark, Shawn, Opi, Ben, Wilma, all banished from his thrashing mind by the memory of that darkness, heavy as coats in the closet.

Simon stomping into the kitchen where Corey was eating his dry cereal, driving the matchbox tow truck around the table and in between the salt and pepper and behind the sugar bowl. Simon furious because he'd just had a fight with Tina, and she'd locked herself in the bathroom. Simon opening the fridge, knocking around the bottles on the top shelf, slamming the door.

"Where's the orange juice? Did you drink the last of the goddamn juice?"

Corey backed up the tow truck and attached the tiny hoist to his spoon. He didn't look up.

"Answer me, you little moron!" Simon grabbed the truck and shook it in front of his face. "I brought orange juice yesterday and the fridge is fuckin' empty!"

Corey's truck disappearing in that big ugly hand, and something inside his head exploding. He lunged at Simon, closed his teeth around hairy knuckles, and bit until he tasted blood. And then he tore out of the kitchen, into the closet in the bedroom, burrowed under clothes that smelled of Tina, and held his breath until his chest felt like it was on fire and his eyes bulged. With a roar ten times as ferocious as the tiger, Simon wrenched open the door, and punched his arm through the curtain of shirts and sweaters. He seized Corey around the waist and dragged him to the kitchen. Again Corey found flesh, twisting his head to lock his jaw around Simon's forearm. Simon bellowed even louder and, with his free hand, swung at Corey's neck. The force of the icy wind almost blew them both back inside the house when he kicked open the sagging basement door. He raised Corey flailing and kicking over his head like a trophy, staggered into the cement stairwell, up the steps. When he got to the top, in a final savage burst of strength, he catapulted Corey into the snowy yard.

Through a swirl of black and crimson, Corey saw the spruce tree coming toward him and clutched desperately for a branch, but missed and sank through the wind-whipped crust of the snow, grazing his shoulder on the scaly bark, resting finally in a curl around the base of the tree.

Corey wrenched his eyes open and leapt up. Something furry scooted out from under the leaves, scrabbled over his foot, brushing his ankle as it ran. He stumbled out of the grass, kicking side to side until he was on a small wooden bridge.

Back to the rock. That's where he'd go. Behind the last jutting piece of stone he'd wait a bit longer. But he wouldn't close his eyes. No. Even though Simon had stormed away as soon as he threw Corey into the snow, he was always lurking. Always in Corey's dreams, Tina beside him.

It must have been Tina who carried him into the house that morning. Tina pacing, smoking, stopping every thirty steps to return to Corey, pat his arm, knee, hair, pull the nubby blue blanket tight to his shoulders. They sent a male cop, a policewoman, and a social worker.

The lady from upstairs came right into the living room, shaking her finger at Tina, clucking at Corey, plucking the policewoman's sleeve. "Like I said on the phone, I don't make trouble. But I worry about the kid. Always alone. And now this man, this monster . . ." She puffed herself up to an angry height, mimicked Simon lofting Corey through the winter morning. She shuddered. "I had to call. Mostly it's best you mind your business, but not when a child is hurt." Her eyes threw one last knife at Tina before she scurried from the room.

He said what Tina had told him to say. That he'd run up the stairs, slid on the ice, went flying across the yard, hit the tree. But she must have known nobody would be dumb enough to believe you could break your arm and crack your ribs by throwing yourself against a tree.

Tina had taught him to lie. This night was Tina's fault. If he wasn't so sick, he'd enjoy the fact that it was Tina he'd conned by lying just like she'd taught him. He took a deep breath, kept his eyes straight ahead, and darted up the hill. When he got to the top, still holding a lungful of air, he bit his lip to keep from panting. His heart pounded so hard his T-shirt bounced with each thud. His chest ached.

35

WILMA'S TEETH WERE CHATTERING SO VIOLENTLY by the time they got into the car, she could barely hear Ben's arguments. All she knew was that he was bent on going home. If the wind could bite through her heavy sweater, how would it feel to a boy wearing a T-shirt as thin as a whisper?

Ben peeled off his jacket and draped it over her like a blanket, tucking the sleeves behind her back. When he started the car and pulled into the traffic, turned the corner toward home, Wilma shucked the jacket aside and seized his arm.

"We have to go to the zoo." She tried to unclench her jaw. Her words wanted to clatter out like ice cubes into a glass. "If we explain what happened to the security people, at the very least they'll keep their eyes open for him." She strained sideways, as far as the seat belt would allow, so that he couldn't avoid looking at her. "We can't leave this to Kristel and the police. They won't even bother to look for him till morning, and the longer he's missing, the more likely it is Kristel will decide to send him somewhere else. Please turn around."

"If he's gone, he's on the run. He's not sitting still. He's not at the zoo."

"And so?" Wilma threw up her hands. "What are you suggesting we do? Go home to bed?"

He nodded, eyes ahead, driving cautiously as ever. "Go home, for starters. Maybe Tina will call back and tell us the whole story. Maybe Corey will call. Maybe Corey's asleep in his bed."

Wilma leaned back and folded her arms across her chest. She closed her eyes and ignored Ben's reasonable assurances for the rest of the drive home. She could not rid herself of the image of Corey crouched between a clump of bushes and the heavy wire mesh of the tiger's enclosure.

The car was still rolling to a stop when she threw off her seat belt, opened the door, and ran up the sidewalk, key in hand.

"Corey?"

Dark. Not a sound but the hum of the furnace, which had kicked in for the first time in days. One hand reached for the phone, the other poised over the answering machine.

Ben walked past her, down the hall to Corey's bedroom, flicked on the light, and stood leaning on the doorframe.

"You didn't really expect to find him in bed, did you?"

He turned and came slowly back to the kitchen, crossing the oblong of light that fell into the dark hallway. "I guess I was harbouring a slim hope." He rubbed his face with his hands, his fingers lifting his glasses onto his forehead. "God, Willi, I never guessed we'd get so wound up with this kid."

Holding up a hand to silence him, she put her ear to the answering machine. Phil's voice was faint, the tape messy with static. "Hey, Mom. You probably didn't get my card yet, so when it comes, ignore the part about me coming home. The job interview's off. There doesn't seem any point in driving out now, so maybe I'll hitch as far as Winnipeg and hang out with Grandma for Mother's Day. Or maybe not. You don't have to call back. I'll phone you next weekend."

Then Tina's message. Not the strident voice Wilma expected, but a husky rush of words that sounded almost like an apology. "Yeah, this is Tina Brinkman . . . "

Out in the dining room, she could hear Ben rummaging in the liquor cabinet. He came around the corner with a bottle of Scotch. "Want something? It'll help you sleep."

Sleep? He was planning to sleep? Wilma hit the stop button and cut her mother off at, "Wilma, you know how much I hate talking to machines?"

"There's not a chance that Glenfiddich, warm milk, or choruses of angels singing lullabies could put me to sleep when Corey's roaming around in the night. Seriously? You're going to bed?"

He shrugged and poured three fingers of Scotch into a glass. "Unless I can come up with a good reason to sit here and watch you worry."

"Shouldn't we call the police?"

He leaned against the counter, glanced out into the dark yard, frowned. "Nope. I think we should try it a different way. Remember that social worker, the one with the piercings and tattoo, telling us that Corey always seems to forget what he's running toward? How eventually he sits down and waits for someone to find him?"

Wilma shook her head sideways so rapidly the kitchen lights flashed a kaleidoscope in her head. That picture of Corey huddled on a bench downtown in Olympic Plaza just before Christmas, waiting, was so cold and sharp she had to shake it away. Ben handed her his glass and she sipped, just to feel the warmth of the whisky.

"Let's give him a chance to come home on his own," Ben said. "He doesn't know Tina phoned us. We don't have to call the police to prove to him that we care. Let's wait at least until morning and see what happens."

"No!" When he tried to put his arms around her, she backed away. "Did you look out the car windows when we were driving home? Did you see who's out there standing on corners?"

"Yeah, I did. And it's not Corey. He's going to hide until it's safe to come out. Christ, Wilma! Give him credit. He has good instincts. He doesn't go looking for trouble." He took a long swallow and slammed the glass on the counter. "There's nothing to be gained by calling anyone tonight. I promise you we'll get out there first thing in the morning. We'll go to the old man's house, wheedle Tina's address out of him, and head Kristel off at the pass. We'll get Tina to say we picked Corey up ourselves. Kristel's already ticked off about working on the weekend. We won't hear from her till Monday. He'll come back on his own, Wilma. I know this. Nobody's ever given him that chance."

She took another step back. "Like Philip will eventually come back on his own? All we have to do is wait?"

Ben stared at her. "This hasn't a damn thing to do with Philip. I'm going to bed now. Are you coming?"

"Good night, Ben." She watched him take off his glasses and rub the dark shadows around his eyes. Like bruises. She felt them under her own eyes. Maybe he was right. Chasing after Corey when he ran was like inviting someone to meet you in the same dark alley where you've already been battered twice. She put a hand on his arm. "You go to bed. I'm going to call Ma, then read for a while."

Ben sighed, his shoulders slumping. "We'll get him back, Willi. I promise we will. You are planning on coming to bed eventually?" He stepped so close she felt his breath part her hair, the shadow of his body brushing hers. Wilma knew he was hoping she'd relax, lean into him, and they'd fit together like pieces of a puzzle. That she'd forget about her mother, forget about phone calls, leave it all until tomorrow.

She tilted her head back, and looked into Ben's eyes. "Stay up while I call Philip," she said.

There was the slightest pause when Wilma sensed the intent rather than the actual shaking of his head, and then the phone rang and they leapt apart. Ben was closest. "Yes?" He exhaled. "Hi, Elsie." He handed Wilma the phone, then, drink in one hand, jacket over the other arm, walked down the hall to the bedroom. "Wake me if you need me," he said and closed the door behind him.

Wilma took a deep breath before she clamped the phone to her ear.

"Ben?" Elsie's voice was testy. "Where's Wilma? Ben!"

"Settle down, Ma. We're in enough of a flap already. Corey's missing. We thought it might be him calling."

"Aw no, poor boy." Elsie clucked a half dozen times.

Wilma imagined her at the square kitchen table, enthroned on a chrome chair, quilted housecoat tented around her, looking like the curly-topped dolls whose plastic heads she glued to crocheted bodies for the church bazaar. Shorter even than Corey, her legs would barely touch the floor while she sipped her Ovaltine, peeked over her glasses at her address book, tried to decide who was still awake in which time zone. By now, she'd have called all three of her sisters, her brother Ed, and Wilma's brother in Vancouver where the night was still new.

"You called earlier, Ma?"

"Of course I did. How else would you know to call me back?"

She let it go, too tired to race her mother around the circle. "Any particular reason?"

"I knew something was wrong. I said to myself, when I was looking in the fridge to decide what I should have for supper and the bacon reminded me of Corey, how he likes bacon and tomato sandwiches, I said, I'll bet it would be a good idea to phone and talk to Corey. You see, I should have phoned earlier instead of yakking to Molly for an hour. She's got another lump, you know. Now what are you and Ben doing at home if Corey's lost? One of you needs to stay home for the phone, but Ben should be looking for him."

Wilma's head was on the table now with the phone lying beside her ear. *Keep talking Ma,* she sighed. There was a pause, a wheezy intake of breath, and then a stifled cough.

"Ma! Are you smoking again?"

"No! I only keep them here for emergencies. Isn't this an emergency?"

Elsie had spent Easter with them, baking hot cross buns, daffodil cake, yeast donuts in this kitchen, drawing Corey into everything she did, coaxing smiles they'd never seen before. "Come, Corey, and help Grandma Elsie do these dishes, and then we'll walk to the store and buy chocolate milk to have with the donuts. They should be ready to fry when we get back." And slipping out onto the back step to smoke, when she thought no one was watching.

Mark, who was home that weekend, ragged her relentlessly about cigarettes, cholesterol, white sugar. "Go away," she said. "I have a new grandson who appreciates my food as much as you did when you were small like him. He's so polite, he'd never hound an old woman about a few bad habits."

" Corey," she said, pulling him close in a pillowy hug—she snorted when Wilma told her she wasn't allowed because of the rules—"I bet you never tried to tell your grandpa what to eat."

Later, Wilma drew her aside. "Ma, how do you know about Corey's grandpa?"

She'd shrugged. "He told me on the way to the store, he used to watch his grandpa bake bread. Early in the morning if his mom wasn't home, he went along to the bakery. How come, I want to know, this baker grandpa's no longer in the picture? Of course I wouldn't ask the child, he's got enough to worry about, and I don't want him to think I'm snooping. How do I know? I listen."

"When you were here at Easter," Wilma sat up and held the phone to her ear, wishing she'd let Ben pour her a Scotch of her own, "did you get the feeling he was unhappy, or that he'd run away again? I hoped . . . we both thought he'd settled in finally, and that he wanted to stay here."

"Of course he wants to stay there," Elsie snapped. "What does running away have to do with wanting to stay? He's like your Uncle Ed. Eddy ran away every two months from the time he was eight years old until he grew a beard, but that had nothing to do with leaving home. He said he got restless and he had to go."

"But this could be our last chance. Corey has a new social worker. I think she hates us. If he runs away she'll probably move him."

"No." Wilma imagined her mother leaning back in her chair, quilted arms folded across her chest, grey curls bobbing with every shake of her head. "That boy is not going anywhere because he belongs in your house. You tell the social worker Corey's been drifting around waiting to find you and Ben. Or give me the phone number and I'll tell her. How come they keep saying they have no foster homes for teenagers? I hear about this on the news so much I've been thinking that I should take somebody. When they get a family like you, they start counting the child's chances like baseball? One, two, three, he's out? Wilma, that's stupid. You get off the phone now so Corey can call and tell you where he is. I'm going to stay up and wait for you to call me back. Goodbye."

And Wilma knew she would. She'd stretch out in the recliner in front of the television, and she'd be there in the morning when the building monitor knocked on her door to make sure she was still alive. At nine o'clock, Winnipeg time, she'd call again, and Wilma would still be sitting here polishing the buttons on the phone with her index finger.

She tiptoed into the bedroom where Ben was flung across the middle of the bed, the air above him reverberating with the constant low-grade gurgle in the back of his throat that drove her nuts. When she sat on the edge of the bed to open a dresser drawer, he stirred, patted the blanket on her side, rolled over. "Sorry," he mumbled. Wilma shook her head. She had him so well trained. So why was he asleep when Corey was lost, and she was out of her mind with worry? Because that was his solution to stress. Sleep on it. It'll make more sense in the morning.

In jeans now, a turtleneck, heavy sweater, and a windbreaker, she followed the light back to Corey's bedroom, and pulled a pair of sweatpants out of the closet. She lifted his hoodie off the hook on the back of the door, folded the clothes, tucked them under her arm, and then slipped out the front door. She drove halfway down the block before she turned on the headlights.

36

TINA DROPPED BOTH TOYS INTO HER PURSE AND looked down at her hands. The imprint of the tow truck showed white on her palm. She rubbed her feet to warm them, nail polish shining black in the murky light, as though her toes were dipped in blood. While she was pulling on her socks, headlights arced across the wall and played on the locked door. Involuntarily, she ducked, arms clasping tight leather around her knees, face pressed to her thigh until she heard car doors, the laughing voice of the guy across the hall. The gay guy who'd tried so hard to be friendly, but was terrified of Simon.

She dug under the couch for her running shoes and tied them quickly. When she heard footsteps in the hall, she stuck her head into the light. "Hey, Lawrence, could I use your phone?"

Lawrence stepped back, wary, peering into the dark room behind her, holding up his arm to stop the man behind him. "Lost your privileges again, Tina?"

She shrugged and tried to smile. "Forever I think. My kid's sick. I want to phone and see how he is."

"Your kid?" He seemed to have relaxed now that he could see the room behind her was empty. "You never told me you had a kid. So who looks after him?"

"The province of Alberta. Look, I'm kinda anxious so can I make one quick call?"

He turned his key in the lock and held the door for her. "So long as you're alone, Doll, anytime."

Tina unfolded the scrap of paper from her pocket and perched on the edge of a leather sofa with the phone in her hand, while Lawrence moved around the living room flicking on lamps, dimming them, finally joining his friend in the kitchen. This suite was at least twice the size of hers. Not a stick of furniture had come from the thrift shop or garage sales like the junk in her place.

The phone rang four times, and once again the smooth male voice on the answering machine. Where the hell were these people who were supposed to be looking after Corey?

This time she ignored the machine, disconnected, then stabbed at the first three digits of Opi's number. No. He'd be sitting in front of the television and would ignore the phone even if he heard it. Besides, what would she say? Hi, Opi. I lost Corey again. Misplaced him at the zoo. Could you come out in the dark and help me find him? Yeah. That was exactly what she intended to do. To find Corey. But she'd have to do it herself.

"Cappuccino?" Lawrence dangled a dainty coffee cup from his finger.

Tina shook her head. "I don't have time. But thanks."

She turned before she left. "Hey, if you hear someone kicking in my door, call the cops this time, okay?"

He raised his eyebrows and shook a finger at her. "Not a chance, Tina. Not even a teeny-weeny chance."

Tina looked both ways down the short hallway before she opened the door to her apartment, locked it behind her, flicked on every light. One more smoke. If she was going to fuck up her no-smoking plan, she may as well do it right.

She paced from the deadbolted door to the kitchen sink to the glass door leading to the tiny balcony, listening for footsteps in the hall, watching for lights in the parking lot. If Simon stayed away tonight, she could risk bringing Corey back here when she found him. But what chance was there that he'd stay away? The longest he'd ever disappeared from her life, except for when he was locked up, was the week after he threw Corey into the snow. When he came back, he was so quiet it was spooky. He moved around her as though he expected her to lunge at him with a knife every time he turned his back. He actually thanked her for not turning him in. So meek and grateful, Tina wanted to puke.

"Yeah, that's what I need to hear, Simon," she'd screamed. "That I stand by my man while my kid ends up shuffling around foster homes where nobody—nobody!—cares about him the way I do."

That was the most important thing Corey had to remember. Nobody was going to love him as much as she did. Not a hard lesson to sell, considering all the shitty places he'd been since they took him away. Every new home promised he'd be there forever, but a few months later they came up with a lame excuse for kicking him out. In a couple of years, if it even took that long, there wouldn't be any homes left. Who was stupid enough to want someone else's teenaged kid? Then he'd finally be able to run to her and they'd let him stay. She'd worry about what to do with Simon when the time came.

She'd hoped that Simon would care less and less about Corey the older he got, but the reverse seemed to be happening. Simon was more jealous than ever. And the older Corey got, the smarter he became. Never again would she make the mistake of bragging to Simon that Corey was a brainy kid and was probably going to go to university and make something of himself. Christ, she sounded like the old man when he used to talk about her. But if Corey didn't quit moving around, he'd end up like her. If he stayed put this time, maybe Foster Daddy with the deep voice could help him with his homework and kick his ass through school. He was probably way beyond Tina already. Imagine having Corey sitting on the futon with his Math book on the coffee table, and the only other people around to help him with his homework were Paulette and Simon. She'd have to send him across the hall to ask Lawrence for help and then she'd worry that some of the queerness would rub off. Now she sounded like Simon, and that was even worse than sounding like Opi.

Tina stubbed out her cigarette, emptied the ashtray into a garbage overflowing with greasy take-out cartons. When she got back with Corey, she'd put him to bed, then clean up this dump. In the morning she'd make him a nice breakfast.

Leaving the apartment ablaze with lights, she opened the sliding glass door to the balcony, stepped outside, perched on the railing, then dropped easily to the parking lot.

37

COREY CROUCHED AT THE END OF THE SWINGING bridge as though he was getting ready to run a race. He was surprised at the depth of darkness on the other side of the river. He'd expected the buildings and paths in the centre of the zoo to be well lit, security people wandering around. Instead, the shadows around the monkey house where he was headed made the dinosaur park behind him look like high noon. Easier to stay hidden once he was across, but the thought of racing that jiggly length of bridge, in full view of anyone watching from either side, was more than he could handle. He sat on his heels, fingertips in the dirt. Finally, he leaned forward on his hands, lifted his head, and began to walk crab style onto the undulating bridge. Below him, the narrow channel of river separating St. George's Island from the dinosaur park, slid by with hardly a ripple of sound.

Halfway across the bridge he made the mistake of looking down, reeled back when the reflections in the water rushed up to meet him. Feet stretched across the deck, spine pressed into the railing, he closed his eyes and took a deep breath, and another. The sway was like rocking in Opi's old chair, only there were no arms around him, no scratchy sweater pressed to his face. His face was ice. A finger of a breeze from the water below reached up and froze the tears that flowed sheet-like down the slopes of his cheeks.

He kicked at the railing on the opposite side, wishing Tina was here so he could push her off the bridge. Her fault that he was on the run again after trying so hard to keep his feet in the right place. If he could tip Tina over the railing into the black water, he'd wave goodbye and hope she floated all the way to Hudson Bay. Last year in Social Studies he did a map and put all the rivers in Canada on it, all wriggling across the prairies to Hudson Bay. He imagined a stick figure with wild hair floating out behind her on his river. Right around Winnipeg was where he'd draw her if he could do that map again.

Corey kept trying to swallow, but there wasn't a drop of spit in him. He had to get to the water fountain outside the monkey house and take more Tylenol. The motion of the bridge was making him queasy. Without thinking, he looked down at the rippling sheet of water, and the nasty volcano in his stomach finally erupted. He spit into the river, tried to wipe a dribble of vomit from the front of his shirt, and lay with his face on the wooden floor of the bridge.

When the tiger roared, Corey lurched to his feet, turned his eyes to the deepest darkest shadows on the other side of the bridge, and ran.

Staggering when his feet hit solid ground, he turned to the right and then stopped, disoriented by the blackness ahead of him, overwhelmed by dizziness when he lifted his face to the orange-tinged sky.

He crept behind a twisted tree and stretched face down on the sloping trunk, arms encircling, eyes closed to shut out the spinning world. Above him, there was a rustling. When he looked up, a dangling fan-shaped shadow slipped sideways, whisked across the top of his head. If he'd been able, Corey would have run. He was paralyzed. All he could do was hold tight and stare up at shining eyes and a crested head. His own strangled scream was drowned by an ear-piercing screech from overhead. A peacock hunkered there, never shifting its malevolent gaze from Corey, not even toward an answering scream from across the path. Corey let his arms drop and slid slowly into a crouch. On the other side of the path, more hulking shadows shifted in the lowest branches of the trees.

He gulped a long drink of the cold night air. Peacocks. Opi hated them. Gaudy, evil-looking birds. Good for nothing, he said. On warm evenings, you could hear the peacocks all the way to his house and he'd jump up and slam the window. Corey wondered why Opi had never told him about this, about peacocks in trees in the dark.

At least he was on steady ground again, and closer to the fence. Even the air on this side of the bridge felt friendlier, warmer. And then, far to his right, as far away as the tiger's cage, twin beams emerged from the dark. He listened hard past the pounding blood in his head. Someone talking to himself? Singing? In the last peek before he pulled tight against the tree and held his breath, he was sure only one head bobbed behind the windshield of the truck. Not until it was almost past did he hear the static of the radio. A second voice from somewhere else in the park. He peered out again at the security guard cruising slowly by the bridge, eyes moving no further than the fringes of the road, humming to himself, slurping from a steaming cup.

Corey exhaled. It was almost worth stepping out of his hiding place to get this night over with. To beg for a sip from that hot cup. But then the truck was past, swallowed by the darkness, and Corey's head filled up again with memories.

Opi holding the heavy mug of coffee to Corey's lips. So black you couldn't see the bottom until the last few slurps, where a layer of sludgy sugar waited for the spoon. Or tea with honey, big globs of honey stirred and stirred until the top of the cup was greasy with sweetness, and then a squeeze of lemon. That was the medicine for a cold. Tonight, so many things he'd forgotten were bursting in his thoughts like bubbles. Ever since the conservatory when he remembered the matchbox trucks, he'd had this weird feeling that he was going backward.

Opi's voice whispering in his head whenever he closed his eyes. "Corey, Corey, Corey, Cor." He used to sing to him in Dutch while he was falling asleep. The only words Corey understood were those repetitions of his name. "Corey, Corey . . ."

He'd wait a few more minutes to be sure the guard didn't turn and come back. Then he'd make a beeline for the tigers.

Burning up and shivering at the same time, he took a deep breath, and resisted the urge to glance backward at the river. His legs still remembered the sway of the bridge. He didn't trust his eyes. Each time he jerked his head too quickly, the night began to spin around him. With his back against the scaly bark of one tree, he braced his feet on the protruding root of another, and tugged the red sweater from the waistband of his shorts. He slid his arms into the narrow sleeves, wrists dangling far below the cuffs. With the wool across his chest, he buttoned between nodding white daisies.

A few more minutes and it should be safe to move. Until then, he'd close his eyes and try to imagine that he was home in bed. From the warmth of that dream, it was a short trip back to another bed. Home in his bed with Tina's stuffed bears keeping watch. Black button eyes on the top of the pillow, the sound of Opi's felt slippers moving around the kitchen. When everything was ready for morning, he'd plod down the hall and sit on the edge of Corey's bed.

Again, in Corey's head, that gruff old voice sang the name song. "Corey, Corey . . ." Tina, always out somewhere when he went to sleep. Just Opi, who went to bed as early as Corey because he was up at four to get the baking done. By the time Corey heard the alarm clock through the wall between the bedrooms, Tina would be home. Sometimes still peeling off her clothes and climbing into bed beside him, but always home before Opi left.

Slowly the swirling memories evaporated, and Corey felt the damp ground under his legs. When he pressed his feet hard, they were prickly with pins and needles and he began a crazy dance against the trunk of the tree.

He should have stayed on the other side of the bridge. If he'd slid down the bank, climbed over the wire fence to the bike path, he'd be outside the zoo by now. Then along Memorial Drive, across the road, turn right at the next corner. He'd bang on Opi's door and he wouldn't go away until it opened.

He wriggled his back up the tree. Winced when a ridge of bark lifted the sweater and thin shirt and scraped bare skin. Stamped his feet until the tingling stopped.

The coast was clear.

38

TINA ALMOST GOT AWAY. SHE'D BEEN LISTENING for the roar of the bike, ignored the footsteps behind her, thinking they sounded like a shuffling old man. In fact, if she'd suspected she was being followed she would have guessed Opi, not Simon. So when she got to the bus stop, fished in her bag for a smoke, and then glanced over her shoulder, she jerked the match away so fast she almost set fire to her hair.

"Jesus, Simon! Don't sneak up on me like that!"

He loomed over her, rocking on the balls of his feet, fuzzy-eyed drunk, but quietly drunk—at least for the moment. If she could get him back to the apartment, he'd be asleep in minutes. She could leave and he'd never know. He sank onto the bench, slapped the wooden slats with the palm of his hand. "You trying to run out on me, Tina?"

"Nah. I'd have waited for you except I'm worried about Corey. I have to find the kid. He lied to me about phoning his foster home."

His eyes focused, now hard and unblinking as snake eyes. "So you thought you'd play Cat Woman and fly off the balcony." He reached up and grabbed her arm hard. "You know better than to play games with me, Tina. Where were you going?"

The pressure on her skin was increasing, like a vise on a soft piece of wood. She flinched, gritted her teeth. "I'm going to find Corey. Just like I said."

"I'm supposed to believe you, right? C'mon, babe, the kid lies cause he learned that from you. A liar like his mama. What'd he get from his old man? His good looks maybe?" His lip curled, but his grip on her arm grew slack. He slumped forward, head between his knees, and retched.

Tina looked away. Good question. It had been a while since Corey bothered her with that one. Are you sure, Tina? Are you sure you don't know who he is? She hated having Corey believe she'd been such a little whore she didn't know who his father was.

Simon looked up at her with bleary eyes. "I don't feel so good."

She felt a flash of sympathy. That sense of obligation for the times he'd held her hand and stroked her forehead. The day she had the abortion, when he'd driven her home, sat on the bed holding her hand while she cried herself to sleep. And the night they first met. She'd been crumpled in a corner of someone's basement, stoned out of her mind, scared to death of a skinny leather-jacketed guy grinning down at her while he unbuckled his belt. Something was whimpering, like a puppy kicked out in the cold. She hadn't known until another arm reached out of nowhere and shoved the leather jacket aside, that it was her own whining she'd heard. "Hey!" Simon had yelled so loud his voice ricocheted off the cement walls, and someone turned off the music. "Leave her the fuck alone. She's a kid."

When the music started again, he slid down the wall and sat beside her. "I don't feel so good," she'd said, and puked on his shiny black boots. He carried her into a shower, let the hot water soak her to the bone while his boots washed clean. When he turned the water off, he sat her on the seat of the toilet, wrapped a towel around her, and then he drove her home on his motorcycle. They pulled up in front of the house just as Opi disappeared down the street on his way to the bakery. Next night, Simon was back, tapping on the door after the old man went to bed, and the next and the next and the next. "You and me, Tina, we're meant for each other. I don't want nobody but you."

And it looked as though she didn't want anyone but Simon. She'd never figure out what it was about Simon that made her wish he was gone when she had him, and hoping he'd come back to mess up her life again when they were apart.

"Come on." She hauled him to his feet, took her keys out of her bag, and dropped them into the pocket of his jacket. "I can't afford another new door. Go home and wait for me. I have to find Corey and stash him with the old man. Then I'll come home and look after you."

He patted the pocket, stuck his hand deep inside, and pulled out a small plastic bag. "You walked out on me before I had a chance to give you your present." He fumbled with the bag. "Hold out your hands and close your eyes."

"Now who wants to play cutesy games? Save it for later."

He thrust his chin at her and almost fell into her arms. With his lips crawling warm under her hair to her throat, she was tempted to go home. She would pretend, as always, that the whole world was in Simon's lips, and his hands on the small of her back. That nothing was more important.

"You don't have to find that kid. What good's that kid ever done you?"

He stunk of vomit. After he'd leaned for a minute, Tina moved carefully away, leaving him to sway gently side to side. "More good than I've ever done him." She could hear the swish of bus tires at the corner behind her.

"Here." Simon slid two fingers into the bag, shook it away and dangled a pendant on a fine chain in front of her, so close the gold oval bounced against her nose.

Without stopping to examine the gift, Tina closed her fist around it. She dropped it into her purse. "That's real pretty, Simon. I'll thank you for it later."

When the bus pulled up, she hopped on. Left him there, shouting after her.

The only other people on the bus were two kids about Corey's age, farting around in the back. They should have been at home. No way would she have let Corey wander around the city at this time of night. Now that was a joke. When she was thirteen, she climbed out her bedroom window as soon as she heard the old man snoring in the room next door. He started baking at four in the morning. Bad luck for her that he went to bed so early. If he'd stayed awake until eleven like normal people, she would've done her homework, gone to bed, graduated from high school, gone to university, and been a fucking lawyer by now. But instead, she was out the window. Jeez, if you looked at that old windowsill, it was probably worn down with footprints—Anna's and then hers. If they'd stayed at Opi's, Corey could have used the same route. Except she would have been there, awake, to keep him home. And she was pretty sure he didn't have friends to meet in the night.

"Hey."

Tina looked up. One of the punks had sidled up beside her. "You wouldn't have some spare change, would you?" Tina glanced over her shoulder. The other kid watched from the back. He'd sent his girlfriend to do the work. Her yellow hair was lacquered into spikes, her skin around the eyebrow ring and the nose ring, had a greenish cast. The smile she was trying to paste on her face twisted sideways. Tina dug in her bag. Corey's change was still in the side pocket, and so was Simon's necklace. This kid looked like she needed the money more than Corey did. Tina dropped a shower of coins into the outstretched hand. She slid her hand back into her purse, tempted for a few seconds to lay the necklace on the grubby palm to see the look on the girl's face.

"Go home," she said softly. "Believe me, kid. I know what I'm talking about."

The girl stared at her, slid the money into the pocket of her tight jeans, and whirled around to join her boyfriend at the exit door. The two of them scurried off at the next stop like rats.

Tina shook her head. Hand still in her purse, she fingered the outline of the pendant, twisted the chain around her finger. When she finally pulled it out, the necklace twinkled in the white light. Very classy. A brushed gold oval with a centre square of white gold, outlined in diamond chips. Ten small diamonds. The sort of necklace a loving husband would give his wife on their tenth anniversary. She held the chain with her fingertips, let the pendant spin. At least the back of this one didn't have "RM" engraved in a heart on the back like last year's locket. Still, she could imagine Simon scooping it off someone's dresser and dropping it in the bag with the silverware, CDs, and the sugar bowl full of spare cash. She wondered if Opi still kept his change in the fancy beer mug in the china cabinet. Loose change in the beer mug, in the bottom drawer of the china cabinet a wad of bills that he fished out every month and sent to the phone company, the gas company, and whoever else he owed. Probably still sending cash. The only man in the universe paying with cash. If she lived there, she could've helped herself to a handful every now and again. Funny she'd never done that when she was a kid.

Her hand drifted back into her purse to the empty wallet. There'd been times when she thought about hocking the stuff in the black leather box. That was before Simon's kid sister, Genevieve, was hauled in for possession when she pawned one of his Christmas presents. Besides, these weren't crown jewels. She'd be lucky to get a couple hundred dollars for the whole fourteen years worth of goodies.

At the next stop, the driver cranked the sign on the front of the bus to 'Out of Service'. Tina glanced at her watch. Aw shit, this was the last run. She'd be walking home. The zoo was only two stops away, but what the fuck was she thinking? Even if he'd lied to her about phoning, even if he was on the run again, even if he was curled up under the bench by the seal tank, he was there because he was pissed off with her. And what kind of half-assed story would she have to come up with to talk her way into the zoo at midnight?

Here she was again, stuck in the middle. Simon at her place, Corey out in the cold. Unless he really was back at his foster home. Maybe they didn't answer the phone after ten o'clock at night.

No matter how hard she tried, Tina couldn't conjure up a picture of Corey asleep in bed. She was stuck with the image of Corey hunched over the bench by the seal tank, Simon towering over him.

She stared into the night. The streets were quiet, the storefronts splashed with shadows. At the next corner, she'd be able to see the bridge and, beyond that, the dark island of the zoo. So many times she'd fucked up by making the wrong choice when it came to Corey. This time she'd listen to the voice whispering inside her head. He's lost. Go find him.

39 BEN WOULD HAVE SLEPT THROUGH THE RINGING of the phone, the slamming of the cupboard doors, the sound of the late night news, and any other racket Wilma might have produced in her agitated insomnia, but when the front door opened quietly, then closed with the same sneaky care, he was instantly awake.

He knew where she going. Flashing the sweet smile with which she'd pushed her way to the front of the cashier's line at the restaurant, she'd have the zoo security squad ferrying her around the dark cages. She'd cup her hands to her mouth and call, "Corey! Where are you, dear?" in that slightly puzzled, flute-like voice in which she'd long ago said, "Ben, it's so very sweet of you to want to marry me, but in case you haven't noticed, I'm going to have a baby any minute."

He pulled on a pair of jeans and a sweatshirt. By the digital display on the clock radio, it was now twelve fifteen, Saturday.

Ben wasn't inclined to act on impulse, like Wilma. Their marriage wouldn't survive if they both barrelled headfirst over every bump in the road. Someone needed to stand back and plot the course. So instead of following Wilma into the night, he took the empty Scotch glass to the kitchen and refilled it with cranberry juice. He leaned against the counter. Phil's Mother's Day card was on display in the centre of the table. Wilma had said she was going to call him back, but Ben was sure she'd left without phoning anyone. Not Phil, nor Carmen, nor anyone else after she'd talked with Elsie.

Whatever Elsie said would have been enough to send Wilma off to prove herself. And now that Elsie knew Corey was missing, she was probably in a cab on her way to the bus depot. By tomorrow night she'd be standing at the counter kneading dough. Maybe the wild list of summer plans he'd flung at Kristel wasn't so crazy after all.

Every summer, for years, Phil and Mark had taken the bus to Winnipeg to spend a week with Grandma. They had donuts and chocolate milk for breakfast, and rode without seat belts in her ancient station wagon to her brother Ed's farm. As soon as their legs were long enough to find the gas pedal, Eddy let them drive the tractor. One summer, they'd tried to float across the dugout on a leaky raft and would have drowned if he hadn't come out of the barn at the critical moment. Back in the city, they traipsed around to bingo and whist games with Elsie. They didn't go to bed until they nodded off, one on either side of her, watching late movies. Some nights they didn't go to bed at all. Elsie covered them with a quilt and slept in the old recliner to keep watch. They were sworn to secrecy, but as soon as they were off the bus they spewed out every hair-raising detail of their vacation and delighted in watching their mother's face on the drive home.

Later, Wilma would go into the bedroom and he'd find her lying there staring at the ceiling. "Do you think," Ben would ask, "that she's a bad grandmother? That we shouldn't let them visit on their own."

"No!" she'd shout and pound the pillow. "Don't you get it? She's the best mother of all, but if I let them do any of the things she allows, horrible things would happen for sure." Ben had been afraid that Elsie might be too much for Corey. That the first time she absent-mindedly patted him on the bum when he walked past, Corey would retreat to his bedroom and not come out until she'd boarded the bus home. The first time Ben was the recipient of one of Elsie's love pats, Wilma had laughed so hard, both Ben and Elsie had shouted at her to calm down or she'd go into premature labour.

"Oh Lord, Ben," she told him later, "if you could have seen the look on your face. Like you were going to swallow your eyeballs."

He'd felt his face go red. "Well of course I was startled. She doesn't get to go around patting men's asses. If a man did that to you, you'd be furious."

"Yeah, I know," Wilma said, "but this is my ma. Get used to it."

Either Corey was used to it by now, or Elsie had tempered her style.

She had definitely cooled toward Ben in the last three years. The first time she visited after Phil left home, she'd sat across the kitchen table from him, reached over, covered both his hands with her own small, well-calloused palms.

"Ben dear, you have to make peace or your family will fall apart."

He'd found it hard to look at her eyes. Behind the thick glasses, she was as unblinking and unsettling as a barn owl. "We're as peaceful as ever, Elsie."

"I'm not talking about fighting—although I think sometimes a good clean fight would do the two of you a world of good. I'm talking about making peace inside yourself. You think I haven't cried a whole river of tears over this? I found feelings I never knew I had inside of me. I hurt so much for all the walls he's going to have to climb. But Philip is still Philip, our same sweet boy. He doesn't need us less. He needs us more." Her eyes had gone blurry behind her glasses. "Do you know how many things I wish I'd said to my Murray before he was killed? We had words before he stomped out the house and got into the car that day, Ben. I never had a chance to take them back. Don't count on 'someday.'"

"What is it you want me to do, Elsie?"

"Phone him, sweetheart. Tell him to bring his friend for supper. Tell him you'd like to see his apartment. I went this afternoon. He's got it fixed up so . . ."

He'd pulled his hands free and walked out of the room. Away from wise, old Elsie.

He wondered how different things would be if Murray, Elsie's husband, Wilma's dad, hadn't died all those years ago. If having a dad around when she was a teenager would have kept Wilma home that Jasper summer. He was sure that he and Wilma were fated to meet, but what if there'd been no Phil? He couldn't imagine their life without Philip.

Ben glanced at the clock. Twelve thirty. Enough of Philip and Elsie for now. He expected that Wilma would come home after the zoo. First she'd circle the surrounding neighbourhood. She might even look up C. Brinkman in the phone book and drive by his house, but by now an old man would be asleep. Wilma wouldn't pound on the doors of any dark houses. If she wasn't back by two, he'd go looking. Unfortunately, the cell phone was charging on the counter. If she'd taken it with her, he could have phoned, pleaded with her not to do anything bizarre, to come home. It wasn't a stretch to imagine her walking away from the security office, then climbing over the fence to do her own search.

Ben opened the fridge. You'd think that having a twelve-year-old in the house would improve the snack situation, but Wilma was still watching his cholesterol like a hawk. Tonight's leftover salad, last night's broccoli, and three flavours of yogourt. Actually, a visit from Elsie might be just the ticket. She baked non-stop.

God, what was he doing? He was thinking about donuts, trying to negotiate a peace with his mother-in-law, when he now had two kids missing. The door to Corey's room was ajar. If he'd been asleep where he belonged, he'd have crept out to the kitchen after Ben and Wilma were in bed to turn on the light over the stove. Ben tried to remember to leave it on. Each time he stood beside the bed, listened to Corey's slow, steady breathing, he hoped the poor kid might make it through to morning without dreaming.

With a carton of vanilla yogurt in hand, he started to close the fridge door, then impulsively shoved the container back onto the shelf. He opened the freezer, pulled out ice cream instead. A sliced banana, a drizzle of chocolate sauce, and he was in business. He had the sundae assembled, his spoon in hand, when the phone rang. Sure that it would be Wilma, Ben shoved the bowl out of sight behind the toaster.

For a few seconds, he thought the squeaky voice was Corey. Then he realized the kid on the other end was asking for Corey. A few days ago, Wilma had mused that no one ever called for Corey. How strange that was, when Mark and Phil had driven them wild with their quarrels over telephone time, and the constant calls. Now, in the middle of the night, a night into which Corey had disappeared, someone was calling. From the traffic sounds in the background, this kid must also be out on the street.

"Corey can't come to the phone. It's past midnight. Who is this?"

"Could you wake him up, please? Tell him it's Shawn. It's kind of an emergency."

159

The name was vaguely familiar. Ben was sure Wilma would remember where Shawn fit in Corey's life. She had an infinite capacity for this sort of detail.

"Shawn, you'll have to find someone else to help you out." The silence was so long Ben thought she might have hung up, until he heard the wail of a siren. "How do you know Corey? Are you a school friend?"

"Yeah, that's it. I'm sort of a school friend."

"From St. Peter's?"

"Yeah."

For all Ben knew, there might be a St. Peter's, but he was sure Corey had never gone to a Catholic school. Shawn was none too bright to fall into that one. The best guess was that she was another runaway foster kid. The kind who'd be easily caught in traps.

"I think Corey's mentioned you, Shawn. If you've got an emergency, wouldn't it be a good idea to get in touch with your social worker?"

No denial or hesitation. "Oh yeah, that's a great idea. Like she's the one I really need to talk to." Her voice cracked and the sneer was gone, leaving the choked whisper of a very small child. "Please, mister, lemme talk to Corey?"

The old man, and now a little girl in tears. Ben rubbed his eyes. "Sweetheart, you go somewhere safe, okay? And call back tomorrow?"

"I dunno where I'll be tomorrow. Forget it."

"Wait! Do you have a pen? Write this address down." He intended for her to get in a cab, tell the driver he'd pay when she got here. Beyond that, he didn't have a clue what he'd do with her. Pray hard that Wilma would be back before Shawn-in-trouble knocked on the door?

"I don't have a pen and I'm not so good at remembering things, so tell Corey I'm going to Vancouver, okay?"

And then she did hang up. Ben slammed down the phone. Goddammit anyway! How many lost kids did there have to be? As if a cab driver would have had anything to do with delivering a scruffy teenager COD.

Even with the kitchen window open, the silence in the house had all the weight of fathoms of water. The wind chime on the eaves hung straight and still, glinting in the moonlight.

The melting ice cream had lost its appeal, but he hated waste. After the final cloying spoonful, he picked up Phil's card, ran his fingers over the embossed print of a bouquet of flowers. The kid who'd never hear of giving his mom any gift but flowers or perfume. Somewhere in the desk in the hall, Wilma's address book would be nestled in a pile of stationery and stamps. Just a few steps away.

Ben turned on the light, knelt in front of the desk, and sifted through a drawer full of old Christmas cards and letters. Philip's name was on the inside cover of the book, the address and phone number crossed out and rewritten five times.

A minute of staring at the numbers and he had them in his memory. Tomorrow, they'd still be there, but by then the need would have diminished.

On the fifth ring, a voice husky with sleep growled, "Yeah?"

"Phil? It's Dad."

"This isn't Phil, it's Greg. Hold on."

Ben winced. Had he expected it to be easy? How could he have mistaken the low timbre for his son? Phil's voice, so like Wilma's, woke his ear like the first notes of a favourite song.

"Dad? What's wrong?"

"Oh, nothing wrong. No, everything's fine, son."

"It's two o'clock in the morning."

"I know. I'm sorry. I forgot about the time difference. Look, Phil, I wanted to tell you that your card came today and your mom was so happy, and then your phone message blew it all away. Why don't you come out anyway? I'll buy the plane ticket."

The silence was as blank as it was deep. No image of Phil crystallized in Ben's mind. Not only was he blocking the picture of two men in bed, but his memory would only retrieve a face that was at least five years younger, an eighteen-year-old face. It had been almost two years since Ben saw his son at the wedding of one of Wilma's nieces. It was not that closed and wary face he remembered either. At the wedding, he'd hugged Phil and talked about seeing him again soon, but time seemed to slide by. And there was still that issue of Ben having to visit first, and someone named Greg.

"Dad, I'll call you in the morning, okay? But let me talk to Mom for a minute if she's still up."

"She's not here. Corey seems to be missing again, and she's gone to look for him. I'm waiting by the phone in case he calls."

Again, he felt the weight of every silent mile that separated them. Christ, that sounded lame. Wilma was out in the night and he was sitting by the phone. Waiting.

Phil's voice was quieter now, almost as though he'd cupped his hand around the receiver. "What's going on there? Dad, I'll come next weekend, okay? I have a ride. I don't need your ticket. Now go find Mom. Please?"

Ben was aware finally that he was nodding. Phil was waiting for him to speak. "Yeah, okay Philip. Glad you're coming. I'll go find both of them."

40 COREY RAN THE PATH ALONG THE RIVER TO THE tigers, not caring about the soft thud of his sneakers on the pavement. Even if the guard was close, he was busy talking and drinking coffee, and not expecting to find a boy hiding in the trees. Corey wondered if anyone else had ever hidden out in the zoo at night. That he might be the first one, the only one, made him smile. He was invisible. Streaking through the oily shadows toward the tigers.

By the time he reached the high fence of the enclosure, his eyes had adjusted and he had a sense of direction. Though his throat was hurting like crazy, he'd ignore it. Things were finally coming together.

He stood, panting, inside the glass shelter where people watched the tigers in their smaller cage. He'd sat on this bench once on Opi's knee and cried because the babies they'd seen on their last visit were gone. The whole front of Opi's shirt was soaked. He could still remember the feel of the cloth and the whiff of sweat that was his grandfather.

All he could see now was the bulky shape of a rope platform, where the mother tiger had been sunning herself when he and Tina stood here in the shade this afternoon. A few hours ago, but it felt like last year.

The moonlight caught a glint of silver below the platform, and then another and another, and from those few feet away Corey could see three tigers watching him. The outlines of their bodies looked drawn in black ink. He leaned into the barrier, sighed when his cheek pressed against the cold glass.

If he could climb into this pen and cross the hard-packed dirt on hands and knees, would the tigers be confused long enough that he could crawl between them, rest his head on the rumbling purr of a big chest? Or would they smell breakfast? They were well fed, and he was such a scrawny kid that, even if they were hungry, they'd probably turn up their noses. But they were cats, and cats liked to hunt and kill things for sport, not just for food. Even Smoky had stalked spiders, pounced, played with them until they were mangled to death.

He closed his eyes, face cooled by the touch of the window, his body protected from the wind by the shelter. Smoky, asleep on his pillow, soft touch of fur on Corey's cheek, tiny kitten motor vibrating against his skin in the night. Simon killed Smoky. Corey was sure of that. Funny though. With the tigers watching him, he felt safe from the nightmare of Simon.

The male was probably curled up in the grass. Even the larger enclosure was a miserable space for a wild animal. When he was little, Corey had imagined setting the animals free, but Opi had told him that they'd die for sure. Try convincing Shawn of that. The day at the zoo with Tina, she'd hatched one of her hare-brained plans while they stood at the entrance waiting for their social worker to pick them up. Tina smoking on the bench, looking at her watch every two minutes.

"Hey, Cor! I have an idea." Shawn wrapping her arms around his neck, pulling him tight against her so she could whisper in his ear. The feel of her hard little tits against his chest. Tina scowling at them. Shawn with that goofy smile she had when she was pretending to be innocent. Staring into Corey's eyes as though their lives depended on her idea. "Say tomorrow night I sneak out of the group home at midnight. It's not hard—they're so dumb they don't even look in my room after I go to bed. And you sneak out and we meet down here."

"I can't do that," he said. "I'd never get out of the house." He was living with Frank and Judy. 'You could think about calling us Mom and Dad,' they'd said, 'after the adoption's complete.' They'd put a lock on his bedroom window after the first time he ran. "And besides, how would we get down here in the middle of the night? The buses quit running at midnight."

Shawn, eyes rolled slightly upward, gnawing at her lip. Big smile flashing across her face. "Hitchhike. I do it all the time. You stick out your thumb and look kinda sad and somebody always picks you up."

He didn't ask her to fill in the rest of the travel plans because they'd make as much sense as hitchhiking. Corey didn't like asking strangers for the time, never mind if they'd drive him to the zoo in the middle of the night.

"And then," she wasn't finished yet, "we bring along saws and stuff, and we open the cages. I bet there's nobody around, and by the time they notice there'll be animals everywhere. Oh man, Corey, can't you see it?"

"Yeah," he said, just as Tina grabbed hold of the back of his new shirt and pulled him away from Shawn, "I can see them everywhere, eating each other and us too."

With the sense that someone was watching him, Corey opened his eyes enough to peek under the fringe of his eyelashes. The pale shape of the mother cat was so close that if the glass hadn't separated them, his knee would have grazed the tiger's nose. Yellow eyes stared hard into his.

Easing away from the glass until the back of his legs touched the bench behind him, Corey lowered himself to sit, then slowly lifted his feet and stretched out on his side, facing the tiger. The cat's huge head rested on its front paws. It yawned, teeth flashing pale in the dark cave of its mouth, then settled again and closed its eyes. Only the flick of the tail every twenty seconds gave it away. Corey knew that if he were to jump up, the tiger would spring up too. Any sudden movement and he'd puke, his stomach was suddenly that sick again. Eyes closed, with long, slow breaths he drew the smell of damp wood into his lungs. This was something Opi taught him. When you were sick, or scared, or couldn't stop crying, the best thing to do was stand on the back step—or better still, be held in Opi's big arms—and take slow, deep breaths. He'd forgotten that advice until tonight. He couldn't remember the last time he'd pressed his nose to a window screen for gulps of night air. Corey, Corey, Corey, Cor . . . So clear, that if he opened his eyes he would surely see cuffed grey pants and the hem of a raggy brown sweater. Why? Did this mean that Opi had died? That he was going to hang around whispering to Corey like an angel in some stupid movie?

Corey blinked and the leaf shadows overhead flickered, a bird darting between branches. But it was too late for birds. He shivered. Moving so slowly that the tiger only turned his ears, he lowered his feet to the ground and sat on the edge of the bench, his head in his hands, elbows on his knees. A few more deep breaths and his stomach stopped churning.

Okay. It was time to get the plan moving, yet he felt safe for the first time since Tina had stalked off into the sunlight at the seal tank.

The night he spent in the hospital, after Simon hauled him out of the closet and threw him against the tree, there was a nurse who'd come in to check on him every half hour or so. Each time, she had bent close and whispered, "You're safe here, dear." Like he wasn't safe at home. Well, that hospital didn't feel safe, and neither did the foster home he went to the next day. All he wanted that night and the next, and the next, was to see Tina—and that was the one thing they wouldn't allow. How safe can a kid be when you won't give him the only thing that would make him feel better?

Now, with bats swooping, peacocks screaming, his throat on fire, he still wanted Tina. But only till morning, and then he wanted to go home.

When he raised his head, the tiger was watching.

"So," Corey whispered, "what do you think of this idea?"

Kristel expected to pick him up at Tina's in the morning. Ben and Wilma thought he was at Tina's. Tina was partying, but eventually she'd go home, she and Simon, and crash like they were dead. He needed Tina, but only her house. He'd wait until the sun came up, then he'd start walking. Streets were easy downtown. All he had to do was follow the numbers until he came to the address in his head. He'd sit on the step until Kristel arrived. Then he'd tell her Tina was sick with a sore throat and pukey stomach, asleep upstairs. And then Kristel would take him home.

Corey pressed his palm to the glass where the tiger's shoulder rested. He was sure he felt warmth and a low, rumbling vibration. "Hey, thanks," he said. Then he curled up on the bench again with his head in the curve of his arm and closed his eyes. Imagining that he really had agreed to her stupid midnight plan, he pretended that his arms were Shawn's and held himself tight, remembering that smell she had like licorice and wet grass, and the silk of her skin against his.

41

WILMA FOLLOWED THE MOON TO THE ZOO. WITH every corner she turned, the cold, white crescent hung directly ahead. Her brain was full of snow. Heavy, wet, clumping thoughts that left her shivering even with the heater blasting, the windows rolled tight.

Since she'd driven away from her dark house, she'd replayed the day and all of the messages on the answering machine. She should have shaken Ben awake, dragged him with her. Ben was the one who could dive into murky problems and come up with a crystal solution in his hand. Except, this time, he'd refused to own the problem. He was giving it back to Corey in the same way he'd handed Phil's life to him when he'd said, "Fine. Do what you have to do. You know where to find us when you need us."

This movie she'd been replaying in her head was meant to have a happy ending. On television, the child would have faced mortal danger by now but, in the end, after the tension and the tears, there would be a resolution that allowed the audience to turn off their sets, content all's well that ends at bedtime. Could it be that Wilma was the only one who believed she and Ben could provide the happy ending to Corey's tale?

After Corey bolted the second time, the social worker said he thought Corey's run of foster homes was nothing more than bad luck. He had a feeling that finally things would turn around for Corey, if Wilma and Ben could cut him enough slack. That he'd probably run again, but eventually he'd settle down. Kristel obviously didn't see things that way. She'd already set the wheels in motion for Corey's next destination. Summer camp would be a way to ease him out of their life. Kristel was probably convinced that they'd be relieved when she called to say he wouldn't be back. Oh, there was a sequel to this story. Kristel Maclean was writing it.

Wilma gripped the steering wheel, clenched her teeth. All these stories were her own damn fault. She'd let Ben write the first chapters in the saga of the wayward son, but tomorrow morning—no tonight, when she got home—she was going to tell him he was fired. She was taking over. Even if Phil didn't come home next weekend, in July she was flying to Toronto. And if she could come up with a better story than Ben, then she could surely outwrite a mere child like Kristel. Okay, that was the mission for tonight—get the bloody ending right.

The further east she travelled on Ninth Avenue, the quieter the streets became. There were none of the spring dawdlers she and Corey had seen when they walked here this morning. Traffic seemed unusually light for downtown.

She could drive brazenly into the security entrance at the zoo, but no matter what story she gave the man at the gate, he'd think she was a few lumps short of a full load of coal, as Uncle Eddy would have said. A reasonable woman didn't wander around in the night, conspicuous as snow in July, if her child was lost. A reasonable woman called the police. That's what the security guard would do. If Corey was behind that fence, there had to be a way to find him from the outside.

She changed lanes to turn left onto Twelfth Street, stopped at the red light. On the other side of the street, a bus rolled to a stop. The lone passenger stood, then descended from view out the exit door.

A few seconds later, a woman appeared. A woman walking toward the corner in running shoes, and a skirt so short only the hem peeked out from under her sweater. Running across the street in front of Wilma's car, even though the WALK light had turned to red.

Wilma turned the corner, drove slowly toward the bridge, her eyes flicking back and forth to the figure in her rear-view mirror. Matching this woman to the one who'd hugged Corey this morning, the voice on the answering machine. 'Yeah,' she'd said, 'this is Tina Brinkman.'

The husky voice on the phone was as incongruous a match for the quick, slight figure, as the quiet purr of the big bus pulling away from the curb. Who could it be but Tina? What other woman would be trekking through the night to the dark zoo? The thought of Tina as an ally, after all these months of hating what she'd inflicted on Corey, was beyond Wilma's capabilities. Tina was the cause of this night. All that had been required was that she look after her son for twenty-four hours.

Across the bridge, beyond the streetlights on St. George's Drive, the zoo was even darker than Wilma's imagining. She'd pictured Corey sick, cold, lonely, lost, but nowhere in her mind had he been so totally swallowed by the night. She kept to the far right, crept along the curb, craning her neck to peer into the shadows behind the fence. Dinny asleep in the moonlight.

In the lot across from the entrance, a car was parked facing the river. Wilma turned in a broad arc behind it, her headlights illuminating a frantic unscrambling of limbs in the back seat. She killed the lights and drove to the farthest corner of the parking lot, the spot closest to the tigers.

She sat squinting, adjusting to the dark. When she looked in the rear-view mirror, other cars emerged, parked haphazardly behind her in the shadows. Off to the right, where'd she passed the first car, another pulled in. A minute later, a shape slid out from behind the trees, approached the car.

Wilma closed her eyes. When she opened them to stare straight ahead into the zoo, to imagine the tiger slinking along the perimeter of his enclosure, a scream curdled the silence, ran like a cold finger down the quivering length of her spine. No telling whether it came from inside the zoo, or from the zoo out here. How could she have forgotten that this place, so benign in the daytime, full of family vans and strollers, popcorn and sunshine inside the gates, turned into another world after dark.

She clicked and double-clicked the button that locked the doors. What now? Sit here in the car, shouting his name? Convince herself that no one in the shadowy landscape behind her was remotely interested in her presence? Get out and pace the fence, shouting? How long before the police arrived, and what would she say? 'I misplaced my foster son. Thought he might be here.'

Finally, she rolled down the window. The night was so still—not even a murmur of voices—she wondered if she'd imagined the screech. If she listened extra hard she might be able to hear the padding of giant cat feet. She'd expected a rush of cold to fill the car, not this warmth, so soft and shy it hung outside the window in a mist. Well, she thought, this is spring, when the weather flips and flops. Ma must be praying hard. She could hear Elsie's voice in her head. Listen God, at least warm the night for a lost boy.

Wilma sat in the car, whispering her own prayers, waiting. Five minutes until she glimpsed the legs, the white face, gliding past trees and rocks. Black hair, black sweater, melting into the leaves. She tried to ignore the thud in her chest like footsteps advancing. Ignore, ignore. She'd been trying to ignore this woman's existence, and now Tina was floating toward her through the night, like the worrying bits of a long day spinning together in a nightmare.

Across from the entry gate Tina stopped, leaned against a streetlight, paying no attention to the cars in the parking lot. So Wilma, too, tried to focus only on the solitary figure under the light. Too far away to be sure, but she thought she could see a tiny dot of red and the curl of smoke.

When Phil, at sixteen, wanted to look for his father, Wilma had asked him what he'd do. How he'd meet him. What he'd say.

"I won't say a thing. I don't want to meet him, only look at him. I'll stand on a corner outside his house and smoke until he comes outside, gets in his car, and drives away. The next day, I'll go back at the same time and sit in my car with a camera. Zoom in on the door, and when it opens—*click*. And drive away. That's all I want."

She hadn't even a picture to give him, to make that standing on corners unnecessary. She'd offered to help when he turned eighteen, to put an ad in every newspaper in Kentucky, but by then he'd said it didn't matter. She didn't believe him. It seemed he was still standing on corners.

Tina ground her heel into the pavement, looked around, shifted the bag from her shoulder to the ground at her feet. She pulled the sweater over her head, arms raised in a languorous stretch. Wilma would have draped it over her shoulders, slung it across an arm, but Tina heaved the sweater onto the bush behind her, where it sprawled and then sank from sight. Crossing the street, she passed the ticket gates, stopped and pressed close to the fence, fingers high above her head in the mesh, toes testing their grip in the bottom loops. Headlights caught her there, a car slowed. She backed away, turned, crossed her arms, and leaned on the fence. The car turned into the lot, cruised quietly to a stop, facing the river. Tina began to walk, dragging her right hand along the wire. As she came abreast of the car, Wilma took a deep breath, and opened the door.

42 TINA WAS SURE, EVEN BEFORE THE WOMAN STEPPED out of the car, that it was Corey's foster mother, the woman who'd hovered over him in the ticket lineup this afternoon. She wasn't at home to answer her phone, because she was out here looking for Corey. Standing beside her car in the moonlight, pale hair curving around her jaw, big eyes locked on Tina, she looked like a ghost who was about to evaporate.

Tina crossed the road. "So, did you see him?" She waited, hands on her hips. But instead of answering, Foster Mama got back into the car, reached across, and unlocked the passenger side.

Oh for Chris'sake, all Tina wanted was an answer, not a conference. She opened the door, peered in. "You're Wilma, right? My kid's foster mother?" The lady looked the way the mother of a twelve-year-old was supposed to look—middle-aged, middle-class, kind of plain, and tired.

She nodded, motioned toward the empty seat. "Why don't you get in so we can talk? Or I'll get out and we can sit somewhere else. It's warm, isn't it? Warmer than it's been all day." She dangled a hand out the window, then brought it back and held it to her cheek. "The ice is gone. When did that happen?"

Maybe, Tina thought, *this Wilma woman was a nutcase after all.* She slid into the car, but left the door open. A plastic pocket on the side was crammed with books and gum wrappers and crumpled Kleenex. Family car. She took a deep breath, exhaled, and turned slightly. She and Wilma might have been chatting on a bus stop bench. "So, where do you think he is?"

Wilma's eyes narrowed. "Until we got your phone message, we thought he was with you. Where he's supposed to be."

"Yeah, well he was sick. He shouldn't have been out at all. I made him phone and tell you to pick him up." If this woman didn't wipe the big smear of nastiness of her face in about ten seconds, Tina was leaving. She sure as hell didn't need a middle-aged broad from suburbia tagging along. She'd find Corey on her own.

Wilma shook her head. "There were no calls from Corey. Not while we were home, and not on the answering machine."

What a surprise. Tina raised her arms to lift the hair off the back of her neck. The car was stifling. "Well then I guess he lied, didn't he? How long have you been here?"

"Only a few minutes," Wilma said. "I thought this would be a good place to start. Close to the tigers. Corey told me he likes the tigers best."

"Yeah, we always have to hang out with the tigers for half the lousy visit." What other things, she wondered, had Corey told Wilma? And what the hell point was there in sitting in the car talking? "So now that we started with the tigers and there's nothing to see but dark, have you got a plan?"

"We could go to the gate and ask if they'll let us in." Wilma leaned her elbows on the steering wheel and stared at the wire fence.

"They won't let us wander around in there. You think he's going to come out if guys in uniforms start stomping around looking for him?"

Wilma sat up straight and drew one arm, and then the other, out of the sleeves of her jacket. The turtleneck underneath bristled with static. The air in the car felt electric. Every time Tina moved her head, her hair crackled on her shoulders.

"We have to find him," Wilma said. "His social worker is waiting for one more run so she'll have an excuse to move him." She tossed the jacket onto the back seat where there was already a small pile of clothes. "She doesn't like us. I think that no matter what we do, or what Corey does, she won't let us keep him."

She was grumbling and mumbling as though she was talking to herself. She dragged the sweater over her hair, flung that into the back too. The shirt underneath was wrinkled and damp looking.

Tina desperately wanted another cigarette. As a matter of fact, Wilma looked like she needed one too. "Don't worry about her. About Kristel, I mean. I'm going to get her off Corey's case."

Wilma folded her arms, slumped down in the seat. "She wants to send him to wilderness camp. A camp for Native kids."

Oh, fuckin' fantastic. So that's where Kristel was going. "Yeah, well," Tina said, "that's because some social worker way back decided that my dad must have been an Indian. Could be. Do I care? But can you imagine Corey in the wilderness?"

"Oh." The foster mother was staring straight ahead, biting her lip.

"Forget it. By tomorrow, Kristel's history." She felt a twist in her gut. She kept remembering Kristel's eyes behind those big lenses. Cameras. Kristel recording everything. Everything stored up to use later.

"I hope so," Wilma said. "I surely do. But it might not be soon enough. I can feel Corey slipping away."

Tina instinctively put her hand on her purse. At the moment, the two matchbox trucks were all that she had of Corey, but they were more than this other woman owned. She felt a swell of pressure in her chest, a rush of blood to her head. She clenched her teeth to stop her lip from trembling. No way was she going to start blubbering in front of Foster Mama. What was the matter with her tonight? She was a freakin' basket case. It was as though Corey's whole life was hanging in the thick air between them. The past—those goddamned little trucks—on one side, and the big, black hole of what would happen next on the other. Tina and this nervous blond woman pulling like crazy in opposite directions. Only there was nothing to fight over but the air. She took a deep breath, cleared her throat.

"Are you gonna keep him?" Still staring out the open car door instead of at the woman beside her. When she didn't answer, Tina swung around. "Everybody says they'll keep him, and then they throw him back. I know you're thinking I don't have any right to ask you what you're going to do, because I'm the one who fucked up his life, but I want to know if you really plan on keeping him or if you're just waiting to bail out too."

Wilma's voice was hard and flat. "We will not bail out on Corey. But we don't get to make the final decisions, or even to vote, it seems. I just told you that his social worker is working on a plan that doesn't include us. Did you know that? Did Corey tell you that if he runs away from us again, he'll probably end up in a group home?"

Tina leaned back and closed her eyes. "Social workers are assholes."

"Yeah," Wilma said. "Well meaning I guess, but assholes all the same." She sighed. "Which doesn't mean that we have to put up with it."

"So, should we look for him?" Tina asked.

"I think we have to."

The two of them swung their legs out of the car, stood, slammed the doors without locking them, and crossed the road together.

43 BEN WAS TEMPTED TO POUR ANOTHER SCOTCH, but his ears still hummed with Phil's voice. And wasn't that exactly what he'd done the night Phil broke the news that he was gay? He'd poured another Scotch and stared at the wall, while Wilma paced and talked to herself.

When Philip finally came home, he'd stood in the doorway to the living room, frowning, his hands shoved hard into the pockets on his sheepskin jacket, shoulders drawn guardedly up to his ears.

Wilma had flown out of her chair, wrapped her arms around his waist. "Oh, Philip, are you sure about this?" She tilted her head to look up at him, and Phil lowered his chin. From where Ben sat, the lines of their two bodies flowed together with such grace, they looked like one of the porcelain figurines on the china cabinet behind them.

"Mom." That was all Phil said, all he needed to say.

She pulled him toward the couch but he wrestled his arm free and dropped down instead on the floor in front of the bookcase, where he habitually stretched out with a pile of pillows, to read. This time he leaned against the shelves, hands clasped around bent knees. He looked from Wilma to Ben, and then back to Ben. "Can't we talk about this later? Tomorrow maybe? Or in a few days when you guys have had time to get used to the idea?"

Ben could still remember that the drapes were open, and when he tried to look at Phil, his eyes were drawn away to the window, black and etched at the corners with frost. It was one of the coldest nights that winter. "No. Let's get it over with, shall we? You've obviously had lots of time to think, to make decisions."

"A decision? Dad!"

Ben held up his hand. "No, you listen. You've also had the floor since you walked in here with that paper. Even while you were gone we've done nothing but try to make sense of this epistle you dropped in our laps. I think you at least owe us the courtesy of answering a few questions."

Phil closed up totally at that point. He stared at the floor, and even though he must have been sweltering, he hunched deeper into the heavy coat.

"Why don't we start with your Mom's question, and it is a fair question. Are you sure?"

Phil looked at his mother, closed his eyes, and began to speak as though he was reciting a well-practised address. "I am sure. There is absolutely no question in my mind. Physically, emotionally, I am attracted to men. I enjoy the company of girls—women—but sexually . . . "

"For the love of God, you're eighteen years old!" Ben shouted. "How can you know that? Have you even been with a girl?"

Wilma threw up her hands. "Stop! Phil, you don't have to tell us this. None of it. All that's important is for you to know that we love you. No matter what." Glaring at Ben, then at Phil, she pressed her palms to the coffee table and leaned forward so that she intersected their lines of vision. "Phil's right. We need time to get used to this, to think it through. For now, let's go to bed."

Philip had flown from the room, but not to his bedroom. Instead, he'd pounded down the basement stairs, and a few minutes later they heard the blare of the television.

Ben had poured another Scotch, his third that night. He shook Wilma's hand off his shoulder when she asked him softly to please come to bed. He sat in front of the window, drapes open, looking out into the winter sky, all those cold stars winking back at him. He heard the thick blanket of quiet drop over the house, doors open and close. By the time he went to bed, Wilma had churned the sheets and pillows on both sides into a rumpled sea. She lay curled on her side, facing the window, the blinds pulled high. She too had been contemplating the stars. When he finally closed his eyes, Ben knew from the absolute stillness of her body that she hadn't slept, and wasn't likely to.

This time Ben wasn't leaving her alone in the dark. He grabbed his jacket from the closet, remembering the frigid wind that had stalked them downtown. Remembered too, that Wilma had said Corey was wearing shorts, and detoured to his bedroom. The favourite hooded sweatshirt that usually hung on the back of the door was missing, but on a hook in the back entry, one of Phil's old sweaters that Wilma wore in the garden was an easy grab.

Halfway out the door, he stopped. He was acting on impulse, operating in Wilma mode, and one soft-hearted woman charging through the night was enough. There was no doubt that Corey was on the run, but tracking him down might take far longer than the remaining fragment of this night. With the social worker ready to swoop down in the morning, the best thing Ben could do was to buy some time. He stepped back into the house, trying to remember what Kristel had said about retrieving Corey in the morning. Kristel Maclean. As though he still held it in his hand, he could feel that business card burning against his palm. He turned on the lamp in the living room, retrieved the card from the coffee table where he'd dropped it in the afternoon. How long does it take to lose a child? In this living room, a few hours seemed to be sufficient. Kristel's home phone number was conveniently printed on the back of the card. He glanced at the clock. What earthly excuse could he give for calling at one o'clock in the morning? People didn't call social workers in the middle of the night. They called the after hours number—the emergency people—and that was one of the numbers that he was sure Wilma would have pasted to the list on the side of the fridge.

The explanation was easy. He didn't want to call their social worker in the middle of the night, he said, but wanted her to know as early as possible that his foster son wasn't with his biological mother tonight. That Corey was sick, so they'd cancelled the sleepover. And while they were telling Kristel that she needn't make the trip to Tina's in the morning, they might want to ask her if she had a girl named Shawn on her caseload. Shawn, it appeared, was on her way to Vancouver, if that was of concern to anyone at Social Services. The tired voice on the other end of the phone thanked him for calling, claimed to have recorded all the details, and promised to relay the message. What time had Shawn called, the woman wanted to know, and did Ben know from where, and did she say how she was getting to Vancouver? When he hung up the phone, Ben had a flash of fear that Shawn was more likely to be found than Corey.

Finally, he was out the door again and driving toward the island of downtown lights. He hadn't actually lied to the emergency worker. What difference would it make tonight if Social Services knew that Corey was on the run? So far as Ben could tell, they'd never actually found him. He just turned up.

Some time soon, Ben would have a long talk with Corey about running, and tell him that he truly did understand. That until he met Wilma, he'd felt he'd be plagued forever with the itchy feet that had wanted to be somewhere, anywhere but the dreary Manitoba farm where he grew up. He had no idea where he was heading each time he walked out of the barn, stared across the field, and felt the pull of the horizon like a magnet to his feet. His dad, his older brother, his grandpa, all happy enough if they could get the baling done by supper time. When he was four years old, he was two fence posts beyond the mailbox before his mom caught up with him, hauled him home.

The same purposeful lack of direction had carried him miles from home when he was twelve, thirteen, fourteen. Eventually, they started sending his grandfather to find him. The rusty green truck would pull up beside him. "Where do you think you're going, Benny?" the old man would holler, and Ben would hop in.

"I dunno, Grandpa. I felt kinda restless, figured I'd go for a walk."

"Okay, but next time, turn around when you get halfway finished and come on back."

He'd never told Wilma about the running. He was afraid of fracturing her vision of a secure future for the baby. Once they were married, there seemed no point in talking about those adolescent jaunts. It had been years since he'd been even mildly tempted by a beckoning road.

Tonight, the only compelling thing about the road ahead was that it could take him to Wilma and Corey. A thermos of coffee would have been a good idea. In spite of the adrenaline that had carried him out the door with Phil's sweater under his arm—the sweater he was still holding on his lap, his right hand slipping from the steering wheel to rest in the nubbly wool—he felt fatigue reclaiming him as the streets slid past. He rolled down the window, hoping the cold would revive him. Instead of a rush of chilling wind, there was a gentle caressing breeze that smelled strongly of apple blossom. Ben shook his head. On a night like this, the road could lead anywhere.

44

COREY WAS JOLTED OUT OF HIS DREAM BY VOICES. He had no idea how long he'd been on the bench. It might be time for the guard to make another run past the tigers. He tapped lightly on the wall of the cage, and the tiger sprang to its feet. Nose to nose through the glass they studied each other.

"Okay," he said softly. "I gotta go now. I'll be back on my birthday." And then he darted back onto the same trail he'd taken to get to the cats.

There was no sign of the security guard on the path, no movement anywhere, no more voices calling. Just Corey making his way cautiously along the fringe of the path, dizzy and feeling sicker by the minute now that he was running again. When he came to the swinging bridge that lead back to the dinosaur park, he slipped behind a clump of shrubbery.

He wanted out of the zoo. This night felt like it had already gone on for a week, and there was no sign of morning in the sky. Unless he got over the fence, he was going to be trapped here between the cages forever.

He needed to find his way to Tina's now and hide in the parking lot, but his head was swimming. The edges of the park were bathed in streetlight. Too open, too bright, too far right now for his jelly legs. From one shadowed corner to the next, he crept down the cement steps at the side of the monkey house. The outside cages were quiet.

Long ago, Opi had brought him back to the spider monkeys over and over again, until he could listen to their chattering without shaking in his shoes. "Corey, Corey." He'd crouched beside him and whispered. "Making noise, but behind a fence, so what's to be scared of?" Then, they'd go into the washroom, where he'd wet his handkerchief, wipe Corey's face. Big blue spotted handkerchief. Probably by now, Opi used Kleenex like everyone else. Washroom. There was a washroom close by.

Corey tried to swallow, but his mouth was as dry as the cement under his feet. Crouching and darting, he covered the distance between the gorilla playground and the giraffe's backyard. Down the steps that led to the main path, then into the shadow of a tree a few metres from the concrete recess of the washrooms. He focused on the sign on the washroom door, the pool of light around it, then pushed himself slowly upward with his fingertips and sprinted. His hand was flat on the metal plate around the handle when he heard the unmistakable sound of a flush. A quick dodge into the women's washroom next door. He held his breath in the dark while the men's door opened, footsteps crunched away. Not daring to turn on the light, he waited for his eyes to adjust so he could find a sink. Head under the tap, big gulps of water, a handful of Tylenol, more water.

Finally, bursting to pee, he pushed open the door to one of the cubicles. The way he was aiming in the dark, he may as well have marked out his territory around the bench by the tiger's cage. He barely had time to feel relieved, when even the darkness tilted and began spinning in sickening circles. He slid to the floor, knelt and puked up the bitter pills.

When he could stand, he went back to the sink. He splashed water over his face, his hands, rinsed out his mouth, took a long drink.

For a minute, he considered stretching out on the floor and staying until morning. Only, Kristel was going to be at Tina's by nine o'clock, and getting out of the zoo at seven in the morning would be even harder than it was in the dark. He opened the door an inch, then another. All quiet. How could an island that had as many animals as a forest, or a jungle, be perfectly silent in the night? The tiger knew he was here. He wondered if any of the other animals sensed an intruder. Did they care?

If he ran straight across the lawn from here, vaulted over the fence, he'd be on the path he and Wilma had followed on their way in. No animals at all along that escape route. The big problem—even if he could make it over the fence without strangling himself in the wire on top—was the security office that had a clear view of that whole stretch of lawn and fence. He needed some cover before the final dash. The good news was that he could think again. The puking, the peeing, the cold water, had fixed him. For now. Pulling the door softly closed behind him, he moved back out into the night.

In a clump of lilac bushes on the edge of the grass, Corey took one long breath, let the smell of blossoms, river, and nighttime wash away the memory of toilets and vomit. He straightened, shoved his hands into his pockets, and marched down the tulip-lined path, across the lawn to the far edge of the conservatory flower garden, and then in a straight line toward Dinny, never taking his eyes off the dark shelter at the base of the old dinosaur.

45 WILMA AND TINA STOMPED ALONG IN SILENCE, side by side. From the west parking lot, they crossed the bridge to Memorial Drive, trudged up the hill along the prehistoric park.

A car slowed, window rolled down. One of the two men whistled and called out in a language Wilma couldn't identify. Definitely not English, but the suggestion was unmistakable.

"Fuck off!" Tina shouted back without breaking her stride.

The car screeched away. "I think," Wilma said, "they took a closer look and decided you were with your mother."

Tina's grin lifted her chin, spread the corners of her mouth, and wrinkled her nose so that she looked exactly like Corey when he smiled one of his rare smiles. How could this mother be mirrored in so many facets of that quiet, serious child? "Excuse the language," Tina said. "Hey, you don't let Corey get away with bad language, do you?"

Wilma couldn't imagine Corey telling anyone to 'fuck off'. In his mind maybe, or with his friends—except he didn't seem to have any—but in front of her and Ben? "No," she said, "it's not a problem at all. He has good manners."

"He always did," Tina said, each word weighted. "I made sure of it." Then she grinned again. "If he ever tells you to *houde uw bec*, smack him. It means shut your mouth in Dutch."

At the top of the hill, Tina crossed the strip of stubbly grass, pressed her face against the wire fence. "Corey!" she sang, and "Corey!" and again and again, her throaty voice bouncing off the wall of rock.

She sank to the ground and opened her bag. Shook out a cigarette. Tossed the empty package over her shoulder. "Now we wait a few minutes, to see if he comes. He won't risk calling back." It was like she was explaining the rules of a game. A game they'd invented and played many times before.

Wilma wandered to the fence and stretched on tiptoes, trying to glimpse the path on the other side, shivering when she imagined the twisty trails, the caves. She looked down at Tina, whose head was back, chin tilted so that she stared up at the sky. Any stars were lost in the dirty orange wash of freeway lights. She wondered if light filtered through to the swamp on the other side of these prehistoric mountains.

"Corey's so afraid of the dark," she said. "I can't stand thinking about him alone in there." Did Tina even know that Corey slept with the light on, wrestled demons in his dreams?

Tina exhaled, smoke rising like a halo around her. Her skin had an exotic copper glow. Wilma was sure her own face looked jaundiced. "He was never afraid of the dark when he was with me," Tina said. Then abruptly, "How many other kids do you have?"

Was this girl confusing her with someone else? Imagining that Wilma had left a houseful of children wide-eyed in the night to come looking for Corey? Surely Corey had told Tina that he was currently an only child. "At home, you mean?"

Tina shrugged. "Whatever." She tossed the cigarette into the grass, and only by turning quickly away did Wilma resist the urge to rush over and stomp it out. She'd also like to throw the shrug and the "whatever" back at Tina. Attitude. One thing that Corey, thankfully, had not inherited.

Or maybe Tina was trying to make conversation. *Whatever*, Wilma thought. "Our two boys are grown up. Phil lives in Toronto and Mark's at university in Victoria."

"Is that why you decided to take a foster kid? Because you had extra space?" She looked puzzled, as though she really was trying to make sense of all this. Eyes like Corey's. Brown with green-gold flecks and sculpted lashes. One corner of her full bottom lip was caught between small white teeth.

Wilma sat down on the grass facing Tina and wrapped her arms around her knees. It seemed terribly important to explain this properly. "We never even thought about fostering kids until a couple of months ago. Ben—my husband—works with Frank Marshall. He and Judy are the last couple Corey lived with."

Tina flicked a hand over her shoulder, lifting the wild mane of hair so that it was gilded with copper light. "The fancy house, trip to Disneyland, designer clothes, people who only wanted him if the package didn't include visits with his mother." Wilma flinched at the ferocity of Tina's voice. "I'm his mother. And for the record, don't ever call me a biological mother, or a birth mother, or a natural mother, okay?" Then, as quickly as Tina had flared, she faded. "Aw shit, what difference does it make? He never called me Mommy anyway." She sniffed and rolled her hand as though she meant for Wilma to keep the tape playing. "So then what? You heard they were bailing and felt sorry for Cor?"

Was that how it had been? "Something like that. And something to do with having extra space. Ben was so determined. I guess he was missing the boys as much as I was." That, at least, was what he'd said, but Wilma didn't believe it. If Ben missed them as much as she did, Philip would have been home for Christmas.

"No kidding. I thought people couldn't wait till their kids left home. I'd feel like that. If I had Corey, I'd be wishing he'd grow up and get his own life." She pounded the ground with her fist. "I would."

"We did too, Tina. We couldn't wait for them to leave." Wilma raised her palms. "They were slobs. They wear size thirteen shoes and they each park three pairs in front of the door. They leave smelly socks in the bathroom, they never put the lid down, even though I've told them for twenty years, and they eat enough to feed the troop of gorillas behind that fence. And besides that, we were excited for them, because Ben and I both remember leaving home. The thrill of it. But I miss them terribly." She stopped, not knowing how it must have been for Tina to leave her home, but the beautiful face showed no reaction.

"Don't they come back sometimes? And then you remember all over again why you're glad they're gone?"

"Not often enough. So having Corey has been wonderful. He's not at all like either of our boys—and they're not like each other—but he's a wonderful boy, Tina. He really is."

Tina stood up so abruptly, Wilma was left feeling as though the lights had come on in the middle of a movie.

"Corey!" Tina shouted this time. No more echoing serenade. She stamped her foot. "Corey! Where are you?!"

The fence here was high, appeared to be inaccessible from the inside, and dangerously visible from the busy street. To Wilma, this was the least likely of all escape routes from the zoo. "Shouldn't we try walking along the fence where he could at least see us?"

Tina looked one way, then the other. "If I was in there, I'd be hiding in the dinosaur park. In a cave maybe. I was sure he'd be up here."

"But he might not be in the zoo at all." Knowing that she sounded exactly like Ben, still she couldn't stop. "By now he could be miles away." As much as she reminded her of Corey, there was something in Tina that was stirring up Wilma's need to contradict, to be on the other side.

Tina's eyes were like a cat's, reflecting the yellow streetlight, unblinking, regarding Wilma with pitying disdain. "I know my kid. He's so close to home at the zoo, he wouldn't run anywhere else." She pointed at the fence. "He's in there. You must have known that or you wouldn't have driven down here."

Here was the Tina the social worker had described. Wilma didn't need this girl in her tiny skirt to tell her what she knew. Reminded again that Tina was the cause of all of this, she started down the hill, not bothering to look back to see if Tina would follow.

When she was halfway down, Tina ran past, her running shoes whistling against the grass. She stopped and waited for Wilma at the corner. "Maybe we should split up and double our chances of finding him."

For a minute, Wilma played that notion in her head, chewing on her thumbnail, trying to pretend that she was breathing easy in spite of the sprint. She didn't want to double any of this night. It was two o'clock. Her car sat open in an empty lot, Ben was at home dreaming that she was asleep on the neighbouring pillow, her mother was awake in Winnipeg praying for warm weather on Corey's night, her son in Toronto would be wondering why she hadn't answered his message, and there was a good chance Corey had climbed the wrong fence and been eaten by the Siberian tiger. Wilma was on a corner, drenched in orange light with the person she'd most feared for the past six months.

46

THE OLD MAN UNBUTTONED HIS SWEATER. FOR AN hour, maybe more, he'd rested against a tree by the river, vaguely aware of the damp seeping through his trousers. His legs ached as though they were weighed down by a coffin's depth of earth. Then, like a curtain opening on a cozy fire-lit room, a peculiar warmth had pushed aside the cold edge of this night.

From a clump of bushes maybe ten long strides away—where a short while ago he'd seen a needy-looking pair of people stamp a nest in the branches, spread a rolled up sleeping bag, and disappear with a small bundle of belongings—there suddenly came a cry as thin as a new kitten's. The bush quivered and parted, an elbow protruding, a flash of white skin, then a face like a full moon peered through the leaves at the old man. A hoarse whisper, another body emerging. A man, so thin the map of his ribs was drawn on the sweat-stained shirt, shambled down the path and stood close, his long arm grazing the top of Brinkman's head. "It's warmin' up, eh?"

"Feels like it is."

"My girl's got a baby there, you know, and we're kinda short."

The bare shoulder shone through the leaves. Brinkman shrugged. He leaned on one hip and pulled a worn change purse from his pocket. The man cupped his hand to catch the shower of coins.

"If you dig deeper, we'll have enough for a bed."

"That's all I have. Lots of beds downtown, especially for a woman with a baby."

The cracked boot swung to and fro over the old man's legs. "Yeah, like she's the Virgin Mary. You think there's room in the inn? Come on, you can do better than a few quarters."

"No." He leaned back, the bark of the tree printing ridges in the thick wool of his sweater. "You think if I was rich I'd be sitting under a tree in the middle of the night?"

The man was close enough now that Brinkman almost gagged at the smell of him. His chest was tight, his heart thumping a crazy beat, quick and then a halt and then quick- quick again. He squeezed his shoulders together, then slowly pulled one arm, then the other arm, from the sleeves of his sweater. Folding carefully in his lap, he held it up like a package to the body teetering over him. "Here. Wrap the little one so he stays warm."

He slumped against the ancient poplar, closed his eyes until the flickering shadow moved away. Instead of back to the woman, the man had gone the other way, toward the inner city lights.

Oh, what Inez would say if she knew he was wandering around in the night. She'd be waving her arms and chittering at him like the white-handed monkeys that had terrified Corey when he was small.

They'd been keeping company for almost two months before he told Inez about Corey. By then he knew the names and ages of all her tribe of grandchildren, nieces and nephews, although he did his best to avoid meeting them. He'd done without family all his adult life and wasn't about to adopt someone else's. What he didn't know about Inez, and probably never would, was her other life. She never spoke of her childhood, of how she and Jorges came to Canada, of what they'd left behind. And yet she pressed him for details of his own flight. Even more, she was curious about Bepp and Anna. He'd kept Tina a secret until she phoned one day. Inez could hear the wheedling female voice from halfway across the kitchen, stood with eyebrows raised, waiting for him to explain. Still he didn't mention Corey, couldn't to a woman who doted on her grandchildren and would surely have thrown herself in front of a bus if someone had taken them away.

Last May, on Tina's birthday, he'd waited in the trees across from the south entrance to the zoo for two hours, hoping for a glimpse. When he saw them standing beside the dinosaur, he'd stared, stunned that Corey, little Cor, was almost as tall as Tina. For the five minutes that he spied from behind a tree, he'd thought of every reason for walking across the road and calling out to them, and of every reason to stay hidden. Suddenly they were gone and his decision was made for him. Not even aware that his face was wet with tears, he'd walked home, opened the kitchen door, and there was Inez. And there was nothing to do but tell her.

"Brinkman, you foolish, stubborn old man." She'd crossed her arms and pursed her lips. If she could see him now, she'd try again to talk sense into his miserable old Dutch head, but likely with as little success. If Inez had answered the phone tonight, that man, the foster father and his wife, would be sitting in Brinkman's kitchen drinking coffee. Together they might have found the boy by now.

The old man turned his eyes to the river. Swollen with spring melt from the mountains, it slid past like a sheet of chocolate, lights dancing on the surface. Deceptively calm and friendly looking here in the centre of the city, yet deep enough for the desperate. Once long ago, he and Bepp on a Sunday walk had watched rescue boats pull a body from the spring river. He'd been carrying Anna, and Bepp had grabbed her from his arms, pressing the baby's face into her breast so that she wouldn't see. A young woman had thrown herself from the Centre Street bridge, they heard later. Single and in trouble, he'd suggested, what other reason could drive someone to such a thing? Bepp had simply stared at him.

It was Bepp who'd insisted they live near the river. At least, she said, if she stood on the bank, closed her eyes, and listened, she could pretend she was at home beside the sea and not stranded in this lonely, landlocked city. When it became clear that she was bent on destroying herself, Brinkman had written to Bepp's mother and asked if he could send his wife and baby back to the family. No, came the swift reply from one of the sisters, Mama was sick too. There was no one to look after an extra child.

Now the woman had crawled out of the bushes and stood beside Brinkman with a bundle cradled on her arm. "Can you spare a few dollars?" Sliding his billfold from another pocket, he peeled out the lone twenty-dollar bill. She snatched it from his hand, and shuffled away in the direction her man had gone.

This, the old man thought, *was enough*. All the helping he needed to do in one night. But when he reached the main sidewalk and should have gone back the way he'd come, he turned in the direction of the zoo instead.

He still needed one more glimpse of the boy. To know he was safe.

Half a block away from the bridge that would take him across to the island, he saw two women, one small, dark, and wild-looking, and the other a stranger, standing under the streetlight. When they stepped away together as though they were listening to the same music, he walked slowly forward to take their spot on the corner.

47

FOR FIVE MINUTES THEY STOOD UNDER THE light debating which way they'd each go. Tina could tell from the panic on Wilma's face every time a car cruised by, that the woman was too damn scared to wander on her own.

"Look," she said, "why don't we wait in your car instead of rambling around. We can keep calling to him from there. He'll hear us eventually and figure it out."

Wilma nodded, practically galloped across the bridge.

Back in the car, slumped in their corners, they'd run out of words. Tina was tired of this. What she wanted was to sleep, but she could imagine Wilma's reaction if she suggested a nap. Still, she curled against the door, legs tucked under, arms resting on her knees. 'Like a cat,' Opi used to tease her. 'You move, you eat, you sleep like a cat.'

"He's wearing shorts and a T-shirt," Wilma said softly. Tina didn't need that reminder. She sniffed, turned toward the window, but Wilma sighed and kept right on talking. "If he moves around, we'll see the moonlight on his skin."

Jesus! Did she have to turn this into a tearjerker? Like Tina didn't know life was one long, sad movie? What was she supposed to do? Confess that it was all her fault, and she'd make it up to Corey when he finally materialized in the friggin' moonlight?

Forget about sleeping. She sat up and considered the fence. If she was alone, she'd be on the other side. Would probably have found Corey, and would be hoisting him over by now. Wilma was a drag—Christ, Paulette would be more help—and Tina had no idea why she'd been hanging with her all this time. Trying to make friends for later? From the time she'd walked up to the car, she'd felt Wilma sizing her up. Measuring against all

192

the things she'd heard from the social workers. Maybe from Corey too. In the warm car, with this timid woman, she might as well tell her own side of the story. She had the feeling she wouldn't get another chance.

"I tried, you know." She kept her eyes on a clump of long grass on the other side of the fence. "I tried to be a mom."

She felt fingertips land on her wrist, cool and light as air. "Tina, you don't have to explain. Not to me."

There was a flicker of shadow in the dark. Then nothing. Tina turned, stared into the wide blue eyes. "Yeah, I do need to explain, because nobody knows, or seems to give a damn what it was like to be fourteen years old and having a baby all by myself. Just me and a worn out old man who didn't need any more trouble." Wilma flinched. Well tough shit. Tina had never whined about this before, never thought it was worth the trouble to try and make anyone understand. It was time she had her say. "I was a kid. But after I had Corey, I wasn't supposed to be a kid again. Not ever."

The air in the car was so still, Tina thought Wilma had stopped breathing. Outside, the pavement and the trees beyond the fence were white in the moonlight. Wilma's hair touched with the same silvery light. Ghosts.

"Oh Lord," Wilma said, "you're so scared when you're that young. I was sure I was going to die." She leaned toward Tina, whispering. "How to tell my mother, and if I even could, what would I do with it, and did I really have to have it, or was there some other way."

Tina untangled her feet, planted them on the floor, leaned in to Wilma's secret, speaking so quietly she was barely mouthing the words. "So, what did you do?"

"I got married." One sputtering gasp of laughter, and as quickly as she'd started, Wilma stopped, put her palms to her cheeks. "I'm sorry," she said. "It's myself I'm laughing at, and Ben, and life."

Tina shook her head. Maybe when she was Wilma's age she'd get the joke. "Well I didn't get married. I figured Corey would be better off without his father, even if I'd known who he was."

"You were braver than I was." Wilma wiped her eyes with the back of her hand. "I got married for me, so I wouldn't have to do this alone. Not for my son."

Tina shrugged. "It doesn't matter why you did it. Your son got to grow up with his dad."

"No!" Wilma seized both of Tina's hands. Touching again. Like they'd known each other for years instead of two hours. "Listen to me, Tina. He didn't. I didn't even know his dad's last name."

Tina threw back her head and roared. "Oh God, that's perfect! You got pregnant by some guy you didn't even know?"

For a minute she thought Wilma was going to tell her that she'd misunderstood. She saw the air in the car quiver between them, squiggly shock lines like in a comic book. Wilma put her hands on the steering wheel and closed her eyes as though she was getting ready to shoot that family car over a mountain of tires. Hands still tight on the wheel, she finally turned toward Tina.

"That was a long, long time ago," she said. "I was very young. It's not important anymore."

"Whatever. But maybe it's important to your kid."

"His name is Philip." She was looking at Tina, but as though she didn't see her, as though she was staring through her to someone on the other side of the car. "I think you'd like Philip." She shifted slightly so that the two of them were knee to knee. "He's coming home next weekend. For Mother's Day. Why don't you have dinner with us? Corey would like that."

Oh yeah, Corey'd be fuckin' dazzled by the idea. If they ever found Corey again, and if Cousin Kristel didn't send him to live on a reserve. What the hell was this Wilma chick thinking? That she was going to line Tina up with her son?

She shook her head. "Thanks, but in case you haven't heard, I'm not allowed on the guest list. You think that social worker doesn't like you now, tell her who's coming to dinner and watch her light up."

Wilma sighed. "Funny how we keep coming back to her. I mean it, Tina. We're going to find Corey, and take him home, and we're not having any more of these ridiculous visits. If you want to take Corey to the zoo, we'll pick you up and drop you both off, and come back and get you, and take you wherever you want to go. And when you miss him the most, phone me and come visit him at home. Have dinner with us and see where he sleeps. No one will know but us."

Tina tried not to sneer. This sounded real, not the kind of smarmy promises she'd heard before. "Wilma, you haven't been in this business very long. That's not the way it goes."

"Yes, it is." She pounced on Tina's arm for about the hundredth time. "We're going to rewrite it."

Tina stared at her, then into the dark again where she was almost positive she'd caught something moving from the corner of her eye. She threw open the car door. "Okay. Let's go find my kid so we can all go home." She cupped her hands to her mouth. "Corey!"

This time Wilma called too.

48 IN A QUICK VAULT, COREY WAS OVER THE LOW barrier and safe in the shadow under massive grey legs. He sat down against Dinny's ankle, scrubbed his face, his runny nose, his hot cheeks with the scratchy sweater, then wadded it into a ball and used it to cushion his head. Knees to his chest to keep the sharp gravel from embedding itself in the backs of his leg, he let his fingers play over the dinosaur's chipped toes. Imagined running his fingertips over Tina's sparkly nails, remembered the bag in his pocket. Tina's earrings. Nope. Not Tina's anymore. He was giving the elephants to Shawn. If he hadn't screwed up tonight, he could have asked his social worker if she'd help him find Shawn—he couldn't remember her name, that woman with the big red glasses. Funny, because she'd been flying around inside his head all night. But now everything was fuzzy. It must be close to morning, and tomorrow—today—he was supposed to be at Tina's. Or was that yesterday and he'd already been away for two nights and really messed up?

He took the earrings out of the bag, swung the elephants gently back and forth with his little finger. Yeah, Shawn was gonna love these if he ever saw her again. Maybe he could hide them and get a message to her, like a treasure hunt. That would be sweet. He could imagine the goofy look on her face.

The ground under Dinny was covered in crushed rock. Corey scraped away the top layer and scooped a shallow bowl into the dirt underneath. He could bury the present here, but if some animal—there were squirrels everywhere in this zoo—chewed through the bag and dragged away the earrings, the whole thing would turn out like all of Shawn's adventures. No treasure at the end. Corey tapped on the porous stone. Unpinning one of the elephants, he chipped cautiously away at Dinny's leg with the sharp post of the earring until it was sunk deep into Dinny's hide. Poor old dinosaur.

Shawn would have taken it one step further. He could hear her chirping away as if she was beside him. "Cor, do dinosaurs have ears? I got the coolest idea."

Shawn was the kind of kid who'd climb the dinosaur right to the top and screw those earrings into Dinny's head. With that bad luck of hers, a big bird, like the crows Opi chased out of his garden, would peck them out and steal them away. She'd bring some other kid to show them this cool thing she'd done and there'd be nothing. 'Yeah, right,' they'd say. Corey pressed the second earring extra hard into Dinny's leg.

He wished he'd worn his watch. For Christmas, Ben and Wilma had given him a sports watch with Indiglo and an alarm. He tried figuring in his head how long he'd been wandering around in the dark, but couldn't even remember what time the sun went down. The night was dark, and quiet, and the earrings were planted. Time to move?

Out from under Dinny's belly, Corey raised his arms and felt air ripple warm around him like bathwater. Earlier in the night, the sweat-soaked T-shirt had clung to him like sleet, but now it was a second skin, soft and familiar. Since he'd fallen asleep beside the tiger he'd been warm. He wouldn't freeze to death behind the dumpster at Tina's place.

He was on the dark side of the dinosaur, hidden from view of the brightly lit security station and with his back to the night skyline. Dinny's sad face, high above him, was ringed with stars.

He leaned against the chipped old hide and took deep breaths. He could do this. Even the line of barbed wire at the top of the fence wouldn't stop him. Tina used to climb all the way to the roof on Opi's house to get in her bedroom window when she was his age. She'd told him this, bragging. If Tina could climb the roof, he could climb a lousy fence.

Then he tilted his head again, measured the height of the dinosaur, and thought about Wilma when she was a kid, standing on Dinny's back with her arms high and the funny smile she had when something surprised her. Like the time he'd been doing his homework at the kitchen table. She was helping him while she emptied the dishwasher. He'd been watching her out of the corner of his eye and in his head he was whispering "Mom," over and over, trying the word. When she looked up and smiled, it was as though she'd heard him. She'd come to the table and brushed the back of her hand against his cheek.

Yeah, he could see Wilma up there on Dinny, smiling. It was the kind of thing Shawn would do too, climbing and climbing all the way to Dinny's head. Sitting up there in the moonlight with her long legs wrapped around Dinny's neck. In fact, he could imagine anyone but himself climbing that old dinosaur without being afraid, or thinking someone might see, or giving a second thought to why they wanted to do it in the first place.

Corey raised his hands to his face, surprised by the slick wetness on his cheeks. He brushed the hair out of his eyes and looked up at the dinosaur's sad face. At all those stars above him.

Never had Corey been anywhere that he'd felt so perfectly alone. Not lonely, or lost, or frightened. Just him and Dinny and no one around to see if he fell or chickened out.

The dinosaur's back was a cinch. Corey stood on the tip of the tail and, like a tightrope walker, made his way up the long curve until he was directly over the hind legs. His head felt like it was floating in front of him, lifting off his shoulders and disconnecting his thoughts from the heavy weight of his feet. He had a clear view across the river to dark houses. Look over his left shoulder, past shrubs and trees, and there were the black conservatory windows. Glance over his right shoulder, through lacy leaves, and there was the dark path leading to the tiger's small world. But best of all, from where he stood steady and tall on the hump of Dinny's back, he could see two security guards floodlit against the back wall of their office. They leaned there, smoking and staring across the park at Dinny. And he knew that they couldn't see him. At last, he was invisible.

Just as Corey returned his attention to the steep angle of the dinosaur's neck, a car crossed the bridge, headlights spraying the lawn near the security gate. He stood with widespread legs, watching the car pull into the small parking lot beside the security office. Ben's car. He was sure of it.

He would have been down Dinny's spine in a minute, tearing across the lawn to Ben, but for about the hundredth time since he'd scrambled behind the rocks in the pink dusk, the roar of a plane filled his throbbing ears. When he tilted his head to the flashing lights, they looked so close he instinctively ducked, lost his balance, and caught himself in time to pitch forward, arms clutching Dinny's neck. In the first few seconds that he clung there, amazed that he hadn't crashed to the ground, Corey was sure he heard a voice sing his name.

He lay there panting, his ears ringing with the echo. "Corrr... eeeeee..." like a bird. Or like Shawn when she teased and teased, trying him to get him to swing at her so that she could dance away and tease some more.

"I'm here!" he shouted, but he couldn't hear his own voice over the scream from the sky.

49

BY THE TIME WILMA CAUGHT UP, TINA WAS AT THE ticket office, her fingers curled around the iron gate.

"Co-rey!" Not so loudly this time, her voice falling on the last note. Then, she stepped away and collapsed onto a stone bench, arms and legs flung wide like a doll thrown there by a careless child.

"Oh shit! Where is he? We haven't got all night."

"Yes we do." Wilma perched on the end of the bench with her back toward Tina, her eyes on the fence. "We have until nine o'clock in the morning, when Kristel is going to call my house to tell me she's on her way to your house." She squinted into the dark beyond the gate. Strange there weren't at least a few lights. Or would it upset the animals, keep them awake if nighttime didn't fall properly? Surely animals raised in captivity would have adapted.

She was so tired she wanted to stretch out on the bench and close her eyes. Just for a few minutes. Just to get some energy back. She tried to focus on what Tina was saying, but the agitation that had fuelled her through the day, and half of this night, was gone. Tina was no longer a mystery. She was this girl on the bench, barely older than Philip, and her motivation right now was no different from Wilma's. Oddly, from this vantage point, Wilma felt as though they'd already succeeded. She tilted her wrist to catch the streetlight. Almost three o'clock. If she'd brought the phone, she could call Ben and tell him to come. It was his turn to wait. And then she'd climb into the back seat of the car and sleep. She stood up, stretched. "I wish I'd brought a thermos of coffee."

"I wish I had a cigarette. You could go get some. Coffee, I mean. There's an all-night place up the hill. And while you're at it, could you get me some cigarettes? I'll wait here."

"No, I don't think so." Wilma sat down again, still scanning the mosaic of shifting shadows. Tina sat with her feet stretched out in front of her, running shoes so small Wilma doubted they'd fit Corey.

She turned back to the trees where black shapes darted and swooped. Both too late and too early for birds. Long ago, on summer nights at Uncle Eddy's farm, her brother, Carl, had teased Wilma about her long hair. Bats loved long hair, he'd said, because they could tangle in it close to a girl's neck and suck her blood. With a bat he'd grabbed from under the rafters in the barn in his gloved hand, Uncle Eddy had tried to cure her of her fear, but the hissing, hideous creature only strengthened Wilma's terror. Not until a summer holiday in Idaho—where she and Ben sat on a dock every night at dusk, Philip and Mark wide-eyed with wonder between them, and watched the incredible radar zigs and zags of the bats feasting on mosquitoes—had Wilma finally graduated from terrified to slightly nervy. But what about Corey? There was still so much to learn about that boy, what he knew, and what he feared. She nudged Tina with her elbow. "We should do something."

"Yeah. But what?"

So they sat there like two thieves in the night, turning the possibilities this way and that, both shrinking into the cold stone when a truck cruised slowly past. Brake lights glowing, it slowed to a crawl before the bend. The man behind the wheel cranked his head around for one last look. Didn't these people, these men cruising the streets, ever go home and go to bed?

"Does Corey know about your kid?" Tina crossed her ankles, arched her back, and tilted her face to the sky. "That he has a different father?"

"Yes." Funny how they kept coming back to her "kid." If only the answer to that one was up there in stars. Wilma couldn't remember exactly how they'd decided that Corey should know that Ben wasn't Philip's biological father. Something to do with Ben's fondness for having his cards on the table, thinking it might make it easier for Corey to live with his own hand. "Ben—my husband—thought it might make him feel more comfortable with not knowing his own dad."

"That's no big deal," Tina snapped. "I explained it to him a long time ago." She sat up straighter, tugging at the hem of her skirt. Even though the night had turned milder, she must be chilly by now. She crossed her arms, scowling at the bushes across the road as though she was trying to remember where the black sweater had been shed. "Does he talk about me?"

Unless he was asked specific questions, Corey rarely spoke of home, and never about Tina. How would a mother feel, Wilma wondered, knowing her child never mentioned her name. "Yes of course he does," she lied.

"It's been four years, you know."

Four years. Six months with Ben and Wilma was a mere one-eighth, 12 percent of that homeless time. But in another six months they'd have claimed almost a quarter, and in another six years he'd have been with them almost as long as he'd lived with Tina. Wilma nodded again.

"Has he ever mentioned my boyfriend?" Now Tina's voice had a sly edge.

"No." And that was the truth. Corey had never mentioned the boyfriend, but they'd heard plenty from the last social worker. A breach of confidentiality, he'd told them in his gravelly voice, but they needed to know about this man. Not that the boyfriend had an interest in Corey, but if Tina ever disappeared he might come looking for her through Corey.

She could feel Tina watching. Wilma was a good liar but Tina was undoubtedly her equal; there's no one better than another liar for sniffing out deceit. "No shit. Well, isn't that a surprise. Simon's been around a long time. Since before Corey was born."

Oh my. The story of this long night was turning into the Book of Revelation. First Wilma's confession to Tina, and now this. Simon. Simon the unknown father? The abusive boyfriend who was considered such a danger to Corey, the court had permanently removed him from Tina's care.

"You don't have to worry about Simon," Tina said. She stood up and raised her arms over her head. Looked for all the world as though she might pirouette, but instead she bent, touched her toes, and then stood up straight. "He'll never come looking for Corey. And for sure Corey will never go looking for him. So don't worry about him, and don't listen to anything Kristel tells you."

Without any warning, she turned and started to walk down St. George's Drive, down the middle of the road toward Dinny. From where they'd been sitting, only the light from the security office at the end of the road was visible, but when she followed Tina, Wilma could see a car parked next to the building, tail lights flashing red.

A few more steps along the narrow strip of grass bordering the fence and Tina stopped again. "Does he talk about anybody else?"

"Sometimes he mentions his grandpa, but he doesn't say much." Wilma was on the verge of telling her that Ben had spoken to him, to Mr. C. Brinkman, but Tina's face puckered with anger.

"Dear Opi. Did Corey ever tell you he could probably be living with Opi if the old fool hadn't tried to pick a social worker up by the throat and throw him across the room? They decided that maybe he didn't have it together enough to look after a kid."

There was movement at the end of the road. Two men stepped away from the side of the building, walked toward the parked car. The car door opened and a tall man emerged and stood talking, one arm draped over the top of the door, the other hand moving in gestures that were instantly recognizable.

50

IT WOULD TAKE EVERY BIT OF STRENGTH COREY had to drag his body up the dinosaur's neck. In fact, he thought, when he dared to open his eyes and look at the long drop to the ground, maybe it took the strength of a different kid after all. The way down was even scarier than the rest of the climb.

With frog legs around rough stone, he stretched and pulled with all his might, hauling up on his elbows, scraping the insides of his thighs, his arms. Every inch of his skin felt wet and raw. Wriggling his heels, he played with the idea of lifting his knees up and under him, crawling the rest of the way, but his ankles would not give up their grip. He clung so tightly, the thick skin of the dinosaur seemed to press all the way to his bone.

Breathe, Corey! Opi's voice sounded so real, so near, he was sure he'd feel those old arms around him any minute. So sure that he waited, licking the corners of his mouth to catch the trickle of tears. There was no embrace, but after two more breaths, he began to feel lighter, as though he was hovering above the cold stone, watching some other boy. A boy so brave he could ignore everything but the need to keep on going. "Breathe," he whispered to that boy. "Look up." He closed his eyes, and when he opened them again there was only the final stretch of neck ahead of him, the sky above. There was a new scent to the night. A tangy mist from the river that he could taste, cold and fresh on the back of his throat. He swallowed, and let his attention wander over the tops of the trees to office towers, then down to the reflected moon on the water.

Finally, he turned his eyes to the guard's office where Ben stood beside his car, two other men with hands on hips facing across the lawn. All he had to do was shout and wave, and wait to be rescued. He didn't have to find his way to Tina's, make up a story for the social worker, prove anything.

Then he heard Tina's voice, real, and so close that if Dinny had dropped his head across the fence, he could've swallowed her. She hadn't seen him yet. If she had, she'd be screaming, not calling, and everyone would be running across the lawn toward him. Tina, Ben, and he knew that Wilma had be close as well. He felt sick at the thought of standing between Wilma and Tina, not knowing which way to turn, what to say. He didn't want to talk to anyone. He wanted to go back to the old tiger and tell her that everything had turned out just the way they'd planned it. But there was one more piece that he needed to tell her as well. He gulped, swallowed another breath of river, and looked up at Dinny's blank eye. He was going to drag himself to the top of the dinosaur.

Searching with his fingertips for each stony ripple that would anchor him, arms and legs so steady he couldn't believe they were his own, he inched his way upward. The higher he pulled, the more gentle the slope and, finally, he was sprawled on Dinny's head.

51

BEN HAD HIS BACK TO THE ROAD, HIS EYES ON the two men who were listening to him skeptically, when one of them raised his arm, pointing over Ben's shoulder, and whistled softly. "Holy shit! What is that on top of Dinny?"

What Ben saw first when he spun around was not the shadowy bulk of the dinosaur, but two people standing beside the fence directly in front of it. One of them was the woman he'd just described to the guards. He would have called to Wilma, had her name on his lips, if he hadn't finally raised his eyes and seen the fluttering around Dinny's head. Something, or someone, sprawled up there, waving.

Ben clapped his hand onto the shoulder of the closest man. "That's him on the dinosaur! And my wife's outside the fence!" He led the charge to the dinosaur without looking back to see if the two guards were following.

Halfway down the path, he could hear all of their voices—Corey, Wilma and the other woman who could only be Tina, all calling. He added his own to the furor. "Hang on buddy! Don't move until I get there. Not an inch, Corey! Hang on!" He was afraid to startle the boy with too many commands, but wanted to reassure, to let him know he wasn't alone. How the hell had this child, afraid to pick up a basketball and shoot hoops in the back alley for fear of failing, found the courage to crawl up a statue almost ten times his height? A smart kid, who must know how disastrous it would be to fall. Or was that precisely why he was up there?

Ben cleared the low fence, circled around to the tail of the dinosaur, and ran up the spine, down the slow curve to the neck, and then stopped, breathless at the base of the neck. From here, all he could see were dangling shoes.

Stroking the grey plaster with his hand, he winced at the thought of those spindly legs sliding the rough slope, but the only other way was with a ladder or a net.

The guards stood below shouting. "Hang on, kid! We'll call the fire department."

"No!" Ben waved them back. "I can get him." He turned to the scraping sound of Corey's feet against the stone. "Go slow, son. Little bit at a time, and hold tight. I'm here to catch you."

Eyes stinging, he held his breath and watched the rest of that fragile body slide slowly into view.

52

ANY OTHER TIME, WILMA WOULD HAVE RUN FOR THE gate, but when Tina went over the fence, so did she. She hesitated at the barbed wire, not sure where to grab, not sure where her foot needed to land when she swung her leg over the top.

"Come on!" Tina sounded as though she was going to stamp her foot if Wilma didn't cooperate. "I'll help you down."

Once the first cautious leg was over the top, and her toe wedged into a hole in the mesh, the second followed as though she'd been clearing fences all her life. She felt for the next toehold, and the next. When she was halfway down, a pair of small hands circled her waist. Not strong enough to hold her if she fell, but reassuring for the few seconds that they steadied her. Before Wilma's feet hit the ground, Tina whirled away, flying across the lawn toward Dinny. There was no point in turning this into a race. Wilma took a deep breath before she trotted after Tina, trying to ignore the stitch in her side and the pounding in her chest, coming in last to stand panting next to the two security guards. She heard and felt the soft whump when Corey slid the last few feet into Ben's arms. Put her hand to her mouth to stifle the gasp.

Tina strained forward as though to take a flying leap at the dinosaur's back. When one of the men put a warning hand on her arm, she shook it off. "Keep your fuckin' hands to yourself. That's my kid up there." The guard looked from Tina to Wilma, up at the dinosaur, then at his partner. The other man shrugged. Both of them stepped back, arms folded across chests.

"Ben?" Wilma couldn't stand it any longer. "Is he all right?" On tiptoes, she watched Ben lower Corey to the curve of Dinny's neck. He paused, teetered, flung one arm over Corey like a brace. Crouched beside him and peered down at the ground.

"You want a ladder?" The guard scratched his head.

"Yes!" Wilma whispered. "Get a ladder."

"No." Ben's voice rang over their heads. "We're doing fine."

So dark up there, tree shadows flickering around Ben. He seemed to ease himself down to sit beside Corey, their two silhouettes melding into one. A minute later, Ben slowly stood, outlined against the sky with Corey's legs circling his waist. Shoulders hunched forward, he looked like a giant. A gorilla walking the dinosaur's back with a boy in his arms. Not until he was almost down the tail, the drop a mere four feet from the ground, did Wilma finally exhale.

In the few seconds it took her to reach the tip of Dinny's tail, she forgot about Tina, reached instinctively for Corey. There was a sharp intake of breath behind her. She dropped her arms and turned. For a moment, she thought Tina was going to spring at her, push her out of the way. Ben looked from one to the other, and seemed to tighten his hold on Corey. And then Tina stepped forward, slid her arms around Corey's waist, and laid her cheek against his back. "Jeez, Cor." She choked on her thick voice. "What were you trying to do?"

Corey lifted his head. "I don't feel so good," he said, and with a long sigh he sank back into Ben's chest. Tina turned away, wiping her eyes and her cheeks with the backs of her hands.

Not daring to look at Ben because she knew she'd be drawn to him, and to Corey, Wilma raised her face to the stars instead. "Nice timing, Ben." All the questions about when and how he knew, she kept to herself. They could wait until Corey was asleep and the two of them were back at the kitchen table.

One of the security men cleared his throat. "So this is your lost kid?"

His hand on Corey's head, Ben held the small face tight to his chest. "Yes," he said, and his voice was as dense as Tina's had been. "This is our kid."

Tina, when she turned, showed no more trace of tears. Her face was closed as tight as when she'd first peered into the car and said, "You're Wilma, right? My kid's foster parent?"

To Wilma, the scene felt oddly in need of introductions, like they'd rewound to an earlier frame. "Ben," she said, "this is Tina."

He nodded. "Yes, I know." As though he were closing a deal, he extended his arm. Tina narrowed her eyes, but finally put her small hand in his. "I think we'll do our talking later," he said. He was in charge now and Wilma felt a rush of irritation. As much as she wanted the night to be over, she felt as though she and Tina were not quite finished. Ben turned toward the fence. "Where did you park the car? We'll pick it up tomorrow if it's somewhere legal."

Legal? Wilma's mind went blank. All she could remember of the past hour was the feel of the mesh that had separated them from Corey. She looked from the fence to the street, shook her head.

"It's in the parking lot on the other side of the entrance. By the tigers." Tina waved her hand in the direction of the downtown lights.

Corey's head came up, his eyes glittering. "Hey, Tina?" She stepped close, held his face between her palms. "Did you see me climb that thing?"

She pressed her nose to his. "Yeah baby, I saw that. But don't ever do it again, okay?"

"Come on then." Ben began walking in a beeline toward the gate.

"Just a minute now." Ben stopped and looked back. The more officious of the two security men held up his hand. "We're going to have a file a report. You can't just take off like that." He motioned to poor old Dinny. "We've got a designated heritage site here, you know. No telling what kind of damage you've done, climbing around up there."

"What!" Tina stepped between the man and Ben. "What we've got is a sick kid. You think the fuckin' dinosaur cares? Get a life!"

Wilma bit the inside of her cheek to keep from laughing. Ben had gone chalky white, stared at Tina, beckoned to Wilma. "We'll sort it out on our way," he said. "Tomorrow if need be."

Wilma did not want to be part of the parade to Ben's car, nor did she want to supply the names and details that would ultimately find their way to Kristel Maclean's desk. "You go ahead," she told Ben. "Get Corey home as fast as you can. We'll be there shortly." Surprisingly, he didn't quibble, but strode away with the one guard fussing along beside him. She could hear Ben's voice, placating. The other man seemed to be waiting to escort Wilma and Tina. Wilma patted his arm. "We'll go out the same way we came in." She jogged to the fence, knowing without looking back that Tina would be right behind her.

53

BRINKMAN KNEW THAT IF ANYONE HAD TAKEN their eyes off the drama on the dinosaur, they would have seen him watching from the other side of the fence. Tonight he didn't care. Not quite daring enough to stand in the open, he sat on a rock on the other side of the road, his back to the river, his attention flying from the child to the mother, and back to the child, until Corey was safe on the ground. Then, he stood and walked slowly back in the direction from which he'd come.

54

THIS TIME, TINA FOLLOWED WILMA OVER THE fence, waiting at the top while she made her cautious descent. When Wilma was finally on the ground, Tina dropped beside her, feeling light as a cat. They watched Ben pat the security guard on the back, open the car, and belt Corey into the passenger seat. As he pulled onto St. George's Drive, he honked the horn and disappeared across the bridge. Shit. She'd love to know how he'd managed that. If she'd been the one with Corey in her arms, there'd be at least two cop cars, a fire truck, and an ambulance in the parking lot by now. "He must be some talker, your husband."

Beside her, Wilma was rubbing her hands on the thighs of her jeans. She grinned at Tina, the first smile the woman had spent all night. "Well, there are ways to get around these people, and Ben is an expert. This is probably the most excitement they've had around here in the middle of the night in ages. I'm sure the word will get out, but let's hope we stay anonymous." She blew the hair off her forehead. "I'm so glad it's over."

Oh yeah, it was over. Tina could tell by the way her teeth were chattering. Any minute now her bones would be dancing too. The same way her body got disconnected from her brain those times Corey was snatched away from her. Her first instinct was to scream and pounce, and try to rip out someone's heart. Funny she hadn't done that yet. But no matter how strong she was when the fight was on, afterwards she fell apart.

All the way back to the car, she kept her arms crossed tightly around her waist to hide the spastic twitching. Wilma padded along beside her, recounting the whole friggin' adventure out loud as though she didn't want to forget a single detail. Tina ignored her, and tried, too, to ignore the chilly cloud rising off the river. There hadn't been a single car since they came over the fence. Probably four o'clock by now. The time that always seemed, to Tina, to be hanging between night and day. The time Opi used to leave for the bakery, and she'd just be crawling into bed beside Corey. She shivered and rubbed her arms.

At the car, Tina stuck her arm through the open window on the passenger's side and dragged out Wilma's sweater. "Can I borrow this?" Before Wilma could answer, Tina shoved her arms into the sleeves. Miles too big, but that was a good thing because the heavy wool wrapped around her like a blanket. "See you around." She turned toward the street, then looked back at Wilma. Felt her face lift in a smile without any effort at all. "It's been a blast, you know."

"Tina, no!" Wilma started to reach for her, but seemed to change her mind. "You can't wander off in the dark. Come home with me. We have a spare bed."

"No, it's okay. That would mess things up even more." The only way to keep from stuttering was to clench her teeth while she talked. She looked both ways down the deserted street. "I'll be fine." Suddenly, she was not fine at all. She sank onto the scrubby grass and clutched her bent legs with her arms, forehead pressed to her knees. Breathe, dammit, breathe. Like Foster Mom needed someone else to look after in the night.

And then Wilma was beside her with another sweater, a sweatshirt, wrapping it around Tina's legs. "Please get in the car. Let me drive you home." She knelt beside Tina, smoothing back her hair to feel her forehead with one hand, the other patting her arm.

Tina shook her head. "I don't think so." When she looked up at Wilma, at the face all crumpled with worry, her cheeks were suddenly wet with another of those damn floods of tears. She fumbled around in her purse for Kleenex, her hand closing instead on the little metal tow truck. With fingertips, she finally pulled out a wad of tissue and swiped at her nose, her cheeks.

"You'd better get home and look after Corey. I'll be okay. I'm not going far." She wanted to give Wilma the toy, to ask her to put it on Corey's pillow so that he'd see it when he opened his eyes in the morning, but her fist would not let go. Instead, she started to hand back the sweatshirt, then instinctively raised it to her face. It was Corey's. She'd know the smell of him anywhere. With the shirt draped once more over her knees, she stroked the fabric with one hand, and let the fingers of the other slip the toy truck into the kangaroo pouch on the front. Folding it carefully first, she handed the sweatshirt to Wilma. "You guys aren't allergic to cats are you?"

"No." Wilma shook her head.

"Good, 'cause I'm thinking about giving Corey a kitten for his birthday." She tilted her head, and studied the tired looking face. "Go home to bed, Wilma."

A few steps down the sidewalk, she felt her energy return. Head back, she ran her fingers through her tangled hair and spread it in a crackling mane across her shoulders. Corey was safe in bed by now. Wilma wouldn't have any trouble coming up with a story for Kristel when she phoned at nine—damn that woman was a good liar! And if Kristel tried to raise any shit, Super Dad could be counted on to head her off at the pass. Tina stopped on the bridge and stared down at the water. There were still dirty drifts of snow along the bank. Until she was ten years old, she'd walked this route with Opi every Sunday, checking the river for signs of the season. In another few weeks, the river would be churning along, high and muddy. But tonight, the water looked icy cold and clear. The thaw had just begun.

Finally, Tina heard the sound of a car driving slowly away in the parking lot behind her. Hands on her hips, Tina watched the tail lights disappear before she turned and crossed the bridge to Memorial Drive.

55

BRINKMAN WAITED SO LONG AGAINST THE LAMPPOST that twice he dozed off, began to slide sideways, and caught himself with a lurch. What a sight he must be to passing cars, an old man leaning drunkenly into the night.

He'd known when he saw those two women on the corner that he should turn around and go home. But as always, instinct prevailed, so he'd followed. Powerless to change, it seemed, as predictable as the animals in their cages. And if, for once, he'd used his common sense? By now he'd be tossing in his bed, regretting the two pots of coffee. Even more, regretting that he'd hung up on the man who called about Corey. It had been months since he'd even said the child's name in his mind, but tonight it played over and over until it mingled with the sound of his blood. All of their names were like bell song: Anna, Tina, Corey. And Bepp, whose name pounded in his ears and woke him in the night.

By the time he'd reached the corner himself, the women had crossed the bridge. He could see them, waiting there in the car. After ten minutes, they got out, Tina running ahead, her legs flashing silver until she disappeared at the bend in the road. The other woman moved more cautiously, stopping to rub her arms and retie a shoe, and even glancing back as though she could feel him watching.

After a few minutes, Brinkman had left his place in the light and followed, stopping in the shadows whenever he got close enough to be seen. Twice he'd heard Tina's voice calling out to Corey with a song as sad as the mourning dove roosting in his neighbour's eaves. Then there were others: a man shouting, and another woman's voice, and the sound of pounding feet. He'd watched until his grandson was safely in arms, then he'd come back to his corner to wait.

She came toward him so slowly he felt invisible. Not until she was standing in front of him, so close the air between them felt compressed into a dense wall, did she finally speak. "Why didn't you come when you heard him call?"

He shrugged. "Did I hear him? Is that what the shouting was about?"

Tina looked at him with disgust. "All you had to do was walk up to the fence and say his name. Just once, so that he knows you care. Goddamn it, Opi! He asks about you every single time I see him."

"It's late," he said, and started to walk away, but then he turned to face her again. "He's okay?" Tina nodded, her lip trembling. Washed in this ugly orange light she was lost child and grieving mother in one face, one small body. His legs were stone, but still he took the two steps back, dragging all of the past with him, and stood in front of her.

Tina wrapped her arms around his waist and pressed her face to his chest. "Opi, don't leave me here."

"No one is leaving you. All you have to do is walk."

When she pulled away, his chest felt cold. She would have turned and crossed the bridge again, but this time he reached for her arms. "Tina, I'll get a lawyer."

"What for? I don't need a lawyer."

"To get Corey back." Her bones felt like a kitten's in his big hands. He'd forgotten how small she was. "He's old enough now, they won't want to keep him. Who wants a teenage boy?" In this light, with gold playing through her hair, there was more of Anna in this girl than he'd ever seen before.

"They do, Opi. Those people who have him now. I think they'll keep him."

He was surprised by the jolt to his chest, like electricity. He'd never imagined anyone wanting Corey. Maybe feeding him, clothing him, sending him to school, but he'd not allowed a picture of someone else claiming the boy as family. "Why should they have him? He's not blood to them." They'd started walking, Tina's arm linked with his.

"Yeah, but the blood hasn't done so great for him, you know."

The street was silent and deserted. Not a single car in sight, but still the traffic light two blocks away turned red to green. In another hour, the birds outside his bedroom window would begin to call, waking each other and greeting the morning until they finally got on with the business of feeding.

"So you're coming home?"

"For tonight. In the morning—maybe afternoon—I'll go see Corey. After that, I don't know. Will you come with me?"

He could imagine, so clearly, the house where the tall man who'd carried Corey down the back of the dinosaur would live with his wife. A nice home with a well-kept garden. He shook his head. "No, you'll go alone. But you'll tell him his Opi was there tonight. Tell him I saw him climb the dinosaur."

Tina raked her cheeks with her knuckles. She sniffed long and hard. "The river smells strange tonight, don't you think, Opi?"

He pulled a handkerchief from his back pocket, unfolded it carefully, handed it to her. She licked her lips before she scrubbed her face.

Brinkman nodded, put an arm around her thin shoulders, and matched his stride to the quick step of her small shoes. "The night tastes of salt," he said. "Your grandmother would have said it smells like home."

ACKNOWLEDGEMENTS

To my family: Robert, for infinite patience and support; Elisabeth, Eric and Stefan, my perfect children who've taught me how to be a mother; my sister, Sharon, whose courage inspires me, and friendship sustains me.

To my friends: the Tuesday morning women, the Edmonton women, the Sage Hill writers, the Alexandra writers. Shirley Black and Ellen Kelly, sister scribes and true friends. In memory, Sharon Drummond, who was such fine company on this path.

To teachers and wise people: Dave Margoshes, friend and mentor extraordinaire, who read this book so many times he is truly "Corey's godfather." The Sage Hill Writing Experience for giving me entry to Robert Kroetsch's novel colloquium and to that wise man for the insight that finally brought the writing to an end.

To social workers and foster parents: Maggie, Wendy, and with deepest gratitude to Alma and Paul Bankert and their family for embodying the real meaning of unconditional love.

To the Calgary Zoo for allowing a nighttime ramble, and providing the perfect setting for a story about a lost child.

To NeWest Press for opening the door; Lynne Van Luven for her fine eye and sure hand.

BETTY JANE HEGERAT earned a BA from the University of Alberta, and an MA of Social Work from the University of Calgary. In addition to being a social worker and a mother of three, Hegerat also teaches courses at the Alexandra Writers' Centre in Calgary and is an avid rose-gardener. Her work has been featured in several literary publications, such as the *NeWest Review*, the *Toronto Star*, and *Alberta Views*, and has won numerous prestigious writing competitions. Hegerat currently lives in Calgary and is working towards an MFA in Creative Writing through the University of British Columbia.